When had his feelings for her changed?

Had it been when she'd become pregnant or had it been earlier still? The first time he'd taken her to dinner? The day he'd held her as she cried?

How had he gone from simply feeling attracted to her as a potential friend to feeling sorry for her and becoming involved with her problem? Looking back, he realized he couldn't name a day or a time that their relationship had begun to shift from one of friendship and mutual purpose to something deeper, more intimate and adult. He'd only known on a subliminal level that it had been happening, not all at once, but day by day, hour by hour, minute by minute, and that this evening when he'd walked in the door and found her, everything had simply fallen into place.

ABOUT THE AUTHOR

Cathy Gillen Thacker is a full-time novelist who once taught piano to children. Born and raised in Ohio, she attended Miami University and after moving cross-country several times, she now resides in Texas with her husband and three children.

Books by Cathy Gillen Thacker

Guardian Angel
Cathy Gillen Thacker

Harlequin Books

TORONTO • NEW YORK • LONDON
AMSTERDAM • PARIS • SYDNEY • HAMBURG
STOCKHOLM • ATHENS • TOKYO • MILAN

Published February 1988

First printing December 1987

ISBN 0-373-16233-2

Chapter One

Jason O'Leary stepped over a bubble-producing lawn-mower and a stuffed dog on a string, and skirted a fallen tower of plastic building blocks.

The hallway was littered with toys. In every room of his new four-bedroom house boxes were stacked waist-high.

A sweet, warm April breeze wafted gently through the open windows, and sunshine was pouring into the spacious living room. It was a perfect Dallas spring day except for one thing: the dancing footsteps, light and slightly uncoordinated, had abruptly stilled. One minute they'd been clattering over the kitchen linoleum, the next scuffling over the softness of the beige carpet. Now he could hear nothing at all. To Jason, utter silence meant trouble with a capital *T*.

Padding from room to room, he called softly in his most skilled and persuasive tone, "Megan, come on sweetie. Come to Daddy. Megan? Where are you, sweetie? Daddy wants to see you." Pause. "Megan?"

Silence, followed by an eighteen-month-old child's infectious giggle.

The sound, brief as it was, was enough to let Jason zero in on Megan's whereabouts. In a minute, he was climbing over the kitchen paraphernalia—which the movers had stacked in the master bedroom while he wasn't looking—to a window seat overlooking the street. Megan was crouched beside it, her hands placed over her eyes peekaboo fashion. He grinned. She always thought that if her eyes were covered and she couldn't see him, he couldn't see her. Perfect toddler logic.

"Megan!" he exclaimed affectionately. "So here you are, you little rascal."

She spread her fingers and peered up at him impishly. "Daddy," she said, still giggling silently, thrilled that her game of hide and seek had been successful.

"Hello, Megan." Jason sighed his relief. Now that he'd found her and knew she was all right, he couldn't resist gazing down at her for one long, loving moment. In pink overalls, a pink, yellow, and white Winnie the Pooh shirt, the white high-topped shoes, with her mass of strawberry-blond curls and enormous blue eyes, she was clearly the most adorable baby he'd ever been privileged to be around. And she was his, all his.

"Lesson number one," Jason muttered cheerfully, tickling his daughter affectionately under the chin. "Daddy should never put Megan down on moving day." He crouched before her and held out his arms.

Megan pushed herself to her feet and toddled into them just as the doorbell sounded. Jason stood up, cradling her in his arms. "I just hope that's the diapers."

"Diapers," Megan repeated, lacing an arm comfortably about his neck. Her tiny elbow rested on his shoulder.

Together they threaded their way through the myriad of boxes, no easy feat. As he picked his way down the hallway, Megan put her head on his shoulder, feeling suddenly shy, Jason guessed. In her view, who knew what stranger lurked beyond the strange door?

Still grinning, Jason opened the door.

For a second he was so surprised that he could do little more than stare at the striking young woman standing on his porch. He guessed her to be a few years younger than he, in her early thirties, and she was undeniably lovely—tall, and slim, with clear light blue eyes and pale blond hair the color of cornsilk that fell in loose abundant waves down her back. Her skin had that sun-kissed, honey tan found only on blondes, and a faint, fading sunburn touched her nose and the elegant curve of her cheeks that gave definition to her oval face. Her mouth was full, sensual, her lips soft and smooth.

She was dressed simply but casually in an emerald, black, and lemon tropical print shirt, a full black cotton skirt and black cotton espadrilles. Her legs were long, very slim and shapely, her waist trim, her breasts small but luscious.

"Hi. You ordered diapers, right?" she said in a cheerful, businesslike tone.

"Yes..." Then Jason saw the bag of diapers sitting next to her on the porch, along with a tall white plastic diaper pail, and the clipboard in her hand. "Yes, I did. Won't you come in. I'm Jason O'Leary."

She smiled warmly. "Carlys Holt."

"I spoke to you on the phone, didn't I?" With one hand Jason lifted the diapers inside. Carlys followed with the pail.

"Right. Sorry it took so long for me to get here, but one of my delivery people is sick today, and we've been taking turns filling in for her." Shutting the door behind her, she took a good look at Megan, who'd come out of hiding just long enough to see who the lady with the lovely voice was.

"So," Carlys said softly, captivated by Megan's cherubic features and wide-eyed glance, "this is the little girl who's allergic to disposable diapers."

"Right. Megan. Megan, meet Ms Carlys Holt. Carlys, Megan."

Megan promptly responded to the formalities by hiding her face in Jason's shoulder again.

Carlys threw back her head and laughed, a delicious sound.

Try as he might, Jason couldn't take his eyes off her. Slightly embarrassed by such a lovestruck reaction to his diaper service, he pushed his glasses a bit farther up his nose. "Sorry. Megan's always been a little shy around strangers."

"I don't blame her. And moving to a new house can't have helped." She looked around at the stacks of boxes. "Is there someplace we could go over the paperwork? I need a little information from you for my service records."

"Oh, sure." Jason led the way to the kitchen. "Just let me put Megan into a high chair and give her a cookie and some juice."

While Carlys set a stool at the ceramic counter—one of the few things the movers had put in the right place—and sorted through her papers, Jason rummaged around in the refrigerator. He swiftly filled a two-handled plastic baby cup to the halfway mark with apple juice, snapped on the lid, then handed it and a teething biscuit to his daughter.

Megan munched and sipped, her eyes fixed on the two grown-ups as they talked. Satisfied that she was contented, Jason propped himself comfortably against the counter, one foot crossed over the other, his arms folded on his chest. It didn't take long to fill out Carlys's form, as he had already given her the basic details on the phone.

"So, where do you work?"

"Data Tech Incorporated—the business center in Las Colinas."

"Oh, I know the place." Carlys looked up at him. "It's quite impressive."

"Yeah, it's a good company." He couldn't manage to stop smiling at her.

"Have you worked there long?"

"Twelve years now."

She scribbled the information down quickly with short, bold strokes and turned to face him, her chin cupped in her hand. "Where did you move from?"

Though he sensed some of her questions were more for personal than for business reasons, he didn't mind answering them. He wanted her to know more about him. He wanted to know more about her. "Houston."

"Ah." She sat up abruptly. Satisfaction filled her smile. She looked like a sleuth uncovering a trail of not-so-obvious clues. "Then you're a native Texan?"

His accent must have given him away. "Mmm-hmm. A city dweller. You?"

"From Dallas. Forever." She grinned, delighted they had Texas in common.

It was a long time since Jason had felt such a rush from simply talking to a woman. He felt himself warming to her more and more. "Ever lived anywhere else?"

Her brows lifted in mock disapproval. "No, sir! And I don't want to, either!" she sang out in a parody of patriotic fervor.

He laughed. "Spoken like a true Texan."

"Amen to that." With an effort and a quick glance at her watch, Carlys got reluctantly back to the business at hand. "So what about your wife?" she asked, dropping her voice to a more businesslike level. "Does she work, too? Will there be someone here during the day to accept delivery on the diapers?" She glanced at him and waited expectantly.

"I'm not married. And yes, there will be someone here every afternoon and most mornings—me. I've negotiated a deal with my company so that I can work on a personal computer at home, at least for the next year or two, until Megan gets a little older. From time to time I'll still have to go in to deliver work and so forth. But most of the time I'll be here."

The last question having been settled, they spent a few minutes talking about Dallas. Carlys was full of warmth and charm; with every second that passed Jason liked her more. And he wasn't the only one. Observing the instant rapport of the adults, Megan, too, was entranced.

So Jason wasn't all that surprised when Megan finally decided that she wanted some attention from their visitor. In a typical bid to get Carlys's interest, she banged her high-chair tray with zeal, waved her teething biscuit and said, "Hi."

Apparently, that was all the invitation Carlys needed to further their acquaintance. She bent down to talk to her. Megan responded shyly at first, then more confidently. By the time they'd finished, Carlys had gotten a smile and a giggle out of her as well as several passionate, garbled sentences neither Jason nor Carlys could quite make out.

"She doesn't usually take to anyone that fast," Jason commented, delighted that the two were hitting it off so well.

Carlys smiled. "I've had a lot of experience baby-sitting. I love children."

"I can see that." And he could see that children loved her.

"Well, I'd better be going," Carlys said, reluctantly gathering up her things. "My people are going to wonder what happened to me."

Jason pushed himself upright. "Thanks for bringing the diapers by so quickly."

"Oh, you're welcome. I know how crazy things can be, especially for single parents." She paused and shot Megan another tender, almost yearning glance. Her eyes swerved to his. "Anyway, good luck. And if you need any more information about Dallas or our little corner of big-city suburbia in general, don't hesitate to give me a call. Okay? My number's in the book under C. L. Holt. I'd be happy to help you and Megan any way I can."

"Thanks."

"Sure."

His eyes still on Carlys, Jason stepped toward her, meaning to walk her to the front door. The moment he moved, Megan let out a wail, sure her daddy was going to leave her and not liking it one bit.

He turned back to his daughter, a chagrined twist to his mouth. *Megan,* Jason thought, *sometimes your timing leaves a lot to be desired.* He'd been hoping to find out a little more about Carlys. Was she single? Was she dating anyone special? He wasn't in the market for a lover—he'd realized shortly after his divorce that he couldn't juggle work and a baby and build a romantic relationship, too—but he was in need of some friends. And Carlys and he had hit it off right away.

Unhappily, Megan's dismay effectively circumvented his mission.

"Looks like you've got your work cut out for you," Carlys teased. Megan's teething biscuit had disintegrated into toast-colored mush, which was smeared not only on her face, hair, hands and clothes but also all over her high chair.

Already reaching for a box of baby washclothes on the counter, Jason grinned goodnaturedly. "I sure do." He made a preliminary dab at Megan, who was now silent again sucking two fingers.

"Well, thanks again for the business. I'll see myself out." Carlys shifted her belongings and groped in her handbag for her keys.

Jason murmured a goodbye.

The last thing he noticed before Carlys disappeared into the hall was the ring finger on her left hand. It was bare.

CARLYS SNUGGLED DOWN under her covers long hours later, the physical exhaustion resulting from a very busy day permeating her bones. Yet her mind was on full alert.

She couldn't stop thinking about Jason O'Leary and his daughter. Clearly he loved Megan very much and she loved him. Being a single parent couldn't be easy at the best of times, and now he had moved to a new city where he didn't know a soul. Yet he seemed to have everything that counted. And he and his daughter were both so happy! Just seeing them together made Carlys feel all warm and content and happy inside, made her feel that anything and everything was possible—if for

Jason, why not for her? Maybe it wasn't so far-fetched for her to be thinking about taking the same route as Jason. Still, she was a bit envious of him; he already had Megan.

Carlys had wanted to be a mother for as long as she could remember. From childhood on, she'd always assumed she would have a baby of her own. Son or daughter, one or ten children, the details weren't important. She had just known parenthood would happen to her by the time she was in her early twenties. But it hadn't happened. She'd dated a lot but hadn't married; with the exception of a broken engagement she hadn't even come close.

Determined to make her dreams come true, with or without a husband, and not just wish her life away, she'd finally begun to look at her situation realistically. She considered her options. She could adopt a child . . . or become a foster mother . . .

And all the while her biological clock was ticking away relentlessly, ticking . . . ticking . . . ticking so cruelly, telling Carlys her time, her chances were strictly limited and getting more slim every day.

It was unfair, Carlys thought, so unfair. If anyone should have a child, she should. A baby was all she really wanted in life, the only thing besides her work that really mattered—and she would be a good mother, the best.

Determinedly she battled the sadness engulfing her, refusing to give in to it. She had to believe everything was going to work out for her, that one way or another some day she would have a baby of her own. Someday soon. She had to keep hoping.

Fortunately, her depression didn't last beyond the night, mainly because Carlys refused to let herself drown in self-pity. Not that she had that much spare time. As usual, she had plenty to keep her busy at work.

And admittedly, there were some very sunny private moments—most of them linked to the man she had just met. To her delight, over the course of the next several days Jason O'Leary called her frequently. He seemed to have a thousand questions about Dallas. Aware that he didn't know anyone else in the area, Carlys gladly took the time to welcome him to the city where she'd grown up. And in the course of those cheerful conversations, they learned quite a lot about each other. Carlys knew, for instance, that Jason hated yard work but considered it a high priority item on the list of household chores, as well as a practical way to stay fit. He knew she loved Tex-Mex food and chicken-fried steak, but didn't much care for Chinese or Thai cuisine, both of which he loved. She steered him to a good grocery store and told him where to go for bargains and dimestore goods. He found a good source of new tires for her car.

On the surface their conversations were mundane, she supposed. And yet Carlys couldn't stop thinking about Jason or help feeling an unexpected camaraderie with him. They were strangers still, and yet in a way not, because she knew instinctively she could depend upon him; she suspected he felt the same about her.

So it came as no surprise that when Jason was called in to do emergency work on a Data Tech computer late at night on his fourth day in town, Carlys was the person he contacted. He needed a sitter fast. Unfortunately, Carlys didn't know anyone he could call at such short notice and certainly not at two in the morning. So she volunteered. It was clear that Jason didn't want to go in to work at all, let alone leave Megan in the care of someone he barely knew. Yet he had no choice. And Carlys was, at that point, his closest friend in Dallas.

Carlys understood both his dilemma and his anxiety. She was certain when she became a parent herself she would be just as protective of her child's safety and happiness. She reassured him that he need have no fears, and recalling the way Megan had taken to Carlys at first meeting, Jason let himself be persuaded.

Feeling oddly buoyant at the thought of seeing Jason and his daughter again, no matter what the circumstances, Carlys got dressed quickly.

The streets were quiet, the spring night chilly. The drive over to his place was easy and fast. Jason greeted her thankfully at his front door.

"Megan asleep?" she asked, noting how quiet his house was.

He nodded and crossed his fingers. "With any luck, she'll never even know I'm gone. If she does wake up, though, there's a drinking cup of milk for her in the refrigerator, cereal and fruit or whatever else she might want if she's hungry. I've left my work number by the phone, so if you have any questions, call. I should be home by seven-thirty or eight at the latest."

"I'm surprised you have to go in to work so soon." Carlys sidestepped around several boxes. Although he'd managed to put up drapery rods and drapes, he'd made hardly any progress with the rest of the unpacking. But then he'd had a lot to do, a baby to take care of, and no close friends or family to help out.

"Normally I wouldn't have to." Jason knotted his tie and tugged at his shirt collar. "Technically, I'm still on vacation and not on call until next Monday, but with the only other person familiar with the system sick, I don't have any choice. Those transactions have got to be run tonight."

Carlys watched while Jason shrugged into a tweed jacket, straightened his tie, clipped a badge on his shirt pocket and picked up his briefcase. He looked very good in his preppy clothes. His dark-brown hair was as naturally wavy as hers, but cut much shorter in layers and left to curl as it liked. He had a Roman nose, a serious chin, a sulky mouth that was wide, slightly bow-shaped, unutterably masculine. His eyes were a dark, mysterious brown behind the round wire-rimmed glasses, his skin smooth and tanned and no matter how close or often he shaved, he would never quite get rid of the faint shadow of his beard and mustache.

Tall, solidly built, his movements graceful and economical, his stride loose-jointed, he was the most arresting man she'd met in a long time. Just from being near him, Carlys felt her pulse quicken.

Jason gestured hastily at the sofa. "There's a pillow, blankets. Help yourself to food and drink."

As he prepared to go, Carlys yawned, sleepiness overwhelming her. "I think I'll just go back to sleep," she said, following him to the door. "Don't worry, Jason, everything will be fine."

And everything was fine. Megan didn't stir until six. She was surprised to see Carlys coming in to get her, but to Carlys's relief didn't cry.

"Daddy—?"

"Daddy went to work," Carlys said, laying her down to change her diaper. "He'll be home soon, and in the meantime, we're going to have breakfast. What does Megan like to eat? Toast, juice, cereal, scrambled eggs?"

Megan said yes to the entire menu and added one item of her own—bacon.

"Something smells good," Jason said, coming into the house fifteen minutes later.

Megan was in her high chair, Carlys was at the stove. Morning paper in hand, Jason put down his briefcase and shrugged out of his sports coat. Carlys was amused by the domestic scene they all made.

"It's breakfast, and you're just in time. Get your problem fixed?"

He nodded. "The system was up and running when I left." His eyes turned serious. "Look, Carlys, about last night, I can't thank you enough. I don't know what I would've done if you hadn't come to my rescue."

Carlys knew he'd have been in real trouble, but she just smiled and said, "Do you have to go in often at night?"

"Depends." Jason poured all three of them some juice, and set the table efficiently. "Sometimes months will pass and I'm not called in at all. Other times, it seems I have to go in at least once a week. It's part of the job and I don't mind—except when it comes to Megan."

"You know, it'll be hard to find someone to baby-sit in the middle of the night."

"Especially on such short notice. But I just have to find someone. I don't have any choice." He turned toward his daughter, smiling as she extended both jelly-smeared hands for a hug.

"Daddy..."

Armed with a washcloth, Jason bent to give his daughter a kiss.

Mindful that she had to go to work, Carlys stayed only long enough to eat breakfast with them. Jason wouldn't let her help with the dishes. After settling Megan in her playpen with a washable book and a heap of toys, he walked Carlys to the door.

He reached for his wallet. "I'd like to pay you for sitting—"

"Jason, no." Carlys, pink with embarrassment, stayed his hand.

"I do owe you," he urged.

She didn't dispute that. "Fine. But repay me in some other way, please. Cut my lawn. Send me a basket of fruit or a box of candy."

"Anything but cold, hard cash," he ascertained dryly.

She nodded. "I did it as a favor, friend to friend."

His eyes held hers understandingly. "Okay. Then would you accept an invitation to dinner with Megan and me as a token of our gratitude?"

Carlys grinned. "Yes—providing, of course, I get to pick the restaurant."

"Done."

"McDonald's in the park?"

"A woman after my own heart."

"You love Big Macs, too," Carlys guessed.

"And their fries. Which, incidentally, Megan is also wild about. Tonight okay with you?"

Carlys nodded her agreement, adding, "If you're sure you won't be too tired after working all night." Looking closely, she saw he did look a little worse for wear despite his show of surface energy.

His eyes glimmered ruefully. "Let's put it this way. As for dinner this evening, I'm going to be up and getting something to eat anyway. And I'll nap while Megan sleeps this afternoon. What time do you get off work?"

Carlys vacillated briefly, trying to decide what would be best for all concerned. "I could meet you here around five. Megan probably likes to eat early, doesn't she?"

He cast her an admiring glance. "You *do* know a lot about children."

And she wanted to learn a lot more. "I have two nephews and three nieces."

"Aha!"

And she desperately wanted a child of her own.

"Five it is, then," Jason decreed.

"I'll see you then."

"We'll be waiting."

Dinner for three at McDonald's wasn't a date, Carlys reminded herself throughout the unusually long day, just a simple outing between new friends. Yet she remained as excited as if it were a date. She told herself it was not so much that Jason was attractive, even though he was the most interesting man she had met in a very long while—he, too, seemed to march to the beat of a slightly different drummer—but because he would understand her desire to have and care for a child of her own even if she had to raise the child alone. His pleasure and pride in raising Megan was unmistakable. And he was a role model for her, combining work and parenthood very successfully, even without a family support system. She knew that if Jason could manage to care for Megan in a strange city, far from family and friends, then she could certainly do the same in Dallas, close as she was to a whole network of devoted relatives.

There was much she could learn from Jason, and she wanted to be close to Megan, too.

Happily, when Carlys arrived at five, Jason was ready to go. Megan, just up from a nap, was lively and excited. Obviously their best plan was to drive together in Jason's new station wagon, and in two minutes Megan was happily strapped into her safety seat, behind them.

While Jason negotiated the streets with understated skill, Carlys gave him a sketch of the northern half of the city and recommended a shoe mender's here, a dry cleaner's there. As they passed it, she pointed out one of her father's stores, a handsome modern red-brick building.

"Your dad owns a chain of sporting goods stores?" Jason looked impressed.

"Yes, Dad has four stores now," Carlys answered, bursting with pride in her father's accomplishment, which was all the more remarkable because he'd never had more than a high school education. "Sometimes he gets one of the Cowboys to come in and do an autographing session for him. It's a lot of fun. You'll have to come and bring Megan."

"I'd like that." Jason smiled, adding, "Although I must admit after living in Houston all those years I'm still an Oilers fan."

Carlys covered her ears, and screwed up her face. "Heresy!"

"Don't worry—" he shot her a teasing glance "—I'll keep my allegiance quiet."

When they stopped at a red light, he looked over at her. "What about you? Have you always been in the diaper service business?"

"No. I'm basically just an entrepreneur. I see a need and create a business to meet the need. Usually when it's up and running well, I sell it, and then go on to something else." The light changed and the car started forward again. "So far I've owned an ice-cream shop, a bookstore that specialized in mysteries, and a carpet-cleaning service."

"And they've all been successful?" They paused at another light.

"Yes—but I can't take full credit for that." Carlys blushed a little under his steady, admiring look. "I was lucky enough to have my parents' expertise and lots of help from the family. Every one of us except my sister Susie has owned at least one entrepreneurial venture. One of my brothers is in men's business apparel and the other's in custom-built home furniture."

"Sounds like a lively crew." Concentrating on the road again as traffic picked up, Jason said off-handedly, "I'd like to meet them sometime."

"Well, maybe that can be arranged," Carlys responded, matching his tone.

When Jason pulled up at their destination, even with her limited experience, Megan knew exactly where they were and what to expect next.

"Donals!" Megan grinned gleefully and pointed to the yellow arches. "F'ench f'ies."

"You eat here that often?" Carlys teased, as they awaited their turn to shout into the outdoor microphone beneath the illuminated menu.

He slanted her a sexy, unapologetic grin. "Looks that way, doesn't it?"

Paper bags piled in the middle of the front seat out of Megan's way, they sped to the nearest park, where they spread a blanket on the grass and attacked their hamburgers. Megan's french fries were supplemented with food Jason had packed in a lunchbox at home: a thermos of milk, a crustless peanut butter sandwich in the shape of a bunny, and applesauce. Their meal finished, Megan happily rolled a ball back and forth with her daddy.

"So how's the unpacking coming?" Carlys asked, eating the last of the french fries. Though the kitchen now looked in order, Carlys had a feeling that the rest of the house had a long way to go.

"Don't ask." Jason moaned and rolled his eyes up. "I've only got three days before I start back to work for DTI on a regular schedule."

"It isn't going, then?" Carlys made a sympathetic moue.

"Let's just say today was memorable for two reasons. I hooked up the washer and dryer, and found my bed frame and put it together. As for the rest . . . I don't know." He frowned, running a hand through his hair, then rolled the ball to Megan again and winked. "You can see how hard I'm working now."

"Mmm-hmm. That's my strategy, too."

"What?"

"When the housework's too overwhelming, cut and run. I hate it."

His eyes glimmered with amusement. "I knew you were my type. Oh, well, the housework'll get done eventually. It always does."

"Want some help?" Carlys wasn't sure why she was volunteering. Getting her own housework done was quite enough for her, and usually the last thing she'd opt for was a struggle with someone else's household, and an unfamiliar, male-run, baby-oriented one at that. Part of her motive was curiosity, she admitted to herself. As a prospective single parent, she wanted to know how Jason coped. Was it something as basic as overall organization that kept his household running so happily or simply his positive attitude toward life that made

Megan such a delightful, well-adjusted child? Thus far nothing had seemed to shake Jason, even his emergency with the diapers.

Admit it. She was fascinated by him. She wanted to get to know him better. She wanted him as a friend, and she sensed he felt the same about her.

The silent moment lengthened.

He gave her a quick, assessing sideways glance, as if wondering why she was so eager to be around a single man with a child, a situation that single women tended to run from.

"It's nice of you to offer..." he said finally, with an uncertainty that was foreign to him.

"But you don't want to impose," Carlys guessed.

He nodded.

Carlys couldn't imagine trying to work, take care of a baby and unpack all at the same time without some help. Whether he realized it yet or not, he needed her to give him a hand, if only for the few days it took to get him settled. "I wouldn't mind, Jason, really."

He studied her quietly, as if debating how close to let her get to him, and vice versa. "Okay. You're on," he said at last, accepting her aid cheerfully now that he had come to a decision. "Want to start tonight?"

"Absolutely. You know what they say about procrastinating—"

In sync with her thoughts, he interjected smoothly, "Never put off until tomorrow what can be done today."

Once back at the house, it soon became clear that Megan, cranky and overtired, needed to go to bed. While Jason bathed his daughter, Carlys began unpacking some of the books in the living room. Jason joined her twenty minutes later. His shirt was damp. He smelled of baby shampoo. Powder dusted his trousers. He looked content and happy. Carlys felt a touch of envy for what he had and then a secret pinprick of joy. Perhaps the same joy wasn't so far away for her.

"That's terrific! You've done all the books and half the record albums already." Jason picked up the stereo and placed it on a high shelf of the entertainment center so that all the fascinating buttons and knobs would be well out of Megan's reach.

"I'm an ace at organizing as well as doing anything domestic," Carlys confided. "My mother had me doing all sorts of routine chores and cooking simple meals by the time I was ten."

"A slave driver, huh?"

Carlys grinned. "She wanted me to be self-sufficient. She wanted us all to be."

"Who's all of us? You said earlier you had other brothers and sisters."

"Twin brothers, four years older than me, and Susie. She's sixteen."

Their hands touched briefly as she helped him hook up the amplifiers. "Is Megan down?" Carlys asked casually.

"She's not only down for the night, but out like a light. I put her in her crib and went back to clean up the bathroom. By the time I looked in on her, she was wrapped around her favorite stuffed animal, with her usual two fingers in her mouth." Finished with the stereo, Jason began putting books into the built-in shelves at the side of the stone fireplace.

"You do very well with her," Carlys said softly, making a start on the bookshelves at the other side of the fireplace.

"Thanks, I... Well, it's been an adjustment." Jason's mouth tightened briefly.

He was leaving too much unsaid. She needed to know more.

"How long have you been a single parent?"

To her relief, he didn't seem to mind her question.

He answered calmly, "I've been raising Megan alone since shortly after she was born, although my marriage was over long before that." His eyes met hers in a way that told her he knew what she was thinking. "I'm not widowed, Carlys. I'm divorced."

Carlys stared at him in stupefaction. "I see," she said finally. But the truth was she didn't understand at all. His daughter was so cute and so adorable that it was hard to imagine any woman walking out on so young a child. Or had it been the other way around? Had Jason walked out on his wife and taken the baby with him, and if so, on what grounds? He didn't seem at all vindictive.

"I was married to Alice Greenway. You may have heard of her."

It took a moment for that to sink in. "Not... The Alice Greenway? The roving correspondent for the network news program?"

"Yep, that Alice Greenway. We met about five years ago in Houston when she was covering the southwest for one of the networks. She was traveling a lot even then, but I saw her whenever she could get home."

"On television she seems very dynamic."

"She's that, all right."

There was no mistaking the pride in Jason's voice or the residual trace of fondness. Prickles of alarm slid over Carlys's skin as she asked, "Are you still in love with her?'' Was he on the rebound? She had to admit she hoped not.

"No." He met her eyes directly. "We're friends." He put a few more books away, then searching for a way to explain, added reflectively in the silence that had fallen between them, "Looking back, I'm not sure why we got married except to cement a relationship that we probably knew in our hearts even then wasn't going to work."

"Why do you say that?"

He shrugged and crossed his arms against his chest. "Because I only saw her once or twice a week at most. Later it was once every two weeks and then once every three."

"You knew it was going to be that way before you married her?"

"Oh, yes."

"And that didn't deter you?"

"I knew how important her career was to her. I didn't resent that."

"And yet, if you were never together—"

"For over two years we tried our damnedest to make a go of it, but you can't build a marriage by long distance. When it got to be brief meetings between six-week separations, we were like strangers. We both decided to go our own ways."

"Then what happened?" And where did Megan fit into all this? When had she been born?

Jason sighed wearily. "About six months into the separation, the initial bitterness and disillusionment we had felt for each other and for marriage in general began to dissipate. We started to talk again, to want to make things easier for each other, instead of the other way around. Anyway, we got together in Houston one weekend to talk about the division of property. Neither of us was inclined to just hand it over to the lawyers, and after all we'd been to each other it seemed silly to go through third parties just to talk. In any case by then ours was an amicable divorce, so we preferred to hammer out the division of property ourselves, then tell the lawyers what we wanted, so as to get the divorce over as quickly and painlessly as possible.''

Carlys could tell by the rueful, slightly exasperated look on his face that nothing had been as simple as he'd hoped. "It didn't happen that way, though, did it?"

"No, not quite. In fact for a while the divorce didn't happen at all." He paused and thrust his jaw forward reflectively. "Maybe because neither of us likes to leave a job unfinished. We both felt an acute sense of failure for not having made our marriage work despite the odds and the separations and the loneliness. At any rate, we decided to give it one more shot." He smiled wanly. "But the problems were still there and weren't going to disappear by magic. The reconciliation ended after only a week, and we decided to go ahead with a divorce, this time with no regrets, only relief on both sides."

He still hadn't mentioned Megan, Carlys thought impatiently.

Jason continued, "About a month later, Alice discovered she was pregnant. She came to me and we talked about it. She didn't want an abortion, but she didn't want to give up her job with the network, either, or commit herself to the responsibility of raising a child. On the other hand I had wanted a family for a long time. So we decided that I would raise Megan and we'd put off the divorce until after she was born."

"And your having a baby together didn't change anything between you?" Carlys asked, thinking, *Surely*

in all that time . . . They had—what?—eight months or
so to reconsider.

"No," Jason said firmly. "By the time Megan was
born we knew the marriage truly had been a mistake
from the beginning and there was no going back. Don't
get me wrong. Megan's birth did bring us closer together, but as friends. Alice sees Megan whenever she's
in town, but she'll never be a full-time mother to her."
His tone as he finished was matter-of-fact; he had accepted the situation as being best for all three of them.
Carlys's respect for him increased. Many men would
have been vindictive or cruel toward their former wife
in a similar situation. Jason was neither. Rather, he still
seemed to understand and respect Alice Greenway. And
Megan was clearly a very happy, cherished child.

"You really enjoy being a single parent, don't you?"

"Yeah. I do."

"It shows," Carlys said softly.

"Thanks." Jason's eyes held hers. "It's not everyone who understands my decision to go it alone."

"Believe me, I do," Carlys said. She understood
better than he knew.

While talking, they'd finished shelving the rest of the
books and had cleared the sofas and chairs. Jason
glanced around the living room with satisfaction.
Though he still had several boxes marked Office to
shift, at least now he could find a place to sit down.

"Do you ever have any regrets about . . . well, making the choice you did? About being a single parent?"
Carlys asked a bit too casually, helping him knock down
the empty boxes. She knew that asking him to confide
in her was taking her into deep water, yet she had to find
out the answer to her question and Jason was the only

single parent she knew. And then he hadn't minded talking to her so far, had seemed in fact to welcome it.

His glance narrowed. He seemed to sense there was a special reason behind her query. Carlys's heart started beating faster.

"What do you mean?" he asked quietly.

She struggled to keep her voice even. He was a nice man, but she wasn't sure how much she could tell him of her plans—or any man for that matter—without alienating him completely. On the other hand, what did it matter? If all went as she hoped, he would know soon enough anyway. And she would have her child.

She tried again. "Do you miss your freedom, not being able to pick up and go when you please?"

"No. Well, maybe a little." He stopped, now sure that something was up. "Why are you asking me this?"

Carlys took a deep breath, knowing that she wanted to tell him before she lost her nerve. Her chin lifted and she faced him courageously. "Because I'm going to be a single parent, too. That is, if all goes well. Jason, I might be pregnant."

Chapter Two

For a long moment Jason didn't say a word. Eyes wide, he stepped back from Carlys.

"Pregnant!" A mixture of shock and surprise washed over his face.

Half her mouth lifted in a wry grin. Her only recourse now was to start talking and keep it up. "I can only hope so," she admitted cheerfully, well used to the reaction her news inevitably prompted. Every single member of her family, from her brothers and sister to her parents, had reacted identically. "Last week I was artificially inseminated."

Recovering slightly, he ascertained in a crisp, distant voice, "You're single?"

Abruptly she felt like an object reserved strictly for Jason's scientific study. "Yes, I'm single and I want very much to have a child, a family of my own." He still hadn't moved. She took a deep breath, preparing to launch into the persuasive speech from the heart that she'd already given family, physician and nurses.

"You don't want to get married?"

"In these days?" Carlys made a joke of what was to her a very painful subject. "Easier said than done. Besides, I've already been engaged. It didn't work out."

Jason was looking at her curiously. After a pause, she added, "In the beginning, I didn't know him well enough, and when I did... Let's just say it was very clear we weren't meant to walk hand and hand into the sunset."

"So?" He shrugged, clearly not understanding her current rush to be a mother. "Carlys, you're still so young. You've got time—"

"Right. I know. All the time in the world." Impatiently she cut short his logical exposition of the standard point of view. That particular speech she really didn't want to hear. She'd already heard it from everyone under the sun. "Jason, I'm thirty-two—"

"So? That's not very old," he interrupted in a quizzical tone.

Her chin lifted a notch at the reproving look in his eyes. "Maybe not for you. But for me, I feel ancient!" Being thirty-two, unmarried, with no prospects made her feel at times like an old-fashioned old maid.

Was it possible that though divorced instead of forever single, Jason felt similarly left behind? "How old are you?" she asked, mimicking his faintly interrogating tone.

He grinned at the mimicry, answering, "Thirty-eight. But let's get back to your situation. What prompted you to do this?" He wasn't judging, he was just asking a serious question.

Carlys shrugged. She hadn't expected him to be quite so interested in her situation. "I guess I feel time is running out for me, or even worse, standing still. Jason, in the past ten years, nothing in my life has really changed except for my businesses. I've been living on my own since I was nineteen. I've been running my own businesses since I was seventeen. I thought by now I'd have a husband and several children as well as my work. Anyway, like it or not, I'm not getting any younger.''

He nodded. ''The old biological clock.''

''Yes. Realistically I don't have all that much time to spare anymore. And I want a child.'' She gestured helplessly when words failed her for a minute. ''Because I'm not married and don't expect to be married anytime soon, artificial insemination seemed the only way for me to have one.''

Suddenly, a whirlwind of motion, he stalked into the kitchen and fixed them both a cold drink, leaving her to follow.

''So that was why you had all the questions about being a single parent,'' he mused, pouring soda over ice.

''I wanted to know what it was like from someone who'd done it from day one.''

Together they carried their glasses back into the living room and sat down.

Jason stretched his long legs out in front of him, and after taking a sip of his drink, said honestly, ''All right, I'll tell you realistically—from one single parent to a prospective single parent—exactly what it's like. There are days when Megan's cranky and I've got work demands piled high and no one to offer relief, and I wonder why I ever thought I could handle this alone. Then there are days when everything is wonderful, no, better than wonderful, and I wonder why I ever thought I couldn't. When Megan's sick, it can be scary. Sometimes I wish for a normal family unit for her—a mother, brothers, sisters—none of which is likely to be provided unless I adopt a second child or hire a surrogate. I guess to sum it up, single parenting is like everything else. You just have to take the good times with the bad and roll with the punches and go on, one day, one moment at a time. And just trust that everything will work out in the long run." He finished on that note of gentle encouragement, then added as an afterthought, "At least you can use the artificial insemination route again if you choose."

Carlys thought she detected a note of envy in his voice, a hint of deliberately subdued longing. "Do you want another child?"

For a moment he was silent. "Yes," he admitted finally, adding honestly, "though alone I don't think I could handle two children simultaneously, at least not with them both in diapers, and at the same time manage to support us all and give them the care and attention I'd want any child of mine to have."

"If it doesn't happen for you...if you don't have another child..." How would he feel?

"Then I'll live with it. I have Megan, after all."

"Yes, you do." Their glances met, meshed.

He leaned forward earnestly. "I understand why you've made that choice, Carlys. If it's any comfort, I admire your courage in going after what you want. After seeing you with Megan, I know you'll make a good mother. You're a natural with children."

"Thanks." Carlys took a sip of her soda. Without really wanting to, she thought of all that still lay ahead of her.

"You look worried," Jason observed softly.

There was such compassion in his face. Of all the people she knew, he best seemed to understand what she was going through; maybe because he was a single parent, maybe because he'd reached his middle thirties without the hope of a child. Whatever the reason was, it drew them together, bonded them like kindred souls. She hadn't felt so close to anyone in a long time, so believed in, revered. His empathy did her good, made her feel stronger and more secure, as if, with his help and understanding, his friendship and wisdom, she truly could weather anything.

He'd poured out his heart to her; it seemed right to tell him what was on her mind. "Deep down, I guess I am worried, Jason. For one thing, I don't even know if the insemination worked and I won't know for several more days."

"What else?" His command was soft but masculinely insistent.

The corners of her mouth crooked up ruefully as she examined her feelings. "I think maybe I've got a type of stage fright peculiar to expectant mothers. I thought about this move for months. I've been so sure that getting pregnant via artificial insemination was the right thing to do. Now that it's actually happening, though... Suddenly I'm so nervous, Jason. And I don't know why."

"Is it the whole big prospect of having a child that's getting to you, the thought of changing your life, or are you just getting edgy waiting for test results?"

"Waiting for test results. I think once I know I'm pregnant and can start making definite plans, everything will be much better. Now, in spite of all my efforts to think positive, I just feel I'm in limbo."

"I know what you mean. I hate waiting, too." He gave her an understanding smile. "I think your impatience is pretty normal. How long before you'll know for sure?"

"The doctor said he'll run a test on Monday." Monday would be two weeks after the insemination procedure had been done. So far there'd been no sign of her period, which was due any time. Carlys had her fingers crossed for a positive test result.

"Well, there you have it. Now all you have to do is get through tomorrow and the weekend."

She groaned comically, contemplating the next seventy-two hours.

"Cheer up, Carlys, the time will pass faster than you think."

"That's what I keep telling myself. And speaking of the time . . ."

It was after ten, and they both had to work the next day, and even if Jason didn't show it, he had to be tired.

"Talking to you has made me feel better," Carlys confessed softly as they stood together in the darkness, her open car door a wedge between them.

He put his hand on hers, his grip warm and strong. "I'm glad."

"WELL, CARLYS, if this isn't a surprise!" Helen Holt looked up from the newspaper and greeted her daughter warmly as Carlys slipped in the back door on Friday morning. "We haven't had you home for breakfast in weeks."

"You know me." Carlys slid into a chair at the long bleached-oak table. "I have this sixth sense about when Dad's fixing blueberry pancakes."

"Translated, I called her to let her know," Susie put in dryly, bounding down the back stairs. She settled in a seat next to Carlys, and to her father's smile of pleasure, began helping herself to a stack of pancakes. Breakfasting together whenever possible had long been a tradition in their family. They took turns at the daily cooking and cleaning up, since they all worked in the family's various businesses.

Carlys walked over to the stove and let her dad fill her plate, though eating was the last thing she felt like doing. Nerves? she wondered. Or good old morning sickness?

"What are you so happy about, Susie?" Carlys took a sip of coffee and turned the attention back to her sister. "Usually you're a grump in the morning."

"I've got a date with Zach Sullivan tomorrow night. He's taking me to the Spring Fling."

"And who is Zach Sullivan?" Carlys asked her exuberant sixteen-year-old sister. Susie had inherited her mother's blond curly hair, her father's light blue eyes, and the tall, athletic frame sported by everyone in the family. There the resemblance stopped. The baby of the family, Susie was the only Holt remotely interested in going to college—although she still didn't know what she wanted to study. She was the only child to plan to graduate from high school on schedule—the twins and Carlys had all graduated early in order to go to work full-time and pursue their various business interests—and to play a musical instrument—the French horn.

"Zach's a drummer in the school jazz band," George Holt said. Methodically he filled his own plate, switched off the stove and came to sit beside his wife. The more easygoing of the elder Holts, he faced life with a steady equilibrium that Carlys often envied. Nothing shook George for long, not Carlys's artificial insemination, not Susie's latest teenage crisis, whereas her mother was more like Carlys—emotional and outspoken when it came to family matters. They all protected Susie fiercely, so much so that sometimes Carlys thought her baby sister's dates were scrutinized more carefully than a candidate for the CIA—a sentiment Susie echoed. However, knowing her family's nosiness was well intentioned, Susie generally gave out volumes of information on her dates.

"He's also in a rock band," she said, around bites of pancake. She then proceeded to name every member of the rock group and the type of songs they usually played.

"I suppose he's cute, too," Carlys hinted when Susie had at last wound down.

"Exactly my type," Susie agreed, finishing with a glowing portrait: "He's tall, dark and handsome. Smart, too. He's probably going to college on an academic scholarship."

Zach sounded like a dream come true. "Well, then, good luck," Carlys said, satisfied.

"Thanks, Carlys." Finished, Susie got up and gulped down the last of her milk. "Dad, if it's not too much trouble I need a ride to school."

"I'll drop you on my way to the office," George promised.

"Okay." Susie's dishes went into the dishwasher. Clean-up at the Holts' was always a family affair. "Just don't forget I have jazz band rehearsal after school, so I'll be late getting over to the store."

George smiled, sending Helen and Carlys a glance that said I hope I live through this latest boyfriend. "I've already adjusted the schedule," George said mildly, carrying his own dishes to the dishwasher.

"Thanks, Dad." Susie disappeared up the stairs.

"So, have you given any more thought to selling your diaper-service business to that group of investors?" George asked, standing at the counter to take a final sip of coffee. With Carlys his conversations usually centered on business. Unless Carlys came to him directly for advice, he left the heart-to-heart talks to her mother.

He hadn't always been so reserved, Carlys reflected, just since she'd turned thirty. Maybe he didn't know quite what to say to her anymore about her personal life. He seemed to have given up hope she would marry, and though he wasn't happy about Carlys living the rest of her life without a partner, he did accept the idea of her as a responsible, mature person on her own. But she also knew that her father and mother both wished her married.

But that state of affairs seemed as far out of her reach as ever. With a sigh, Carlys concentrated on business and her father's question.

They all knew Carlys became passionately involved only when building a business; once the initial work was done and the venture was established, she lost interest. The diaper service had been doing well for the past year and a half. She could take the money now and run; she hadn't.

"No, Dad, I haven't thought about selling."

"Any reasons why not?" Helen asked, putting her newspaper aside. She was just as ambitious and restless as Carlys, whereas George had operated the same chain of sporting good stores for years.

"I still don't know what I want to replace it with." More startling still, she didn't have a clue to what her next venture would be.

Her father looked amazed. "That's not like you, Carlys. Usually you know months ahead of time what you want to do next. You hardly get started on one project before you're thinking ahead to the next."

"I know." Lately she'd been so busy thinking about babies and families and longing for what she didn't have and wanted very badly that Carlys hadn't given her professional life more than a passing thought. In contrast to single parenthood, her business life had seemed extremely inconsequential. After fifteen years of working she knew she would always be able to support herself, but having a child alone—that was another story entirely.

Susie was back, books under her arm and tapping her foot. George also had to go. Goodbyes were said briskly. The back door slammed. Carlys and Helen were left alone.

Helen got a second cup of coffee, then with her customary directness got straight to the point. "How are you feeling, dear? I notice you haven't eaten much breakfast." Searching her daughter's face, she inquired gently, "Are you pregnant?"

Carlys sighed. After meeting a man like Jason O'Leary, part of her hoped she wasn't pregnant. Part of her still wanted to have her original dream of husband, home and then child, through regular and romantic methods. The more practical part of her wanted very much to be with child, however scientifically the condition had to be accomplished. A miracle was a miracle. A baby was a baby and would be hers to love and to nurture. As for daydreaming about handsome men, she was through with that. She'd done it too often in the past, to no avail. Time after time she'd put her desire for a child on hold, hoped with all her heart the man of the moment was the right one, only to discover later that they were separated by fundamental differences or that the chemistry didn't last. Then she'd feel disappointed and stupid for letting her overactive imagination and wishful thinking steer her into a dead-end reality.

Since she'd decided on artificial insemination, she'd sworn off dating and emotional involvement altogether, figuring she had to do one thing at a time. For

a while that approach had worked very well. But Ja
son's unexpected entry into her life had disrupted her
mood of calm determination. She caught herself wishing that someday she could see him socially. Yet she also
knew intellectually that if she let even one more man,
one more hope of marriage, steer her from her destiny
she'd never forgive herself. She could live without a
steady man in her life, but to give up all hope of a child,
too? No, she wouldn't let that happen. As attractive as
Jason was, as fascinated by him as she was, she had to
be content with having him as a friend. Besides which,
Jason had made it clear he was interested in her as a
friend only.

"I'll know Monday. Right now, I think I'm just too
nervous to eat."

Helen nodded and lifted her coffee cup in a silent
toast. "Well, here's hoping you are pregnant, darling." Her eyes misting up, she said with unexpected
emotion, "This family could use another grandchild."

Carlys blinked, too shocked by her mother's unher-
alded change of heart to say anything for a minute.

She remembered all too well the heated argument
they'd had several weeks previously over her desire to
be artificially inseminated. Since then, as close as she'd
always been to her mother, she'd been almost afraid to
bring the subject up. Helen, knowing there was no
changing Carlys's mind once it was made up, had been
equally close-mouthed.

Finally Carlys sputtered, surprised, "But you
said—"

"I know what I said. I know what your father said.
We've discussed it at length since then and—"

"Mom, please, no more lectures."

"Who said anything about a lecture?"

No one. It was that now, dear, I'm determined to have my say look. "I don't want to fight with you," Carlys insisted stubbornly. Carlys hated fighting with her mother; it always made her feel so unhappy.

"I'm not going to fight with you."

"You say that now, but—"

"Carlys, we were *wrong* not to be more supportive. If you want a baby now and are certain that's the right path to take, then of course—" Helen paused and swallowed hard "—we're happy for you."

Shocked into momentary silence, Carlys studied her mother. "You wouldn't be embarrassed that I'm single and pregnant?"

Helen wouldn't go as far as that. "Well . . ."

"You would be."

"It would be awkward, there's no getting around that. To preserve your reputation we'd almost have to explain."

"And that would bother you, wouldn't it?" Carlys demanded, annoyed that this discussion had been allowed to begin when she and her mother already knew they disagreed radically.

"No. Yes. I don't know. I guess it would bother me having to explain your condition." Silence. "Look, if anyone asks us—" Helen sighed heavily again "—we'll just tell the truth. We'll say that you're a very modern woman who's decided on a very modern medical procedure in order to have a family. The important thing is not what other people think or whether they approve or disapprove, but for you to have a family of your own."

Carlys still couldn't shake the feeling that her mother still disapproved though she seemed so calm, so maternally protective. She was putting on a brave front so as not to hurt her feelings.

They'd never let anything fester between them before, she didn't want to let the problem go now. So much as she hated familial confrontations, she felt she had no choice but to remind her mother of her earlier stand. Better that they should have it out in the open now than let it get worse and come out later, to their even greater distress.

"I thought you said I'd ruin my life if I went ahead with this."

Helen cringed. "You would remind me of that."

"I also seem to remember you saying that if I did this, then I'd never get a man, that raising a child without a father would be unfair to both the child and to me. Have you changed your mind about that, Mom? Because if you have..." Carlys wanted to know, needed to know.

"I'm trying to come to terms with it," Helen said, after a moment, "And I...well, I think I am." Helen thought she'd be able to manage quite well if Carlys would quit pushing her for blanket approval. "So your child won't have a father in residence. Your brothers and father will fill the gap. After all, essentially the situation will be just the same as if you were widowed or divorced. Whether your father and I like it or not, we have to accept that life just isn't predictable. And sad as it makes us both, you just haven't met that special man. Maybe someday you will, I certainly hope so, and I know your father does, too. But there's no point in your putting the rest of your life on hold, waiting incessantly for what might never be." She took a deep breath. "As much as I hate to admit it, Carlys, you were right. Everything you said was true. As your mother, I just haven't wanted to see that the times are changing, that marriage isn't necessarily in the cards for someone your age, and may never be."

Helen stopped at the sight of her daughter's smile, which was strained rather than victorious. Her brows drew together suspiciously as her maternal radar zeroed in on Carlys's peculiarly introspective mood and the probable reasons behind it.

"Darling," she asked after a quiet moment, "is there something wrong? Are you having second thoughts?"

Yes, she was having second thoughts, Carlys admitted to herself with a sigh. And all because of Jason O'Leary and Megan, who had made her remember all her earlier romantic dreams of husband and family. They had made her yearn to find her dream again; not just part of it, but the whole dream. Was it possible Jason might someday translate that dream for her into real life? She didn't know. Finding that out would take time, and time was one commodity she didn't have.

With effort, she pushed the alluring image of Jason from her mind. She gritted her teeth stubbornly, reminding herself that she'd been through all this agony, had fought off fantasy and held on to reality, countless times. She knew better than to let her daydreams guide her life. So dammit, why was she suddenly so confused again? Why the relapse into fruitless yearning? What was wrong with her? Was she so impressionable and easily distracted? Or just too disappointed that she hadn't met her dream man and been swept off to live in some castle and have a dozen, perfect, beautiful, impeccably behaved children?

"Carlys?" Helen's tone was unmistakably worried.

Carlys coasted down to reality.

"I'm not having second thoughts, Mom. I still want a baby more than ever."

She had to put first things first. Having a child alone didn't mean she would never marry. It just meant she would have a child, a family, she would at last have the opportunity to be a mother, to love a child, and be loved in return. She had to hang on to that thought and block out everything else. Nothing else mattered.

"I HOPE YOU DON'T MIND my dropping in," Carlys began informally as Jason opened the door early Saturday afternoon. She held up a typed paper for his perusal. "I brought over a list of baby-sitters for you."

"Hey, great!" Jason said enthusiastically.

"You're sure it's not a bad time?" Carlys knew darn well she should have called ahead, but for reasons she didn't want to explore hadn't done so.

"Not at all. Come on in." His glance moving over her — with mesmerizing intensity, Jason gestured freely toward the living room.

Carlys edged obediently past him. Without warning, despite her previous determination to be sensible, she was acutely aware of him in the age-old man-woman way. And why not? In soft faded jeans and blue denim workshirt, his hair boyishly disordered, he was the epitome of rumpled masculinity. The mossy scent of his after-shave clung to his jaw. He was handsome and approachable, maybe too much so for her own good.

"You've finished unpacking," Carlys noted approvingly as she walked into the living room and admired the cathedral ceiling. The boxes had disappeared, leaving an impression of space. Twin tuxedo sofas in beige, blue and white stripes formed a conversation area in front of the fireplace. The room was well babyproofed. Nothing dangerous or fragile was within Megan's reach. A combination rocker and lounger that she'd bet was

Jason's favorite place for reading and watching television sat in one corner of the room.

"Almost. I have a few cartons to go. I've hidden them all in the guest room."

"You look very pleased with yourself."

"Yeah, I am. I think I set a new record for efficiency, but then I was highly motivated yesterday and today. I wanted to get as much done as possible before I had to go back to work. And then, too, Megan has taken a couple of terrific naps. I guess all this moving business has finally tired her out."

"I'll bet. Speaking of the little darling..." Carlys glanced around inquiringly again. "Where is she now?" The playpen was empty. Jason was speaking in hushed tones.

"Still napping."

"Ah, I should have known." Carlys felt disappointed. Belatedly she realized that her reason for coming over was as much to see his delightful daughter as to see him. "Well, I don't want to intrude, so I'll just leave this list with you and consider my good deed for the day done."

He took the list she pushed at him, then caught her arm before she could do more than pivot toward the door. Surprised by her sudden shyness and unwilling to see her go, he said gently, "Carlys, come on. You don't have to rush off."

Carlys knew that to protect her emotional safety, she should run like the devil. She was breathless, enthralled. "Jason, I—"

"I'm almost done for the day," he continued persuasively, relaxing his light hold on her arm. He moved a casual distance away from her, once again only a friend. "Besides, I could use the break—and the company."

Carlys wondered suddenly what he would look like with his glasses off, then forced a halt to her waywardly romantic thoughts. Struggling to gain time and reestablish her equilibrium, she said admiringly, "Your house looks great."

Exerting all her willpower, she turned her attention back to his surroundings and peered into the den which opened off the living room. "Is this your office?" She stopped in the doorway and took a closer look. The office was simply furnished with a personal computer, several bookshelves, a desk and a comfortable chair. It was safety-gated off so that Megan couldn't possibly get in, which was a wise decision, Carlys decided, looking at the expensive computer, stacks of computer listings, and heavy manuals, not to mention the modem Jason had attached to the phone.

He came over to stand next to her. Despite her determination to calm down, her heartbeat quickened.

"Like it?" Hands on hips, he seemed to be waiting for her answer with real curiosity.

She leaned against the doorway, turning sideways to face him. Damn, but he was sexy! And such a nice man, too. She had trouble swallowing. "Looks ideal." Her voice was unaccountably husky; she had to fight an urge to clear her throat. Was he suddenly thinking of her as a whole lot more than a friend, or was her imagination running away with her again?

"Having an office here in the house is convenient," he continued casually.

"I know what you mean.... I work at home, too." Long seconds passed. He watched her, his eyes never wavering from hers. She hadn't a clue as to what he was thinking.

Eventually, with great reluctance, he ended the staring match and studied the list of sitters she'd thrust at him earlier. "Most of these are married women," he mused, after a moment.

"Or widows. I asked my sisters-in-law. They're very fussy about who they get in to watch their children. They assured me everyone on the list is dependable and very good with kids."

Jason nodded slowly. "Thanks. Ten names." He rattled the paper in his hand appreciatively. "I know how stingy people can be with the name of a good sitter. It must've taken you a while to compile this."

Three quarters of a day spent on the phone, a lot of wooing, a lot of markers called in. But Carlys hadn't minded. The effort had taken her mind off her own dilemma, and in any case she wouldn't have wanted him to leave Megan with just anyone.

She glowed with pleasure at his appreciation. "Don't give it a second thought. As far as I'm concerned it was time well spent. While I was making the calls, I came up with the idea for another business."

He blinked and adjusted his glasses on the bridge of his nose. "You're kidding."

"Dead serious. I have entrepreneurial blood."

Clearly his interest in her deepened immediately. She had an impression that he was so intent on keeping her there, she wouldn't have been able to get out the door if she tried.

"So tell me more about this business." A hand lightly cupping her elbow, he led her over to the sofa.

"It's simple, really." Carlys sat where he directed, aware that her arm was tingling long after he had taken away his hand and that she had that rubbery feeling in her knees again. "More women are in the labor force than ever before. Everyone needs sitters, but there's a shortage of them. Many of the professional services aren't as reliable as one would like. Basically, what parents want is the good old-fashioned quality care for their kids given to them by their grandparents or close relatives and family friends. I'd like to develop a training program for baby-sitters and full- or part-time nannies, and then run a service that people can depend on."

Briefly, some emotion she couldn't quite decipher flickered in his eyes.

"You're ambitious." The words were unexpectedly clipped, his jaw taut.

"Yes, I am," Carlys admitted openly and without apology. Silence fell between them, and she realized from the brooding expression on his handsome face that he had withdrawn into some past or present unhappiness. Was he thinking that his former wife had elected to pursue her career instead of sticking to her husband and raising her daughter? she wondered. If so, she could hardly blame him for looking unhappy. Alice Greenway's decision must have been devastating for him, and maybe someday Megan, too, would feel abandoned, unwanted.

With effort, Jason changed gears. He relaxed against the cushions, draping one arm across the back of the sofa, and recovered his former genial ease. "Well, as a prospective client, let me tell you the idea sounds terrific. I wish you luck with your new venture." His eyes were bright, his smile sincere. "What are you going to call it?"

"Nannies Incorporated, I think. I'll have to see." Ahead of her were months of research and organization. But she could handle them.

In the distance, a baby laughed and banged a rattle against a crib. He stood up. "That's Megan, up from her nap." He made for Megan's room. "Come on in and say hello," he called over his shoulder. "I know she'd love to see you."

Carlys laughed. "The feeling's mutual."

Megan greeted them both with enthusiasm. When she was freshly diapered and clothed, Jason lifted her up in his arms.

Carlys didn't want to leave Jason and Megan, but she had a long list of errands that she'd promised herself she would do. "Well, I'd better get going." Carlys walked with Jason into the living room, very aware of his nearness and Megan's angelic vivacity. "I promised my sister I would help her get ready for a big date."

For a minute he seemed inclined to ask her to stay, but the moment passed. Megan cuddled against her daddy's chest; Jason shifted his daughter affectionately closer. "Thanks again for finding me the sitters," he said genially.

Clearly he wanted to be friends. Carlys was a little disappointed he didn't want more than that, yet she knew that at this point, her life was simply too complicated for anything other than friendship. And if she was pregnant, as she hoped, it was bound to get even more complex. Would Jason be able to handle that?

She wondered. Glancing up at him, she knew she had to ask him. The social embarrassment was going to be hard enough for her to handle without her worrying about important friends. "Do you feel comfortable seeing me, Jason, knowing I might be pregnant?"

"Sure. Why? Is it a problem for you?"

"No."

"Well, good." Megan had been tugging at a lock of his curly brown hair. Gently, he disengaged his daughter's hand, curling his fingers around hers. "After all, we have a lot in common, now that you're going to be a single parent, too."

Carlys smiled. "You're right."

"Friends, then?" He held up his palm to her.

She pressed her fingers to his. "Friends."

Chapter Three

"Bad day?" Jason asked with soft sympathy, looking down into Carlys's pale face. Unless he was mistaken those were tears still drying on her thick blond lashes, and the red nose and puffiness around her eyes indicated she had been weeping a good long while. He wondered what was wrong. Today was to be the day for Carlys's pregnancy test. Could her tears have anything to do with that?

"Oh, Jason, it's everything...." Carlys could manage only a tremulous whisper. She wavered in the doorway, her shoulder sagging weakly against the glossy white frame, the back of her hand pressed to her mouth.

Of all the people to show up on her doorstep early Monday evening, clearly she had not expected him. Jason felt a moment's guilt for not calling, then was glad he hadn't. His heart went out to her. She probably would have begged off if he'd called and she looked as though she'd been through the wringer. He was simply glad he was there for her to lean on.

When she said nothing more, he held out the bunch of daisies in his hand. "I just dropped by to bring you these." Ignoring her embarrassed, averted gaze, he pressed the flowers into her unwilling hand, curling her limp fingers around the stems. Mildly, he continued, "They're a token of our appreciation—Megan's and mine—for all you've done for us. The baby-sitter list you compiled was terrific. In fact, the first sitter on the list, Mrs Fitzgerald, is with Megan now."

Still not quite meeting Jason's gaze, Carlys swallowed hard and forced a smile. "You like Mrs. Fitzgerald, then?"

"Oh, yes. And Megan went to her right away." He paused, shoving his hands into his trouser pockets. "I can't tell you what it means to me to know I have someone to leave Megan with when I need to go out and run a few errands or go in to work unexpectedly for a few hours. A parent's biggest worry is always—" New tears were streaming down Carlys's face.

Jason stopped. "Carlys, what is it?"

Shaking her head in mute denial, she whirled and ran back into the house. Without hesitation, knowing she needed him maybe more than she would admit even to herself, Jason shut the door and followed her.

He found her in the living room. Her back to the room, she was standing in front of glass doors that led out to a patio. Still not acknowledging his presence, though he could tell by the tense set of her shoulders that she knew very well he was there with her, she wiped her eyes with a tissue.

Giving her a moment to compose herself, he surveyed the pretty living room—the white stone fireplace at one end, louvered white wooden shutters covering the windows in lieu of drapes, peach-and-white-flowered tuxedo sofa and two peach wing chairs were grouped around a glass coffee table covered with glossy magazines, plants and silk flower arrangements. Family photos were everywhere.

"I'm sorry." Her voice was muffled by the tissue.

Jason closed the distance between them with slow, sure steps. "Because I saw you crying?" His hands touched her shoulders lightly.

She refused to turn around and resisted his attempt to sway her toward him.

"It's just that I hate weak women!" Self-directed anger laced her voice. "And now I'm acting like such a wimp!"

"Carlys, you're not weak and you're not a wimp."

Silence. "Barren, then."

The shock of what she said made him catch his breath. "Carlys—"

"The test was negative," she interrupted tiredly. "I'm not pregnant."

Which meant, he supposed, with relief, that her emotional condition was temporary, not permanent. "I'm sorry," he said finally.

"So am I." Her voice was thick with tears again. And then she did turn. Without warning, she was in his arms, sobbing as though her heart would break. Unexpectedly Jason felt tears come to his own eyes. He knew what it was like to want a child. Carlys had been counting on being pregnant. Her loss was deep and heartfelt, the phantom child she'd hoped to have irreplaceable except by a very real child. Suddenly, he wanted that for her, wanted it desperately.

And still she cried, the sobs deep and soundless, detectable only from the shaking of her body. He held her wordlessly, his hands moving gently, compassionately over her back, offering what comfort he could. Eventually, a long time later, the storm ended.

Having cried herself out, she pulled away from him slightly.

"Carlys, I meant what I said. I'm sorry the insemination procedure didn't work." Jason draped his arm around her shoulder and held her companionably close, his breath warm against her hair. "I know how much you were counting on it to be successful."

"Too much so, maybe." Shakily she wiped away the last of her tears and smiled weakly. Taking his hand, she led him to the sofa. They sat down a friendly distance away from each other, and after wiping her eyes once again and blowing her nose, Carlys continued knowledgeably, in a much calmer tone, "I keep telling myself I should have been better prepared for this eventuality. My doctor told me at the outset that statistically it takes anywhere from three to six tries before the average woman conceives via artificial insemination." She paused and took another deep wavering breath, all the while mangling the crumpled tissue in her hands. "I guess I was hoping to be one of the lucky ones who manage it the first time out." Frowning, she sighed and corrected herself wearily, "Actually, it went deeper than that. I went in knowing the odds up here." She touched her head. "But in here—" her hand fell to her heart "—I refused even to consider the doctor's warning that the procedure might not work."

"You can try again, though, can't you?" Jason asked, aware that on some level he was as concerned about her conceiving as she. He felt a natural empathy as a parent for what she was going through and would probably go through again in the future.

"Oh, yes. I can try again." Carlys sighed her relief, thankful for that much.

"Are you going to?" He was watching her closely, searching for...he didn't know what, except maybe reassurance that she would somehow find the happiness she deserved to have.

"I think so," Carlys confided cautiously, biting her lip with uncharacteristic uncertainty. "I went ahead and made an appointment, anyway. I've got two weeks to think about it."

Needing for his own reasons—gallantry, ego?—to comfort her, he took her hand in his. Her fingers were cold as ice. Wanting to transfuse some warmth into her, he started to rub them. "You sound like you're having doubts. Why? What's changed for you since the last time we talked?" Perhaps if they discussed her problem on a purely rational level, he could help her. And he really wanted to know.

She gestured limply with her free hand, making no effort to withdraw her other hand from his brotherly ministrations. "Well, for one thing, my parents have never really approved of my decision to be artificially inseminated." She compressed her lips together unhappily.

"So? That didn't bother you yesterday or the day before, when you thought it would take," Jason countered easily, playing the role of devil's advocate. "What's changed? Be honest with me, Carlys. What's going on? Tell me what you're feeling."

Carlys knew she could trust him; yet her next words came with difficulty. "I've started thinking a lot about the biological father. Before...I don't know—I guess I just blocked...him...from my mind."

He hadn't thought much about the donor, either. He paused momentarily, mulling over her problem, then asked, "You don't know who it is that's donating the sperm?"

She shook her head. "No, that was part of the agreement. I knew the sperm was from a healthy doctor or student at the medical school. That was it. That was all I thought I'd need to know then."

He tightened his grip on her hand, feeling unexpectedly tender and protective, not altogether what he would feel for any female in need. The feeling was different. How, precisely, he couldn't say. After the hellish years of his marriage, the hurt of having his wife put everything and everyone ahead of him, he wasn't anxious to repeat his failure or even attempt to get involved with a woman again, casually or deeply. Yet, like it or not, he was very attracted to her physically. But it was an attraction he had no plans to move on. Her friendship and her companionship were what he considered vital.

Abandoning self-analysis, Jason turned all his concentration on Carlys. "You're worried about medical history, is that it? Do you think that the baby might inherit some genetic problem or familial disease?"

"No, they assured me that was fine." Now she became aware of the daisies she had dropped on the coffee table and traced a petal lovingly with her fingertip. "I guess it was seeing you with Megan that made me really start to think. She adores you, Jason. I feel guilty realizing I'll never be able to provide my baby with a father, never be able to talk about him—not even a picture. And it—well, suddenly my idea of family just seemed so empty, so...lacking. Still, I was determined to continue with my plan." She took a deep, emotion-filled breath. "Then I went to the doctor, found out the results, and—well, you know the rest. I haven't been able to stop crying since. The result of too much anticipation, I guess. Too much emotional stress."

"I've had periods of guilt, too, Carlys, for not providing Megan with a full-time, live-in mother."

"But she's so happy!" Carlys protested, overcome by a fresh flood of tears.

"Right. And so would your child be." He paused long enough to let his argument sink in, knowing Carlys didn't need persuading as much as simple reassurance that she was doing the right thing.

"So you'll know little about the biological father," he continued. "That doesn't mean you won't marry someday—"

At that, Carlys laughed humorlessly. "Please, let's not kid ourselves, Jason." Her eyes met his directly. "The simple fact is that available men are getting scarcer all the time. Even the magazine articles say so."

"Not all of them say that," he disagreed. "On the contrary, some articles, the more reputable ones, in my opinion, say the doom-and-gloom headlines are irresponsible and misleading." Her brow furrowed, and he explained the depth of his knowledge dryly. "I read the women's magazines when I'm standing in the grocery line." And he had been secretly rather pleased, from a strictly vain point of view, to find himself in a supposedly shrinking pool. However, he hadn't taken those statistics to heart. "Personally, I can't believe there are any fewer available men than there are available women. Now, it could be true that both groups are shrinking in size. Most of the people of my age that I know are married."

"Exactly my point, Jason. I've spent the last fourteen years waiting for Prince Charming to come along, and he hasn't appeared. Whether I want to face it or not—and believe me, I don't—I can't base my life anymore on the hope that someday miraculously everything will work out." She crossed her arms at her waist and hugged herself defensively. "I've done that too many times for too many years already, and I'm no closer to getting a family of my own. I want children, a sense of family, even if I don't have it via the regular route."

"Then go for it."

"I would, I will. Except for the—"

"Question of the biological father." He paused. "Is it really that important to you?"

"How could it not be? Jason, could you really imagine having a child with a stranger? The more I think about it, as much as I want a child, I can't *help* having second thoughts."

"Are you thinking of abandoning the idea altogether?"

"Yes—no—I don't know." She stood up and started to pace the room restlessly, admitting finally, "If I do decide to go through it again, I guess I'm just going to have to accept the limitations and think of this child as strictly my own."

"Can you do that?" Jason had to ask the question for her sake. It was crucial for Carlys to understand and accept beforehand what she was getting into. If she didn't, and went ahead anyway, the results for both the child and for her could be disastrous.

"I don't know," Carlys said finally. "I guess I still have some soul searching to do."

Silence fell between them. "If talking to me is circumventing that . . ." Jason said, not liking the anxious look on her tear-swollen features or his own feeling of helplessness.

"No," she was quick to respond. "I need someone impartial and uninvolved to talk to. Please. Stay just a while longer."

"I'm glad to help," he replied honestly, only too glad to be able to repay her for all the aid she had already given to him.

Carlys made some coffee and they talked for over an hour.

When he left her, she was much calmer. Although still undecided about what she was going to do, she had stopped crying and on the surface at least had quelled her disappointment to a manageable level.

Try as he might, Jason couldn't get Carlys's problem off his mind. Over the course of the week that followed, he thought about it while he did the dishes, when he rocked Megan to sleep, when he got her up in the morning. He thought about it every time he saw a little of his former wife's *joie de vivre* in Megan's face, heard his own laugh echoed in hers, saw Alice looking out of the blue eyes. Whether anyone wanted to admit it or not, and he felt that few people were actually frank enough to do so, part of the joy of raising a child was in seeing the inherited similarities, in discovering which traits had been passed on and which hadn't. While adopting a child was wonderful, it couldn't possibly compare with raising a child who was biologically part of the parent. For Carlys to miss the experience because of reservations about the donor was unthinkable. Yet short of donating the sperm himself, he couldn't see any way...

Why not?

There were countless reasons why not, he counseled himself, more than a little irritated he was even thinking this way, number one being that Carlys would want to raise the child alone, or at least with no paternal interference. Could he handle not seeing, not knowing his own child? Realistically? He doubted it very much. On the other hand, should there prove to be a way for him to share in a mutual offspring's life without interfering unduly...

The idea had possibilities.

He was crazy as hell.

He was ... intrigued.

"HI, JASON, I'll be ready to go in a minute." Despite her impeccable manners, Carlys was unable to prevent herself from shooting him a curious if friendly second look before going in to get her purse.

Following her in, Jason knew how she felt. His behavior *was* odd. They hadn't talked in a week, yet he'd called and asked her to dinner, friend to friend, in a grown-ups-only setting. Sounding more cheerful than the last time he'd seen her, she'd hesitated only momentarily before agreeing to go, yet he knew she had questions. Was this a date? An attempt to ease into dating? Something more? Something important?

If she only knew, Jason thought wryly, aware that his mouth was a bit grim around the edges, how crucial this evening might later prove for both of them.

Blissfully unaware of the magnitude of his thoughts, Carlys was distractedly choosing which things to transfer from a handbag to a small evening purse. Keys, compact, lipstick, billfold...two rather crumbled looking tissues...

"Just one minute more."

"Take your time," Jason said. Suddenly he found he wasn't in any hurry. She looked so ravishing in the demure black evening dress, sheer dark stockings and heels. With her hair soft and loose, her cheeks and eyes aglow, she'd never looked more stunning.

"There, all done." She snapped shut the clasp on her purse and faced him with a smile, her eyes scanning him with the same veiled appreciation that he'd been bestowing on her.

He relaxed, letting her satisfy her curiosity and get a view of him in formal clothes. In dark suit and tie, he knew he looked his best. He'd spent half an hour making himself ready, all in preparation for the talk they were going to have.

"If I didn't know better, I'd think you had something up your sleeve."

If only she knew, Jason thought on a wave of uncertainty.

She stopped unexpectedly at the door. Her eyes were soft, serious, affectionate. "However, I know you're just trying to cheer me up, because of the disappointment and doubts I had last week." In a low voice and with a slightly formal tone she continued, "Your efforts mean more to me than I can say. I want you to know that." Before he could respond with a suitable disclaimer that didn't disavow his friendship, she stood on tiptoe and brushed her lips against his cheek.

He wasn't prepared for the desire he felt at her soft, fleeting touch. For a moment, he was stunned, confused. His heart pounding, he wondered briefly if he should either amend what he was going to say or better yet forget the whole plan.

What? Are you crazy? Forget everything because of one little flash of desire? Face it, Jason, you've been living like a monk. This reaction is probably long overdue and more physical than emotional.

Desire was fleeting. A child was permanent, an endless source of love given and returned. He had only to remember that, and her yearning for a child of her own, to go on.

He waited until they were seated at a secluded table in the best restaurant in Dallas and the wine poured before he laid his thoughts before her. "I've been thinking about what you said about not knowing the father. I've been thinking about my wish to have another child, too, and about Megan needing a brother or sister." He paused and took a deep breath. "Carlys, would you consider having my baby?"

Chapter Four

Carlys was speechless, more pale, more shocked than he'd ever seen her.

He rushed into his explanation. "I know this sounds impulsive on my part. I assure you it isn't. I've given it a lot of thought. I'm willing to act as the donor, but only on one condition, that you let me be part of the child's life in a limited way." He held up his hand before she could protest, continuing convincingly, "I'm not asking you to marry me. I'm realistic enough to know that would never work. But if we could somehow share the child a little bit—if I could be given some visitation rights, see the child on some holidays and birthdays, let the child know Megan, it would mean so much to me and to her."

Carlys was silent after he'd finished. Her eyes were huge and soft in the candlelight. He noticed she wasn't refusing outright, as he had half feared she might.

"Why would you do this for me?" she asked finally, tapping her fingers against the edge of the table.

"Because I know how much you want a child." Because he wanted her to have the same chance to parent he'd been given. Because he felt sorry for her and wanted to help.

"And that's all?" She searched his face for clues. "That's the only reason?"

"I'd like to have another child. Son or daughter, I'd feel equally blessed. I know I couldn't take care of two small children full-time and work to support us, so there'd be no question of my asking for custody. You'd be sole guardian of the child at the outset. And just so there'd be no confusion later on, we'd sign papers beforehand that would spell this out legally along with the limited visitation rights. As I plan to stay in Dallas permanently and you live here, too, we could see each other and make visits easily. We'd also both have back-up support if we needed it. And I know a child of ours would be loved and cared for."

She sat back, thoughtful. "What if the artificial insemination continues not to work?" As she spoke of the possibility of failure, her voice was tense, nervous.

Jason shrugged. "Then it doesn't. I'm willing to try as long as you are." He remembered the depth of her pain when she'd found out she wasn't pregnant before. His demeanor gentled as he thought of the joy a child could bring. "Carlys, I think you owe it to yourself to give the artificial insemination a chance to work."

She smiled faintly, lowered her eyes and fingered the spoon beside her plate. "That's what the doctor said."

"I don't expect an answer tonight."

She grinned and let out an unsteady breath. "Good thing. I don't think I could give you one." Her eyes met his.

There was a silence in which their vulnerability—their proposed vulnerability to each other—became apparent. It wasn't an unpleasant sensation, certainly not the uneasiness he generally felt when confronted with loss of control, especially in questions concerning his child.

Jason wondered at the depth of his sympathy for Carlys, the ease and speed with which they had become close. What was different about this woman? What made their relationship different from the other friendships and love affairs he'd had in the past, all unsatisfying? Perhaps the difference lay in their being friends first and only friends, perhaps in her being such a caring individual, so generous when it came to giving herself, so easy with children, so clearly enamored of Megan. He knew instinctively that she would make a caring and compassionate mother, and by the same token, an equally fair coguardian to a mutual child. Whatever happened, Carlys wouldn't shut him out of his child's life.

He broke into her thoughts gently. "You would need to decide before the next scheduled artificial insemination."

"I agree. This isn't something that can be left unresolved for very long." Her head lifted. Serious and excited, she looked as though she was already making lists of pros and cons. Smiling, maybe already knowing in her heart what her answer would be, she asked softly, "Would tomorrow be soon enough?"

For a moment he was so surprised and relieved by her receptive reaction that he couldn't speak. She'd expressed no aversion, had not been insulted at the idea. He reached across the table to link hands with her. There was no suppressing his joy. "Tomorrow would be fine."

LONG HOURS LATER, Carlys was still awake, her mind awhirl with thoughts. She'd been both stunned and touched by Jason's offer to help her have a child. She'd known he understood her and her desire to have a child of her own, married or not; indeed from the very beginning they'd seemed to have an enviable sympathy that extended to almost every aspect of their lives. But for him to be willing to go through the difficult, possibly embarrassing procedure of artificial insemination with her, for him to give his heritage, his life, himself, was truly an extraordinary act on his part. Yes, Jason was a very special man, a friend to treasure. And he'd come into her life at exactly the right time.

Of course, Carlys reasoned, he would benefit from the arrangement, too. He would have another child, possibly even a son. And her child would have a flesh-and-blood father, a role model, two nurturing parents.

Truly, Jason's proposal was a dream come true. It eliminated the need for an anonymous donor and hence the majority of her worries. To know he would share the experience with her made her feel less alone. Furthermore, he understood her need to satisfy her parents.

Carlys knew she'd be a fool to refuse him; and she'd never been a fool.

"I'VE DECIDED to accept your offer," Carlys told Jason the next evening.

His face lit up with the intensity of his pleasure. "That's great, Carlys, really great." Impulsively, he threw his arms around her and gave her a hug. She returned his embrace happily. He could feel the life brimming in her, the excitement, the hope for the future. Though not surprised by her answer, he still had to be sure she wouldn't change her mind. Releasing her, he said slowly, searching her face, "You're certain this is what you want?"

"Yes." Carlys nodded, moving away from him slightly. Her arms were folded at her waist, her posture defiantly erect. "I want a child. Knowing you'll be the biological father takes away the majority of my fears."

"Just the majority, hm?" Jason teased, dropping relievedly onto the sofa.

Carlys colored slightly but responded with a laugh. To Jason her husky laughter was a warm and welcoming sound in the sleeping-child silence of his house. Neither of them could stop grinning now that the decision had been made.

"A little worry is good for the soul. Keeps you on your toes."

"Well, heaven knows we only want what's best for you." He cleared his throat. "Have you told your folks? Are you going to?"

Carlys sobered immediately. "I think it's best if I—we—level with everyone from the outset, so yes, I do plan to tell them."

"You're probably right," he agreed after a thoughtful moment. "How long are you going to wait?"

"I plan to talk to my folks later this evening." With Susie out on a date, tonight was the perfect time for her to talk to them alone, without interruption.

"Want me to go with you?" Jason asked.

"No. I'll go it alone."

Another pause. "How do you think they're going to take it?"

"The truth?" Carlys gave a perplexed sigh. "I don't know."

Jason had a feeling that Carlys feared the worst, but as she was determined to handle her mother and father herself, he had no choice but to let her go alone. "You'll call me if you need me? I mean it. I can get a sitter, or your parents can come here."

"I will, but I doubt it will be necessary," Carlys said, searching through her handbag for her car keys.

"Just as long as you know I'm here for you."

Carlys looked up, her face aglow with the radiance of an angel. "I do."

"YOU CAN'T BE SERIOUS!" George Holt said, a scant hour later, his appalled, incredulous tone making Carlys wish she'd taken Jason up on his offer or waited until after her pregnancy was a fact before making her announcement.

Helen was as white as a sheet. "Carlys, being artificially inseminated with sperm from a sperm bank is one thing, but to have a child with a man you barely know, that's insanity, bound to cause all sorts of problems later on. Why—"

Knowing how long-winded her mother could be when upset, Carlys cut her off with an urgent wave of her hand. "Don't you see? That's the beauty of it. We're not emotionally involved. We're just friends." In Carlys's view, that made everything so much simpler.

"You won't be 'just friends' for long if you have a child together," George prophesied curtly.

"What's that supposed to mean?" Carlys shot back, aggravated by her father's resistance to what she felt was a terrific idea.

"Having a child together brings you closer together," Helen intervened smoothly.

"Well, then, that'll be nice," Carlys said finally.

"What happens if he changes his mind later and decides to take the child from you?" George asked.

"He won't do that. We've already agreed that I will have full custody of the child, he will have visitation rights, and we'll sign legal papers to that effect before the child is born.''

"He might change his mind later, once he sees the baby in your arms or his," Helen countered quietly.

Carlys felt a moment's unease; determinedly she pushed it away. She wasn't going to let her parents talk her out of this. "I think that's unlikely, Mother. As I said, he already has an eighteen-month-old child and he has his hands full just working and taking care of Megan." Besides, she trusted Jason to keep his word to her. He was an honorable man. Her instincts about people rarely failed her.

"Then why would he want another child?" George asked.

"Because this is the only way he can have one. Don't you see? We're in the same boat, both of us unmarried, both of us wanting children."

"I still don't like it," George harumphed, packing tobacco into his pipe.

Helen looked equally dissatisfied, but maybe because of her earlier arguments with her daughter—arguments that had driven them apart—she was more willing to look for a compromise solution. "I suppose if we met him . . ." she suggested, frowning thoughtfully.

Carlys was quick to agree. "I'll bring him over." Thank goodness Jason had missed this first go-round, otherwise he might have been scared off. In his position Carlys knew darn well she would have retreated in the face of such hostility.

"Let's make it soon, tomorrow maybe," George decreed.

Helen agreed with her husband's unusually imperious request, giving Carlys no chance to hedge. "I think that would be wise, dear. The sooner we can arrange a meeting, the better.''

Carlys let out her breath, suddenly aware she'd been holding it in her lungs for far too long. "All right," she said finally, looking from the face of one concerned parent to the other. She knew when she had no choice. "I'll bring him over tomorrow."

"YOU SURE ARE BRAVE, Carlys, bringing Jason over to meet the Big Meanies."

Carlys grinned at the name the two sisters had coined years ago for their thirty-six year old twin brothers, Matt and Mark. Built like linebackers, the two had managed to scare off or turn off every one of the males Carlys and Susie had brought home to meet the family. The girls were used to their big brothers' affectionately motivated interference, even in some limited instances had enjoyed watching them in action, but there were also times when they tired of the twins' inherent machismo and wished for a little brotherless peace.

"I figured it was now or never."

"Yeah, but considering what the two of you... well... you know..."

"The fact that we're going to have a child together?" Carlys sighed. "We figure it'll be easier in the long run if we just talk about everything openly now, even though it's tough for both of us."

"I guess so." Susie slanted a glance over her shoulder. "The twins have taken it well, don't you think?"

Knowing Matt and Mark, Carlys could imagine how they would be behaving if they'd taken it badly. They were Neanderthals compared with her father. "I don't know how they reacted. I wasn't here when Mom and Dad told them."

"Yeah, but you saw them soon afterward. They didn't say *anything*."

"That's what worries me." Carlys stopped distributing napkins around the table. "They've always been so traditional, you know, almost a throwback to our grandparents' generation. And for them not to even try and talk me out of it . . . It's weird."

"Do you *want* them to talk you out of it?" Susie asked.

"Mercy, no. It's just . . . I don't trust this calmness of theirs. I would've half expected them to be reading Jason the riot act for even agreeing to think about helping me out."

"And they aren't."

"No." Carlys wandered over to the window. She could see Jason talking genially to the twins as if the three of them were old friends. To her surprise, her brothers seemed to like him.

Perhaps everything would work out after all. Bored with dwelling on her problems, she turned to Susie. "Enough about me. How was your date with Zach Sullivan last night?"

"Dreamy."

"Going to see him again?"

"I hope so."

"If he makes you happy, then I hope so, too." Carlys gave her a hug.

"So what do you think of Jason?" Carlys asked her mother later, while they were carrying the dinner into the dining room.

"He's very nice. And his daughter Megan is adorable."

"I like him," George Holt added cautiously.

"Then you approve of my decision to have a child with him?" Carlys asked evenly.

George and Helen exchanged a glance. "Give us time," her mother urged honestly.

Carlys nodded, a little disappointed that her parents hadn't given her their blessing, yet knowing how protective they were of her and all their children, she wasn't surprised.

"What I don't understand," Matt said, walking in the door with Jason and Mark, "is why the two of you don't get married first if you're so hot on the idea of having a child together."

So here it came, what Carlys and Susie had both been expecting all along, the attempt to get Carlys in line.

Leave it to her brother to make mincemeat out of a social situation that should have been handled with kid gloves, Carlys thought, blushing. But then she should have expected that. Matt was the more aggressive of the two brothers and was always the first to jump into everything, whether it be a swimming pool or a race. Mark, on the other hand, stood back a bit, watched for a while, and then had his say—usually just as bluntly, to Carlys's dismay.

"We're not doing what's normal—that is, getting married—because we're not having the baby the normal way," Jason said with a grin.

Carlys sighed her relief. She had to hand it to Jason. He was handling all this so well, including an hour-long game of volleyball with her brothers, their children, and their wives in the backyard.

"We know that," Mark said, picking up where his twin had left off. "It's just… Don't you want your child to have your name?" He looked pointedly at Jason.

"Mark, Matt, I know you mean well, but I don't want to get into this now," Carlys said quietly.

"I think I'll help with the children's dinner in the kitchen," Helen said, fading out of the room. Susie followed, leaving Jason, Carlys, her father and her brothers facing one another. In the room beyond, culinary commotion and laughter reigned, drowning out the silence in the dining room.

Mark was the first to understand the depth of her dismay. As was his habit, he jumped to Carlys's defense first and urged his brother to back off. "Look, Carlys's right. This is none of our business."

"Who says it isn't?" Matt turned on him. Strong and square-jawed, he looked like a Nordic giant in jeans and a striped rugby shirt. "Carlys is our sister."

"And she's old enough to make up her own mind," Mark countered, lacing a protective arm about Carlys's shoulder. "Besides—" he lowered his voice to a tactful rumbling whisper that the whole room could hear "—it's not surprising she wouldn't want to jump into marriage. You know how upset she was over Drake.".

Jason's eyes widened. Carlys knew Mark was trying to help, but his mention of her former fiancé made her want to fall through the floor.

Mark continued persuasively, "It's only natural she'd want to take her time, be supercautious. If I'd been through the humiliation of being left at the altar—"

"All right, guys! Enough!" Carlys snapped, her face flaming scarlet. She clenched her jaw and took in a tormented breath. "Jason isn't interested in this."

But he was; his expression said so.

Matt and Mark exchanged stunned glances. Her father coughed delicately.

Matt continued with his usual lack of finesse, like an elephant tramping through a flower garden, "You mean you haven't told him?"

"No. And I—"

"All right." Helen came through the door with a smile, a platter of barbecued beef in her hands. "The children are all settled." Her daughters-in-law followed with Jell-O, potato and tossed salads. "It's time we sat down and ate, too."

Matt's wife, Mary, smiled. "Before the munchkins are up and about again."

"You'll get no argument from me there," Jason concurred, with a backward glance at the living room and the playpen where Megan still slept. He didn't look at Carlys; but he still wanted to know about Drake.

Carlys felt Jason was getting to know everything negative about her first: how overprotective her family could be, how ineffectual she could be about heading them off, and now he'd see her a jilted woman, too. Bad enough to have a humiliating romantic past without having to talk about it.

"Shall we be seated?" Helen said, taking her place at the head of the table.

George faced her at the opposite end. "Absolutely. Matt, would you say grace?"

"So who was Drake?"

"I knew you were going to ask that," Carlys said a few hours later at Jason's house. Megan had awakened long enough to eat dinner, play her heart out with the other children, make it home, get bathed and tucked into bed. Not surprisingly, Jason had asked Carlys to stay, ostensibly to talk about her family's reaction to him. As yet, that hadn't even come up.

"He left you at the altar?"

"Yes." Carlys looked away. What a nightmare that had been!

"Look, if you don't want to talk about it, I won't pry."

"I don't, to be truthful." But she also knew that Matt and Mark were bound to bring the story up again in their version. She'd rather Jason heard her version first. "But you might as well know all about it. Now that we're going to be mother and father to the same child, I doubt we'll have many secrets from each other."

"I hope not." He waited, relaxed and patient as always, making it easier for Carlys to begin. "I was twenty-six when I met Drake. He was a CPA and successful in his own right, but never as successful financially as I was. Still, we had a lot in common. We were both interested in the stock market, we liked to play racquetball. He was very charming. He did and said all the right things. He knew all the right romantic moves to make, and I...I guess a part of me needed that." She'd needed to feel feminine and alluring, and for a while, despite all their problems, Drake had given her that. She'd mistaken physical passion for love. "The twins never liked him, though. They thought he was a jerk. From the start they did everything possible to scare him off and dissuade me from marrying him."

"But everything failed?"

"Drake didn't like being...bullied, if that's what it was. I'm not really sure. They were just protective, just trying to find out what kind of man Drake really was." Beneath the surface ease, Drake hadn't had a lot of depth to his character. It had taken years and a lot of pain for Carlys to grow up enough to realize that.

"It's easy to see how much your brothers care about you," Jason commented encouragingly. "Personally, I think you're lucky to have such a caring family."

"Thanks." Carlys sighed and ran a hand through her hair. Back to Drake. "Anyway, we were engaged for two years."

"That's rather a long time for an engagement, isn't it?" Jason interrupted.

Carlys held back a wry grin. "That's what the twins thought." And secretly so had she. She'd wanted to be married right away. "But Drake wanted everything to be just so before we got married. He thought it would be easier."

Jason watched her closely. "And that didn't bother you?"

"Yes and no. I was so aggravated by the twins' disapproval. I figured time would ease their objections."

"It didn't?"

"How did you guess? No, it didn't, not at all. I don't know... Maybe if they had resisted my marrying Drake less vehemently, I wouldn't have been so determined to have him."

The corners of Jason's mouth curled up; his brown eyes glimmered with amusement and understanding of her stubborn, one-track, thoroughly romantic nature. "You had your doubts all along, though, didn't you? You knew it was wrong."

Just as he'd known his marriage to Alice would never work. "In my heart I guess I did," Carlys said softly. "I just couldn't admit it to myself." That was a bleak, roller-coaster time in her life. Up one minute, as she planned the ceremony and the details of the honeymoon and reception, down the next as she tried to please her fiancé. "Drake asked a lot of me. He felt that in a marriage one person had to be boss—president of the company, if you will, and the other, vice president. I wasn't convinced of that. I didn't see why we couldn't be equal partners, with me overseeing the details of one area, he the details of another. But . . . I was young and in love, I thought, and ready to do anything to make him happy. He wanted his career to take precedence over mine. I sold a business to make him happy." She stopped as the bile rose in her throat. "I tried to make myself less so that he could be more. The funny thing is, I really thought I'd done it. I'd reduced my income to a third less than his, which was in retrospect a very stupid thing to do. I bowed to his every wish. And still he was uneasy all the time, not comfortable around my family or friends. That should have clued me in but it didn't." And she'd been so miserable, more miserable than she'd ever been in her life, before or since.

"What happened?" Jason watched her with compassion, all trace of humor gone.

Carlys related curtly, "He backed out the morning before the wedding. I knew something was wrong at the rehearsal. I thought it was nerves. I was wrong. He came to me in tears and told me he couldn't go through with it. He told me he didn't love me and he didn't think I really loved him, that we were just doing what we thought we should be doing at that point in our lives. The really sad part was he was right. We both wanted marriage and a family so much that if he hadn't come to me and told me his feelings, I would have married him."

"And lived to regret it."

"And divorced."

"His ending everything at the last minute must've been very hard on you."

"It was. You can't imagine the half of it. My parents and I had to make all the calls. We had to tell guests the wedding was off. We had to return all the gifts."

"What about Drake? Didn't he help in all this?"

"He'd been too afraid, too humiliated. He told his family, and that was about it. My brothers wanted to kill him."

"I can imagine." Jason seemed to share the sentiment.

"Anyway, Drake was smart enough not to hang around. He left town shortly thereafter and took a job at his firm's branch in Chicago."

"Have you heard from him since?"

"No, and I don't want to."

"I'm sorry he put you through that."

Carlys sighed wearily and forced herself to look at the bright side. "At least I learned what I don't want."

"And that is?"

"A marriage for all the wrong reasons. I played a part in the fiasco, too. I never should have agreed to marry him just to get married, to have a family. As soon as I had the feeling that something was wrong, I should have backed out."

Jason nodded, agreed, shrugged. "Hindsight is always better."

"True." She looked down briefly. "So. What do you think of my family?" After the way Matt and Mark had acted she would hardly be able to blame him if he wanted to cut and run.

The corners of Jason's mouth twitched, "Your brothers play a helluva volleyball game."

Talk about self-restraint! Jason qualified for sainthood. "You probably noticed they're, uh, resistant to the idea of our procreating scientifically."

Jason took off his glasses and tossed them onto the coffee table. With finger and thumb he rubbed the bridge of his nose. "Yeah, I noticed."

The low, thoroughly male laughter reminded Carlys that the more time she spent with Jason, the more susceptible to him she became. As it was, she'd known him—what?—a couple of weeks, and already she was imagining something more than a practical arrangement.

"But if you think that's bad, just imagine what they'd think of the romantic alternative," he said dryly.

Carlys burst into helpless laughter. No way would her brothers go for that. No, given a choice, she was sure they would opt for the scientific alternative for her, rather than an illicit affair with pregnancy in mind. "Good point, Jason. Remind me to bring that up the next time we see them."

"Oh, please, spare us that," he groaned, and they burst into a second round of laughter.

As they subsided into cozy companionship, Jason assured her confidently, "Don't worry about your brothers. They'll come around."

"What makes you think so?" Carlys asked, with only half her attention on the question. She had wanted to know what Jason looked like without his glasses. Now she could see more clearly the precise strength of the bones and his eyes' velvety depth.

"Because they love you, and they want to make you happy."

"Then you weren't put off by their meddling?" Carlys asked, holding her breath as she waited for his answer.

Jason linked hands with her to seal their partnership in the venture. "At this stage, nothing could discourage me. Not wild horses. Not Matt and Mark."

Carlys sighed her relief. Her hand tightened within the warm circle of his, "I feel exactly the same." Exactly...

Chapter Five

"Nervous?" Jason asked as they walked into the doctor's office.

"A little," Carlys admitted, glad he was with her. This appointment was more nerve-racking to her than the first, maybe because she had so much at stake now, maybe because she wasn't the only person involved anymore, the only person who might be disappointed. And maybe because she'd begun to want to have Jason's child more than she had expected she would. Catching his solicitous glance, she forced a courageous smile. "How about you? How do you feel?"

"I think extremely nervous about covers it." Jason clenched and unclenched his hands at his sides. He leaned toward her and whispered in her ear. "I feel the way I did on my first job interview."

"That bad." His breath was a warm caress on her cheek. Suddenly Carlys's heart was beating wildly. It was Jason who was shredding her nerves, not altruistic concern for his possible disappointment.

"That weird." He checked her with another glance before signing in for them both on the tablet next to the receptionist's window. Finished, he took her elbow lightly and escorted her to a quiet corner of the small waiting room, adding casually, "And that assured everything will work out for us in the end."

"I hope so," Carlys said nervously, smoothing her skirt over her knees. If the tension she felt today was any indication, she didn't think she could stand a second attempt.

As it turned out, she needn't have worried. Her doctor reported to her that Jason had done his part routinely and without a hitch, and her insemination minutes later in a separate examining room via sterile syringe was as quick and painless as a pap smear. After the insemination, the doctor placed a plastic-covered sponge, similar in size and feeling to a tampon, in her vagina to help the sperm stay in place. For thirty minutes afterward, she remained on the examining table. With instructions to remove the sponge after twelve hours, she was permitted to dress and go home.

Jason met her in the reception room. She hadn't seen him since they'd parted for their separate examining rooms. He looked fine. He didn't seem to like the way she looked, however.

"Do you feel all right?" he asked, cupping a protective hand beneath her elbow and leading her out to his car. His movements were easy, almost fluid. In contrast, Carlys felt as though she was wobbling along on a shaky pair of stilts.

"You look a little pale."

She felt pale. But she insisted, "I'm fine." She wouldn't embarrass them both by behaving like a ninny. She absolutely would not burst into tears, which were close to the surface for reasons she couldn't begin to fathom. After all, wasn't this what she had wanted? She was happy about the possibility of having Jason's child.

So why was she feeling so weepy, so weak and ineffectual, almost let down?

The hand closed caressingly around her flesh. His eyes darkened to the brown of bitter chocolate. His features were softened by the depth of his concern. "You're not in pain?"

She blinked, shutting her eyes briefly against the dazzling sunlight, against all the emotions she saw in his face. He cared about her, friend to friend, as potentially the mother of his child, but that was all, she reminded herself firmly. And with what they were doing, that was all there could ever be between them. Friendship. Anything else was just too complicated.

But what did she *want*? She'd started out wanting a friend. Somewhere along the line, bit by bit, that had begun to change. She still wanted Jason as a friend but she also wanted a deeper level of intimacy between them, a closeness that wouldn't be erased by time or other changes in the fabric of their lives. So why did that suddenly seem impossible? Because what she was describing was halfway between friend and lover? Or because she was also almost unconsciously beginning to hunger for a physical intimacy, too. If only she could be sure she wouldn't alienate him by a hug or a touch. If only she could be sure he felt the same, as she sometimes suspected he did, for however brief a moment....

Jason was still waiting for a reply. "No," she said, swallowing hard around the sudden huskiness in her voice. "I'm not having any discomfort. I'm just a little tired, the result of all the excitement, I guess."

"It was an ordeal for you, wasn't it?"

Yes. "Wasn't it for you?"

He let the silence stretch a little before his eyes met hers directly. His smile was slow in coming, but heart-warming when it appeared. "Not exactly the way I thought I'd be having another child, if I'd ever have one," he admitted with rueful finality.

Carlys nodded wearily. "I know what you mean."

His eyes twinkled. "But this way was probably quicker."

"True." Quicker and passionless. A fresh wave of disappointment rushed through her with tidal force. She looked down and away to hide from him the dejection she knew showed in her face.

"Ready to go?"

When she didn't look at him immediately, he touched her shoulder lightly.

She pivoted toward him. Her head tilted back.

For a second, she thought—hoped—he would take her into his arms and just hold her close. If she'd ever needed to be held, this was the moment. But the second passed and he didn't.

So they were friends. Good friends to be sure, but that was all.

"Yes, let's go," Carlys said, forcing a smile.

Traffic was heavy. Consequently, they said little on the drive home. Gallantly, he insisted on seeing her into her house. As they entered her foyer and shut the door behind them, Carlys's feelings about his chivalry were mixed. Part of her wanted to be fussed over, the other half wanted to be left alone to come to terms with her sudden confusion, her surprising feeling of vulnerability. And not just to Jason, but to the whole world.

"You're sure you're okay?" he said, unwilling, unable to leave her.

"I'm fine, Jason." *Depressed, but fine.*

"Carlys, I can tell something's wrong. If you'd just level with me—"

She could have taken anything but tenderness at that moment; tenderness was her undoing. To her dismay, she felt tears welling up in her eyes, brimming over onto her cheeks. There was no way he could ignore them or she could hide her humiliation. She was crying again. Carlys, who never ever cried! And certainly not in front of any man! Hand to her mouth, she turned away just as her control broke and a low, anguished sob escaped her throat. In an attempt to regain at least surface composure, she held her back rigidly straight. Yet the tears she'd been withholding all afternoon poured in rivulets down her cheeks, dripped over her chin, and soaked into the collar of her blouse.

In one fluid step Jason reached her, turning her and pressing her against him. His voice was a low soothing lullaby to her ravaged nerves. "Hey...hey, it's okay. Carlys, you can talk to me." When she would have pulled herself away, his arms were wrapped more tightly around her. He drew her against his chest possessively, his body warm and solid against hers. She felt the depth of his masculine determination to help, and her shyness fled in the wake of such strength. It had been so long since she'd let herself lean on anyone else, so long since anyone had offered to stand by her, and never so unconditionally.

He murmured against her hair, "You can tell me what's wrong." Leaning back, he tucked a finger under her chin, forcing her to look at him directly. "And don't you dare try and deny it again! There is something wrong or you wouldn't be crying."

Carlys got hold of herself with effort. The tears halted momentarily. Jason released her slowly.

"I'm not sure I can explain—"

"Try." His low tone brooked no argument.

"All right." She supposed she owed him at least that much. Wordlessly, she led him into the living room and sat down on the sofa. He sat beside her, an arm draped across her shoulders, and then simply waited.

It took her a moment to catch her breath. Unable to look at him directly, she stared at the floor.

"This is all so ridiculous . . ."

"Keep going."

"I just feel so sad." She raised both hands in a helpless gesture, then pressed them to her chest. "I don't even know why, except . . . maybe that my doing this, going through the artificial insemination procedure in order to have a child, also means I'm having to accept deep down the loss of a dream that I've had for a very long time." Restless, she dropped her hands to her lap and twisted them together.

"The dream of finding that special someone, settling down . . . ?"

"Yes." She met his gaze frankly, happy that he did understand, maybe—just maybe—even felt the same.

His arm tightened around her shoulders, urged her back against the sofa cushions. She let herself relax in the circle of his arm, let herself feel safe and cosseted, if only for a moment. As the seconds drew out Jason was quiet, too.

Finally, he admitted in a low tone, "I feel let down, too, Carlys. I'm not sure why." His arm tightened around her momentarily, as if he needed her as much as she needed him. "Part of it is what you said, the loss of the dream. But it's more than that for me. Perhaps it's the uncertainty of the outcome of all this, fear that you

won't conceive or my sperm won't be adequate, that
we'll have to go through this whole procedure again.''

Carlys was silent, reading disinclination in his face.

"Oh, Jason, it was awful for you.''

He laughed huskily, turned a little red, then made a
comically pitiable face. "Lady, you can't begin to
imagine... I felt like... No, I... Scratch that. I never
felt like that.''

"Back to adolescence?'' she guessed.

"Worse.''

She laughed through her tears. Poor Jason. Of the
two of them, he had definitely suffered the worst of it.
Her part was passive. All she had to do was lie on the
table and wait for the doctor to complete the medical
procedure. Jason's activity, however, was more of a
participatory character, not to say personally embarrassing. "Well, for the record, I hope we don't have to
do it again,'' she said, blushing.

He grinned, massaging her shoulder with brotherly
affection. "I hope not, too, kid.'' He sobered momentarily, then took a more positive view. "But just think
of the result of all this—another Megan running
around, causing chaos, getting into everything.''

He made Carlys feel the whole arduous business was
worth it. Her spirits lifted. "I do want that.''

"Then you agree it's worth doing again, if need be?''

"Yes.''

"Good. I think so, too.''

The emotional exhaustion Carlys had felt earlier
seemed to have fled. She felt close to Jason, incredibly
close. His free hand reached out to touch her face. With
infinite tenderness, his finger traced the line of her
cheek.

"Better now?'' he asked softly.

"Better," she affirmed in a voice that was, from sheer willpower, remarkably level and composed. Meanwhile, her pulse was racing to beat the band....

Jason smiled and slowly dropped his hand. Realizing that he still had his arm around her shoulders, he withdrew it awkwardly, glanced at his watch, cleared his throat. "Speaking of the little darlin', I'd better get home. I promised my baby-sitter I'd be back by five."

"Tell Megan I said hi, I'll come see her soon."

"I will."

"And, Jason? Thanks—for everything." Hands in the pockets of her skirt, Carlys showed him to the door.

He bent, brown eyes glimmering, and impulsively kissed her on the temple. "You'll see," he said softly, touching the silky hair falling across her brow, "in a few months, this will all be worth the trouble."

His reassurance meant more to her than she could say. "More than worth it," Carlys added. "If we get a child."

"We will." His voice was soft but firm. Jason touched her shoulder lightly as he passed her and headed out the door. He turned and gave her a mock salute before breaking into a broad, easy smile. "I'd stake my life on it."

At that moment, so would Carlys.

JASON RETURNED HOME exhausted from the ordeal of the day, wanting only to spend time with his daughter, read the paper and tumble into bed early. Unfortunately, the rest of his day wasn't quite as uneventful as he had hoped.

Later that evening, Jason had a call from Alice's mother. Mrs. Greenway, out in Arizona, was concerned that Alice wasn't spending enough time with

Megan, She urged Jason to talk to Alice. He didn't relish the task, but finally agreed. As was usually the case, though, it took him several more days to locate his former wife. And when she realized why he had called, she was none too happy.

"Jason, having one person nag me is quite enough!" Alice grumbled irritably, at the other end of the long-distance line.

Remembering his promise to her mother to try to get Alice more involved in Megan's life, Jason put steel into his voice. "There's only one way to put an end to it, and that's by visiting your daughter more often."

Alice sighed shakily. Closing his eyes, he could almost see her face. She'd have that helpless look, much like the one Megan put on when she didn't know how to work a new toy or was perplexed by something she saw on Sesame Street. Alice, like Megan, was out of her depth.

"Jason..." The pleading note was back in her voice.

Jason thought of Megan's welfare. He refused to let Alice's pleas for mercy sway him. In the past he had gone easy on her because he understood how unmaternal a woman she really was and also because he hadn't wanted to get involved in a struggle over their only child. Now he knew that encouraging the distance between mother and daughter, however passively, had been a mistake. Soon Megan would be old enough to ask questions. Answers about Alice, Jason didn't have. "I mean it, Alice. If you don't start becoming a little more involved with your daughter, you're going to find phone messages and telegrams waiting for you at every turn."

At this threat she became equally obstinate. "They'll never catch up with me."

"Maybe not, but I'll die trying to reach you. Let's see. There's the network, the network affiliates, and all the places you visit all over the world...."

There was a brief silence in which he knew he had won that round.

"You'd do it, too, wouldn't you?" Alice asked bitterly. "Humiliate me like that."

Protectiveness surged through Jason with volcanic force. "I don't want Megan hurt. Your continuing neglect will hurt her badly. There's only so much explaining I can do. And frankly, Alice, I don't understand your distancing yourself from her."

"Maybe not, but in the past you've been only too happy to let things go on that way and you only called me because my mother got into the act!"

Jason was silent. What could he say when he knew she was right? There was a part of him, the part that was angry and hurt by her continuing coldness, that wanted nothing more to do with Alice for himself or his daughter. The other half, the half that knew Alice better and knew what she had to give, wanted mother and child to come together.

He'd been apathetic far too long. Mrs. Greenway was right. If he wanted Megan to have even a shot at being a truly happy child as she grew up, he had to get Alice to see her regularly.

To that end he employed every weapon he had.

"Look, Alice, you don't have to cooperate with us. We certainly can't make you get to know your daughter. But I think you should be warned that if you don't at least start making a token effort, I'll be on your case constantly. Your mother will be calling, too," he continued smoothly.

Alice groaned and muttered something unprintable. "Tell me about it. You're not the only person she's been talking to, Jason. She's also enlisted a whole crew of others—my brothers and sisters, my Dad, even some of my old college chums." She sighed again. He waited. Finally, she demanded in the same irascible tone, "Promise me this, Jason. If I do visit—say this weekend—you'll get off my case and persuade everyone else to do the same."

It wasn't the maternal excellence he sought, but what the hell? It was a start. "Provided you stay at least twenty-four hours, sure."

She gasped. "Twenty-four . . . Jason, you're out of your mind! I can't stay a whole day!"

"You've already missed the first year and a half of her life. You owe her at least that much time, Alice. You owe yourself."

"Jason, even if I am there, nothing magical is going to happen in the space of twenty-four hours."

Jason looked at the picture of Megan on his desk. "Maybe not," he agreed. But he could always hope, and for his daughter's sake, hope he did.

"I've talked to Alice. She's coming for a visit, and when she does, I want you to meet her."

Jason dropped by the diaper service to see Carlys the next afternoon. There was no urgent reason for the visit; he could have waited and called Carlys at home. He hadn't wanted to. He needed a friend. Now. Carlys was not only the first person he'd thought of, but the only person who had a prayer of understanding his unusual situation. The only person who really seemed to understand him.

Unhappily, Carlys wasn't thrilled about the idea of meeting his former wife. She toyed with a pencil, her face abnormally pale. "I don't know, Jason. I'm not so sure it's a good idea."

"I am." Jason reached across the desk and briefly captured her hand between his. Just touching her made him feel warmer, more confident. Releasing his hold on her, he sat back and continued his argument persuasively. "The two of you have a lot in common. You're about the same age, both from the southwest. You have large families that care about you, though Alice lives far away from hers now. You're both career oriented." His voice trailed off. He watched as she diligently restacked perfectly neat paperwork on her desk and then got up to close her office door.

No doubt about it, Carlys was tense about this. Why? he wondered. Why would it be so threatening to her? Normally, with the exception of the insemination procedure and resulting waiting game, nothing threw her. Could it be that she was beginning to care about him more than she let on? He knew he was having an increasingly difficult time maintaining his distance from her. Whenever he was with her his need to touch her, to be physically close to her was almost overwhelming.

When he wasn't with her, he found himself wondering what she was doing. Sometimes he even dreamed about her at night, and the dreams were erotic. He was living a monklike existence and she was a beautiful, giving, available single woman. And the chemistry was there. But she was also his friend. And their situation was far too complicated and volatile for him to be even thinking of messing it up by letting the smallest hint of sex or romance into it. Because if either of those elements were to go awry, it would be harder than hell, if not damned near impossible, to resurrect their previous friendship from the ashes of a failed courtship. Losing Carlys at this point was a risk Jason just wasn't willing to take.

Fortunately for his erratic emotions, Carlys's mind was only on Alice and the peculiar difficulty that might be involved in meeting her.

"Does she know about . . . what we're trying to do?" Carlys asked, still restless after pouring them both a glass of juice from the small refrigerator in the corner.

Jason took the paper cup she handed him, trying not to notice how soft her skin was when their hands touched briefly. So she had slender perfect hands, with short practical nails that were polished pink. So she had hands that would caress a man gently, touch but never claw. . . .

God, what am I thinking?

Deliberately, he sipped his apple juice. It was cool and tart, the perfect remedy for his parched throat and overactive pulse. Alice. He had to think about Alice and Carlys. Why did he want them to meet? Not to make Alice jealous, as Carlys now seemed to think, but rather to let Carlys know she had nothing to fear where his former wife was concerned. Seeking to reassure Carlys, Jason quickly invented a definite plan that would almost force her to be with him when Alice arrived in Dallas. "That's another reason I want you to meet Alice," he continued smoothly. "I intend to tell her when she comes. I know that when I do she'll want to meet you." For Alice had always been, if nothing else, insatiably curious.

For several seconds, Carlys didn't move. "How do you think Alice will feel about our plan to have a child?" Her hands were shaking.

Jason's first reaction was to go to her and hold her, but remembering how close he had come to kissing her the last time he'd done so kept him rooted safely in his chair. Pretending an indolence he didn't begin to feel, he gestured offhandedly and crossed one ankle over his knee. "With Alice there's no telling, but I think she'll be pleased. Relax. You've got nothing to worry about."

Carlys's teeth raked across her lower lip. "I hope not, Jason."

"There's no hope about it," he countered evenly. "Believe me, the two of you will get along fine."

"WHEN JASON TOLD ME what he and you were trying to do, well, I'll admit I had my doubts," Alice confided to Carlys several days later in their first moments alone. "In fact, I thought he was crazy. But having met you, I understand. I want you to know I'm very happy for you and for Jason. I know he's always wanted another child. And Megan deserves to have a brother and sister."

The two women were alone on the back patio. After a full day of play, Jason had taken his tired but happy daughter in for a bath and bed. Later, the three adults, having hit it off well from the start, were planning to grill steaks for a late-night supper on the patio.

Carlys had found Alice to be much prettier in person than on television, gregarious, easygoing. Her only shortcoming, if it could be called that, was in dealing with her child. Content to sit back and watch her daughter from afar, she seemed not to know how to talk to Megan. Although Jason hadn't said anything, Carlys knew he found Alice's hands-off policy disturbing. Yet by the same token, she knew Alice wasn't deliberately trying to hurt her daughter. She was simply a woman who was awkward and uncomfortable around children, who kept her distance rather than do or say the wrong thing.

"I thought you might object to our plan," Carlys confided honestly, "especially since we're going about it so unconventionally."

Alice forced a sad smile. "No. Watching you and Meg and Jason together, I know it'll work out. Besides, what right have I to object? There's nothing between Jason and me anymore. I haven't exactly been a stellar mother."

Carlys didn't know what to say to that. There was a moment of awkwardness between them.

Alice leaned forward earnestly. "I know I have no right to ask you this but I'm going to anyway. Would you do me a favor and watch out for Meg? See that whenever she needs a woman's guidance or view, she gets it?"

For a moment, Carlys was too shocked to respond. "Of course I will," Carlys reassured her at last, knowing that if the situation were reversed and Alice were able to do something for Carlys, she would. However that didn't change the fact that Alice was continually sidestepping her responsibility for her daughter's welfare.

Normally Carlys didn't butt into other people's affairs, but watching Alice watch Meg and hearing her plea, she had become aware that Alice loved her daughter, even if she didn't very often show it. Not usually a meddler, Carlys wanted very much to help Alice find a way to be more open in expressing that depth of caring for her daughter. For everyone's sake, she was determined to try.

"You could do that yourself," she suggested in a calm, neutral tone. "You could watch out for Meg."

Alice smiled. Then, in a faintly accusing voice said, "Now you sound like my mother."

Now wasn't the time to pull any punches. Carlys took a deep, bolstering breath. "Maybe she's right."

Alice didn't think so. "I'm not cut out for motherhood." She stood up and prowled the length of the patio restlessly.

"How do you know that?" Carlys asked, curious about this deficiency in confidence in such an otherwise worldly woman. Persuasively she continued, "Why are you so quick to resist? I've seen you on television. You've been everywhere—riots in Miami, the streets of Iran, on foreclosed farms out in Iowa. You've got a gutsiness that's unequaled by any other woman on network news today."

"Thanks for the vote of confidence." Alice forced a smile and sat down beside Carlys. She looked at her hands for a long moment. Her head lifted. "Has Jason ever talked to you about Meg's birth?"

"No."

Alice sighed. "I'm not surprised he doesn't talk about it. When they brought Megan to me in the hospital and put her in my arms... I don't know how to explain it except to say I felt nothing. I expected a miraculous bonding between us. I got a stranger who cried whenever I held her."

"So maybe you weren't so good with her right off the bat," Carlys interjected helpfully. "I'm sure mothering, like anything else, can be learned."

"That's what I thought until I saw how inept I was. Carlys, it didn't get any better. I was in the hospital for three days. I was miserable the whole time. Megan was miserable. Megan cried whenever I held her. Only with Jason was she quiet and content. He has the touch. I don't.'' She held up a silencing hand when Carlys would have interrupted. ''As much as I hate to admit it, I have no feel for parenting, Carlys. I'm just not maternal. And besides, what good would it do for me to get close to Megan, to let her begin to count on me, when I know I'm going to have to take off again?'' Stubbornly, Alice finished, ''I don't want my child crying herself to sleep at night because I'm not there to tuck her in or because I got called away on an assignment and missed the school play I promised I'd attend.''

''And you think if you remain a stranger Megan won't miss you?'' Jason asked harshly, in a voice laced with barely restrained contempt. Neither Carlys nor Alice had heard him come up, but apparently he'd heard most of the conversation—heard it and hated it. Carlys had never seen him look so very angry.

Alice stood up. She looked at Jason and held her ground. ''I know you disagree with me now, but believe me it'll be easier on her if I keep my distance.''

''On her or on you?'' Jason shot back acerbically. ''Megan needs you, Alice. She needs a mother in her life.''

''I know that!'' Alice volleyed back between tightly gritted teeth. There were tears shimmering in her eyes. ''But when are you going to listen to me? When are you going to understand? Face it, Jason! I just don't have what it takes—''

Jason interjected roughly, ''Bull! You've never given yourself or Meg a chance.''

The tears fell in rivulets down Alice's face. Her shoulders shaking, she covered her face with both hands. ''I don't want to hurt her.''

Jason moved closer. His eyes were wet, too. Touching Alice's shoulder, he lowered his voice to plead. "Then let yourself love her," he said softly. "You don't have to be here all the time. But she does need to know you."

Jason's words were cutting too close to the bone. Alice collected herself and responded in a steely tone full of anger, "I'm not going to let you make me feel guilty about this, Jason. I'm not abandoning Meg by giving her over to you to raise. I'm merely doing what's best for her."

At Alice's rebuttal, Jason's lips curled in disgust. She backed away from him as he advanced on her furiously. "When are you going to grow up and stop playing games with yourself and with me and our child?"

Theirs was an intensely private fight. Carlys wanted to go, but there was no graceful way she could leave. Besides, the two of them looked as though they needed a mediator, and like it or not, because she was there, she was elected.

"I'm not playing games!" Alice cried, whirling away from Jason. "You're the one playing games, asking me—no, demanding that I turn into something I'm not! I don't need this guilt, Jason," she shouted angrily, then with effort lowered her voice. "I don't need you and my mother haranguing me."

"Then do something about it," Carlys said calmly, moving to stand between the two of them. Tempers were raging too high. Serenely she advised Alice, "Get to know your daughter. Give it a chance. It's the only way you'll ever escape the guilt."

Alice looked back at Carlys, quicting at the understanding she saw in her face. "I'm afraid," she whispered harshly.

Carlys had no chance to answer; Jason intervened.

"I'm afraid, too," he said with biting sarcasm, "but only that your distance from our daughter will continue, and that as a result, she'll be emotionally scarred for life. So think about that, won't you, the next time you're off doing some live and exciting on-camera report from halfway across the country. Think about what you're doing to Meg. And ask yourself if it's really worth it."

"DON'T YOU THINK you're being too hard on Alice?" Carlys asked, a few hours later. Alice had left soon after the argument, reneging on her promise to stay for dinner and see Megan again the following morning. Under the circumstances, Carlys could hardly blame her. Jason was far too angry to be dealt with.

"Maybe I am being too hard on her," he acknowledged, as he put the finishing touches to two steaks instead of three. "I don't know. I do know that in the past I've been too easy. Look where it's gotten me. And Megan. A big nowhere. Zero. Zilch."

"Do you think she'll come around?" Carlys moved next to him. She knew how much he was hurting. Her heart went out to all three of them. For Alice and Jason were both right. There was no easy solution. Megan needed a mother and a father. She needed more than just a woman's influence in her life occasionally. Though Carlys would do what she could for the adorable little girl and assume the role of guardian angel, she would never be able to take Alice's place in Megan's life, nor would she want to.

"I hope so," Jason said more quietly, allowing himself to think that the situation might be resolved at some point in the future. Letting his anger die, he turned toward Carlys. "Have I thanked you for being such a good friend to me tonight?"

Carlys smiled. This was the old Jason, a man she could deal with, a very dear friend. "No, but that steak you're grilling looks like adequate payment. A porterhouse, isn't it?"

"It is."

"My favorite."

"I know."

Both were smiling again. There'd been a storm; it had passed. They were still together, still friends, with everything to look forward to.

As if echoing her thoughts exactly, Jason's eyes dropped to Carlys's still slim waist.

Carlys grinned. Hope. That really was what life was all about.

Chapter Six

"I can't believe it! Jason, it worked!" Carlys shouted, bolting out of her car. "The first time! It worked!"

Jason had been dutifully cutting the lawn and Carlys caught him pulling the lawnmower into the garage, grass and dirt clinging to his old work clothes. He started toward her to greet her with a hug, but in view of his work-mussed state, contented himself with surveying her glowing, radiant face.

He put his glasses up on top of his head. One corner of his mouth crooked up hopefully. "We're pregnant?"

"Irrevocably." Carlys grinned. She had driven over to Jason's house as soon as the doctor had called her, wanting to give him the news in person. From the expression on his face she had made exactly the right decision.

"Carlys, that's wonderful!" His dusty state forgotten, he picked her up for a giant bear hug and swung her around and around, squeezing her tight. In the process, the glasses he'd shoved on his head tumbled to the ground.

Sticking to his priority, Jason made no move to release her.

"I can't believe it!" Jason murmured wonderingly. "A baby!" Looking down into her face, he relaxed his hold.

"Jason, your glasses," Carlys prompted laughingly, still tingling everywhere they had touched.

"Right." He bent to retrieve them.

Just past noon, Megan was down for her afternoon nap, the front lawn had already been cut, they had nothing to do but be deliriously happy. Carlys was blinking back tears of sheer bliss. "Oh, Jason, it's so wonderful."

"Isn't it though?" he murmured happily.

Impulsively he gathered her to him for another hug, softer, more tender. Contentment rippled through her; she belonged in his arms. Against the odds, everything had worked out.

They swayed together in the scent of fresh-mown grass.

"So what do you think?" Jason said at last. "Girl or boy?"

"Oh, Jason I don't care. I'm just so happy I could perish!"

He enveloped her until her ribs almost cracked. "Me, too."

"LET'S SEE NOW," Jason said that evening as Carlys, Megan and he prowled the grocery store aisles. "You've got your vitamins and iron. Plenty of milk. Lean meats. Vegetables, fruits…" One by one, he checked the items off his list.

Carlys, feeling more a spectator than the principal actor, pushed the full cart. Megan, safety-belted in, sat in the child seat, playing with Carlys's fingers. She didn't understand much of what was going on, but everyone was happy, so she was happy.

To Jason, Carlys said, "You're really going all out on this prenatal care, aren't you?" He made her feel so cosseted, so cared for. Being looked after by a man was a novel experience; Carlys found to her surprise that despite her independent nature she rather enjoyed it.

"Yeah, I am." Jason tilted his head to study the cereals, then finding what he wanted, tossed the box into the cart, put down his list and slanted her an inquiring glance. "Do you mind?"

He wasn't likely to stop even if she did mind. Carlys had the feeling that the same solicitousness coming from anyone else would make her feel smothered, but she didn't object to his. "No, I don't mind your taking care of me. It's nice, knowing you feel the same way about the baby as I do."

He touched the tip of her nose playfully. "I know I'm behaving laughably, like a sitcom father. I can't help it. I think having a baby together is a very special time for a couple. I intend for us both to enjoy every second of it."

His tone was dreamy, almost romantic. Carlys felt hope flood her senses. Ever practical, though, she forced herself to come swiftly back to earth.

So he had hugged her thoroughly that afternoon and she had enjoyed every minute he'd spent doting on her since. He wasn't saying he loved her, or even that he might someday possibly care for her as a woman, just that he loved having a baby with her.

Not that she was sure she'd ever come to have an enduring love for Jason either, but she was sure that she still wanted marriage. She wanted deep, enduring commitment from a man.

Jason said, "This baby of ours is going to be so loved by you and by me."

"I know." No one could love a baby more than she. Except . . . except maybe Jason.

"But . . . ?" Resuming his trek down the aisle, proving himself to be as intuitive as ever, Jason prodded, "Okay, 'fess up. What's wrong?"

"Did I say anything was wrong?" Carlys hedged, hoping he'd change the subject. He didn't. "Okay, so I'm a tiny bit bothered about something," she admitted. "It's nothing."

"Carlys, confess," he instructed her gruffly.

Frissons of sensation shot through her. How could she have thought she could avoid telling him anything he wanted to know?

"All right, I'll tell you, but don't blame me for spoiling the moment." Because not a soul was within earshot and Megan was preoccupied with a display of sodas, Carlys felt free to say, "I keep thinking about Alice and her memory of not having maternal feelings for Megan. What if the same thing happens to me?" Carlys swallowed hard, feeling ridiculous and at the same time so damned scared. "What if they bring me the baby and . . ." She was unable to finish, unable to meet his eyes. Just the thought of incompatibility with her child filled her with unspeakable dread. Alice's miserable experience had been unsought. And if it could happen to the supersuccessful Alice . . .

Jason clearly felt she had nothing to worry about. Both hands on her shoulders, he turned her to face him. They were standing toe-to-toe, so close they were almost touching.

"That won't happen to you," he counseled firmly.

Carlys sagged with relief. Still, because of Alice, there remained a small doubt. They went on up the aisle, Jason pushing the cart and leaving Carlys to wish she had something solid to hang on to. As it was, she felt acutely aware of him, aware of herself and the ever-dwindling physical and emotional distance between them.

"I want to be a good mother," she said firmly.

"You will be."

Yes, but how did one really know? When you found out you weren't good enough, it was already too late.

Carlys picked up a jar of peanut butter, her secret midnight snack for when she couldn't sleep.

Jason knew there was something else bothering her. "Tell me the rest of it, Carlys."

Even though she talked to Jason more easily and honestly than she ever had spoken with any man, Carlys had to struggle with herself before she could say, "It's occurred to me I don't know very much about mothering. I mean I make a fine babysitter, but—"

Jason looked down at Megan, who was now twisting around in her seat, trying to pull groceries into her lap. "The responsibility is awesome," he said, taking a can away from Megan and giving her a light box of breakfast cereal instead.

"Well, it just hit me." Carlys took his place and gave the basket a push.

"That's not surprising." Jason reached behind Carlys, his arm just brushing her hip, and added a jar of crunchy dill pickles to their load. "It hit me too when Alice was expecting Megan, but in my case it wasn't until I actually went out alone to buy the layette. I had no idea what to buy. Alice didn't want to find out or get too heavily involved in the planning since she'd already agreed to give Megan over to me.''

"So what did you do?''

Jason shrugged, the movement sculpting the lines of his plaid cotton shirt to his broad shoulders. "I went to the library and read every book on parenting and babies I could find.'' His lips compressed with remembered humor. "And in general panicked a lot, especially late at night.'' He tossed some rolls of paper towels into the basket. "Look, I've got an idea. Why don't you pack a suitcase and stay with me for a couple of weeks? You can help take care of Megan or just watch. Either way you'll pick up a lot.''

The idea sounded like heaven to Carlys and a great way for her to learn how to parent. "You wouldn't mind having me there underfoot constantly?''

"To tell you the truth, you'd be doing me a favor. I'm going to be on call for the next three weeks. It would be a relief to have someone in the house all that time so that if I'm called in, I won't have to worry about finding a sitter to come over and stay with Megan until morning.''

The arrangement was so practical. Indeed, the only thing holding Carlys back was the chemistry between her and Jason. If she thought she was physically attracted to him now, could she handle seeing him at all hours of the day and night? She didn't know, but she wasn't about to pass up this opportunity. Becoming the best, the most knowledgeable parent she could possibly be was her first priority. As for the physical attraction, well, she would just have to keep it on hold. Maybe living with him, seeing him at his worst as well as his best, would lessen it. At any rate, Jason's plan was worth a try.

"I could use the practice," Carlys said finally, still battling her doubts and her desire.

"Great, then it's settled. Saturday morning okay with you as a move-in-date?"

Heavens, the man didn't waste any time. "Yes. Saturday's fine." The truth was, Carlys couldn't wait.

Jason nodded agreeably, looking utterly pleased with himself and with her.

"Which means we've only got one problem," he said, looking down at their basket.

"What?" Carlys stared at him, perplexed.

"Which of these groceries are yours and which are mine and Meg's?"

"THE GUEST ROOM IS YOURS," Jason said late Saturday morning as he led her back into her temporary domain.

"Oh, Jason it's lovely," Carlys said, looking at the mint-green drapes and matching bedspread. The closet was open and empty. He'd obviously been polishing the furniture. The room smelled faintly of lemon.

"You can put your things in the dressers. The closet, drawers and bathroom cabinets all have childproof latches. Please don't leave anything out, like electric rollers or makeup or even your shoes, because if you do Megan will be sure to get into it."

"Peanut butter and jelly on my pumps probably wouldn't do. Okay. Thanks for warning me. I probably wouldn't have thought about it."

Jason grinned understandingly. "Neither did I at first. I learned quickly. Fortunately, she didn't start out at a run, which meant I had plenty of time to figure out what she wanted to do before she was physically able to do it and cut her off at the pass before it became dangerous."

"Megan's lucky to have such a devoted daddy."

Jason grinned and pushed his glasses higher on the bridge of his nose. "She thinks so."

"And modest, too."

His eyes glimmered affectionately at the teasing note in her voice. "Right." He made a sweeping gesture of invitation at the door. "After you."

Carlys led the way out to her car. Together she and Jason brought in two suitcases, several dresses on hangers, and a cardboard box of toiletries and her hair dryer.

"Good thing you're only staying three weeks," he teased, pretending to stagger under the weight of her last suitcase.

"Right. Otherwise you'd really have a lot to carry," Carlys bantered back. This was going to be fun. Already she was having a good time.

"I don't even want to imagine." Jason put her belongings into the closet, slid the doors shut, secured the childproof latches and turned back around to face her. "So what do you want to do first? I've got a little work to do on the computer yet."

"Would you mind if I entertained Megan for a while? I brought some crayons and paper. I thought we might try our hand at coloring."

"That sounds fine. But, uh, Carlys, she's only twenty months—"

"A dexterous twenty months. I've been watching her hand-eye coordination. She seems remarkably able-fingered for someone her age. Anyway I'd like to try it."

"Okay, just make sure she doesn't eat any of the crayons."

"I promise I won't let her out of my sight."

An hour later, Carlys was beginning to think she had underestimated her own drawings, though they seemed quite unimaginative when compared with the fiercely impressionistic pictures done by Megan.

"Cah-lee," Megan said, accidentally on purpose dropping another crayon from the side of her high chair onto the floor. "Cah-lee—" Megan pointed to the crayon again, then uttered an infectious giggle and ducked her head.

"So you want your crayon," Carlys said, bending down from her chair to get it. "Here you go."

The crayon was promptly dropped again. Megan grinned expectantly, her eyes dancing with the depth of her delight.

"I thought this was a game," Carlys sighed. Picking up the crayons, she put them into a box. "Ready to go outside?" she asked her charge.

Megan nodded, and was already trying to lever herself up.

Carlys lifted her from the high chair. "Let's go tell Daddy we're taking a fresh-air break."

Jason was deep in thought behind the computer screen when Carlys entered his office. "Jason? We're going to go out in the backyard for a while."

"Hmm?" Distracted, he finally looked up, blinked and slowly came into the present. "Oh, Carlys. I was so busy concentrating... I guess because it hasn't been this quiet around here in a long time. How did the coloring go? Did Megan like it?"

Carlys nodded happily. "She did some great pictures. We left them on the kitchen table. You can look at them when you're done."

"I look forward to it. Backyard, you say?"

"Just for a little while."

"Okay." Jason went back to his papers, pausing only to call over his shoulder, "Megan can have some juice if she wants. You, too, Carlys. Just help yourself to whatever we've got."

The truth was, Carlys was already feeling quite at home. The feeling intensified as the day continued.

"Come on, it can't have been that exhausting," Jason said, knowingly several hours later. Carlys was lying on a chaise longue set in the shade on the back porch. "You were only with Megan—what?—two or three hours?" He sat beside her, his hands clasped between his knees, the crisp cotton of his shorts barely brushing her thighs.

"A very busy two and a half hours," Carlys corrected, smothering a yawn with the back of her hand. She knew she should get up, at least shift farther away from his tantalizing presence, but the simple truth of it was she was too tired. And now with Megan in bed, taking her after-lunch nap... No, Carlys didn't want to move, wasn't going to move.

"Did you at least get something to eat?" Jason stood up and shoved his hands into his pockets.

"Plenty. And we left a couple of sandwiches for you in the fridge. Megan didn't know your favorite so we guessed and left you ham and cheese."

"That is my favorite."

"Mine, too." Carlys yawned again. "I don't know what's the matter with me."

"It's the pregnancy," he answered quietly, his devoted look enough to stop any heart at one hundred paces. "You'll probably be feeling tired a lot during the first trimester, if my memory serves me correctly."

Carlys felt herself blush a little, embarrassed because she hadn't figured it out herself, but pleased that he was still so protective of her. "Oh, yeah, the doctor said something about that. I just forgot."

"You need your rest now more than ever." Jason was suddenly solemn. "The drowsiness is probably just your body's way of telling you so." Leaning forward, he touched the side of her face gently with the back of his hand. Softer still, as soothing as any lullaby, he said, "My advice is just to go with the fatigue... close your eyes... let sleep take over...."

Carlys nodded. He didn't need to encourage her further. All she had to do was close her eyes, take another deep, slow breath, and fall into a deep dreamless sleep.

CARLYS AWOKE later in the afternoon, feeling refreshed and anxious to master the art of motherhood again. Megan, also awake and brimming with energy, was only too glad to take part in Carlys's well-planned experiments.

"Okay, Megan, touch the grass. Feel how soft and thick it is. Yes, isn't that good? And now let's feel the bark on this tree. Ooooh. Isn't that rough and scratchy?" Carlys asked. Kneeling, she was at eye level with a standing Megan.

"Oooohhh," Megan touched the bark and then the grass and then the bark again. Aware that Carlys was watching her every move, she mimicked her teacher, furrowing her brow, summoning up an expression of deep concentration. They went on to explore the silky petals on a wildflower and the cold water from a fountain.

Turning from the water, Carlys found Jason studying them both with fascination.

"That's a very sensuous exercise," he observed, impressed. "Absorbing, too. I don't think I've ever seen Megan that entranced."

"Thanks. I got it out of a book I've been reading."

"Is that where you got the idea to color?"

Carlys nodded. "The author said every child should be coloring by eighteen months. According to him, Megan's already a little behind schedule."

Obviously that was the wrong thing to say. Jason's brows lowered like twin thunderclouds. Tersely he said, "Megan's ahead of schedule on all the charts, and even if she weren't I'd be happy."

Carlys studied him curiously; in some strange way she seemed to have insulted him. "You're against teaching her?"

"No, not at all. The coloring was fine. So was examining the out of doors. I am against pushing any child too hard. I don't want her frustrated because she can't read at age two or do multiplication tables. I think she ought to be able to develop at her own pace. The time when she has to fit in with someone else's time-table will come soon enough."

Carlys thought that over. She agreed at last, then hastened to add, wanting no misunderstanding between them, "You're probably right. Anyway, Jason, I didn't mean to imply she wasn't bright or that she hadn't been taught enough—"

"I know. I think your teaching her is great. I'm all for making the world around her as interesting as possible. So what else have you been reading?" he asked genially, sitting down Indian-style on the grass beside Carlys and Megan. He laughed as Megan continued to stroke the grass and say "ooooh" and "ahhhh" with increasing vigor. Carlys laughed too, and Megan, who had no idea what was so funny, joined in.

"What other books?" Jason asked again.

"Um, a book by Dr. Brazleton, who I really like. Spock, who I like less, because some of his advice; for example, the sections on working mothers, seems really old-fashioned, just not in step with what life is like today. But that's a personal opinion."

Jason nodded. "One I share. And listen to Brazleton. He really makes sense. Plus, he's raised kids of his own."

Carlys raised her fist in a cheerleader's victory sign. "Two cheers for practical, hands-on experience."

Jason stretched out beside her, his legs looking long and muscular against the softness of the grass. "Want my advice?" he asked lazily.

"Always."

He reached over to twine his fingers with hers. "I think when it comes to parenting, the safest course most of the time is to just follow your gut instinct. Be firm but loving. Just talk to Megan as you would an adult as much as possible. She'll absorb a lot of it. Scheduled activities are also nice, but I don't expect you to turn every minute you spend with her or the new baby into a work session."

"I know."

"Carlys, you don't have to work to impress me with your parenting skill. You already have. You're a natural."

She smiled, feeling happiness glide through her in long waves. "You think so, hmm?"

"I know so."

Megan broke up the discussion by rolling over and burying her face in Jason's legs. "Da-dee."

He touched his daughter lovingly. "Hi there, sweetheart." To Carlys he proposed, "So dinner out tonight?"

"Actually, the three of us already have an invitation," she admitted.

"Really? Where?"

"My folks. They want to know more about you."

Jason grinned. "I don't blame them, especially now." His eyes drifted to the still-slim lines of her midsection. "What time are we expected?"

"If you're sure you want to go..." Carlys had no intention of pushing him into the family inquisition.

"I'm sure."

Carlys breathed a sigh of relief. "Six."

"Megan and I will both be ready," he promised.

Fortunately for Carlys, the twins were absent from the Holts' dinner table. Her father and mother were both welcoming, if a little on edge, and took to Megan with enthusiasm.

"So, Jason, how are you finding work?" George asked, passing the bowl of mashed potatoes. "Everything going smoothly?"

"As smoothly as it ever does in the computer business," Jason replied with a suitable degree of respect for George's years.

"I know how that can be," George commiserated, passing the peas to Carlys. "I remember one time when our whole computer system went down. We were days getting it fixed. Boy, I'll tell you if that didn't make it hard to do business.... And the customers—to say they were irate doesn't begin to describe it. We had delay after delay after delay."

"So where's Susie?" Carlys asked, when the computer stories had wound down.

"She had jazz band practice this afternoon at school."

"On a Saturday?"

"They have a big end-of-year contest coming up. She said they were going to rehearse until the band had everything down pat, and not to wait dinner for her because she was sure to be late." George looked at his watch. "She should be home by now, though. I wonder what's keeping her."

At that instant, the back door slammed.

Helen smiled. "And speaking of angels...Susie, darling, we're in here."

Susie came into the doorway. She looked, to Carlys's eyes, rather disheveled. Her blond hair was in disarray, and damp at the ends. The color in her cheeks was very bright, yet the rest of her skin very pale. Carlys would have bet her bottom dollar something was very wrong. Helen and George came to the same conclusion.

"Susie?" George asked, his eyes narrowing with concern. "Everything okay?"

"Sure, Dad." Susie looked at her mother. "Okay if I eat later? I'm kind of tired."

"Well, yes, but—"

"Nice to see you, Carlys. Jason." Susie forced a bright smile and whirled to go.

"Susie, do you have a date tonight?" Helen interrupted, stopping her flight.

Susie turned around slowly. She wouldn't look at anyone for more than two seconds at a time. "Uh...no."

"I thought you were going out with Zach again," George interjected, perplexed.

"I was, but... well, practice ran so late. We're all tired. I begged off."

"Was Zach angry?"

Susie waited a fraction too long before she shrugged and said, "No, he wasn't."

About that, Carlys was sure she was lying.

"Did you and Zach have a fight?" Helen asked.

For a second Susie looked as though she was going to cry but recovered admirably. "What is this? An interrogation? No, we didn't."

Behind her the phone rang. "I'll get that," Susie said quickly, disappearing into the kitchen.

George and Helen exchanged worried looks. From the distance, Susie could be heard.

"No. Listen...no...I already did! What more do you want? Leave me alone!" She hung up with a crash and ran up the back stairs.

After dinner, Helen went upstairs to see what was going on with her younger daughter. "I can't get anything out of her," she admitted with a frustrated shrug when she returned several minutes later. "She says it's a fight with one of her girl friends, but..."

"Let me go," Carlys said. "Maybe she'll talk to me." But her luck was no better than her mother's.

"Carlys, look, I know you mean well but this is something I just have to handle myself, okay?"

"If you need help—"

"I know I can come to you," Susie said firmly. "Or Mom and Dad. But I'm also a big girl. Trust me, Carlys. I'll handle it."

Susie was adamant. She still looked about to burst into tears at any second, but more on account of the good intentions of her family than anything else.

"All right. If you're sure." Carlys hugged her and dropped a kiss on her forehead. Susie smelled and tasted of toothpaste.

"Susie—"

"Carlys, enough!" The look on Susie's face forbade even one more question.

Carlys knew when to retreat.

"SO WHAT HAPPENED with your sister?" Jason asked later, when they were back at his house, with Megan in bed.

"I don't know," Carlys said tiredly, collapsed in an easy chair across from him. "I didn't get much out of her." She gave him a quick sketch of Susie's state.

"Well, if she's anything like you, I'm sure she can handle it."

"I'm sure she can, too." But Carlys still wore a perplexed frown.

"You look pretty worried."

"It'll pass." Carlys straightened, forcing herself to shrug off her low mood. At least she had Jason to come home with this evening. More and more, he was like a port in a storm to her. She was getting to be far more dependent on him than was good for her. "I just need to get my mind on something else."

"Ever played any games on the computer?"

"Uh, no."

"Next question. Do you like murder mysteries?"

She smiled, warming to his pitch, whatever it was going to be. "As it happens, I adore them." Leave it to Jason to cheer her up regardless of the circumstances.

"Then I've got just the thing." Aglow with possibilities, he hustled her into his office. "You sit here."

Having settled her in his swivel chair, he positioned a straight-backed one for himself.

"Sure you don't want this chair? It's bound to be more comfortable."

"No, you take it, after all you're the one who's pregnant."

"All right," Carlys swung reluctantly to face Jason's computer screen. Between a man and a woman she liked things to be on an equal basis one hundred percent of the way.

"If I get too uncomfortable, we'll switch." Reaching around her, Jason switched on the computer and inserted some disks.

"Deal. So where do we start?"

"At the beginning."

A picture appeared on the screen: a mansion.

Two hours later, they were completely worn out and not even close to solving the mystery. "I can't believe we spent so much time getting out on the upstairs terrace," Carlys said with a laugh.

"Especially when all it took was a simple command to open the door first."

"Maybe next time." She stood and stretched her tired muscles. "At least then we'll know not to sample the medicine."

"Well, not all was lost." Jason started to massage her shoulders gently.

Magically, the cramped muscles in her neck unkinked, a fluid warmth melted through her.

"We were searching for poison. We found it."

Carlys twirled around, her finger raised. "Ah, but our victim died of a knife wound in the neck."

He wrinkled his nose in response to her nit-picking. "True. But then again discovering where the poison came from was important. There was that tea cup—"

"And the unexplained stain on the rug. And the cup and saucer having been washed after the victim died. We make a lousy detective duo. Now I know why people become glued to their terminals."

"Computer games are dangerous. Working a game, you tend to forget the time completely."

"Spent many nights up until two trying to solve one?"

"More than I'd like to count."

For a moment, they were both silent. Abruptly, she had the sensation his thoughts were drifting erotically, as were her own.

Carlys struggled to keep her mind on what they'd been talking about. "Do you have any other games?"

Whatever trance held her also gripped him. Softly, in a distracted voice, he murmured, "Yeah, I do, although I've already solved all of them. So it wouldn't be as much fun for us to work them together. I haven't bought much amusement-oriented software recently. Megan keeps me pretty busy. I'd like to get some games, though, for us to work together."

Was it the shadowed lids, the pressure of his knee against her, or the dark glow in his eyes that made her think Jason was conjuring up a more intimate scenario in his mind? A scenario that wasn't centered on a computer screen and their mutual mental efforts to defeat the game makers, but just around them. Jason and Carlys. And why couldn't she stop noticing how soft and mussable his hair was, or stop thinking how much she wanted to take off his glasses and keep them off.

"Playing a game has never been so much fun," he said slowly at length, clearly reluctant to let her go but resisting the force that pushed him on.

Carlys's heart was pounding. He was very near. "Nor for me."

"Then you'll do it again sometime?"

"If you ask me." *If only you'd touch me.*

He read the desire in her eyes. It was mirrored on his face, in the sensual set of his lips, his erratic breath. With a low groan, he capitulated to what he was feeling and took her into his arms.

"Carlys, I—"

His lips were on hers, searching, discovering, telling her everything he felt, everything he'd been holding back. Never had she been touched so tenderly, so reverently. Carlys was awash in sensation from her head to her toes, completely caught up in his spell.

Helpless, she responded ardently to the changing warmth and pressure of his mouth, the urgent invasion of his tongue. Her hands glided over his ribs and around his back. Her pulse thudded erratically and she swayed against him as the kiss deepened and he drew from her every response she could give.

Long moments later, he lifted his head. They stood quietly, gauging each other's reactions to the sweetly tumultuous embrace.

They were crazy. It was dangerous. They needed time to assimilate what had happened and discover if they wanted it to happen again.

"I promised myself I wouldn't do that," Jason whispered shakily. There wasn't a trace of remorse on his face.

"So did I." Momentarily, she buried her face in the solidness of his shoulder, loving the feel of him, the smell. Strong, caring, he was the perfect man for her....

"It could ruin things."

Or make them better. She smiled, still trembling, yet filled with an inner happiness she hadn't guessed could exist. With a composure she didn't feel, she said dryly, "I think this is where we say good-night, Jason." If they didn't part, if he kissed her just one more time, she knew she'd end up in his bed. He knew it, too.

He touched his lips to her brow; she felt the kiss all the way to her soul.

"Good night, Carlys."

"Good night."

They embraced chastely and then she left him, knowing that her dreams that night would be not only of the moment, but the man, and the possibility of them sharing a future that extended far beyond the child they had made.

Chapter Seven

"Oh, sweetie, what's the matter? Can you tell Carlys what's wrong? Did a bad dream wake you up?"

Eleven o'clock at night. The house was silent save for the sound of Megan's heartrending sobs. Carlys lifted her from the crib and cuddled her close, her hand moving in soothing circles over Megan's back. "It's all right, sweetie, it's all right."

Eventually, the sobs dwindled to a single hiccup. Still cuddled against Carlys, she started to put her fingers in her mouth, then on the verge of crying again, wreathed her arms around Carlys's neck and held on tightly.

Meanwhile, Carlys had no idea what was wrong. Jason was at work. She could call him, of course, but that wouldn't help, as he could do nothing over the phone but share her worry. No, this time she was on her own.

"Are you wet?"

Megan was.

Cradling Megan against her, Carlys used her free hand to gather up diaper, baby washcloth and powder. Laying her down on the changing table, she put her into fresh clothing, talking to her gently all the while. By the time she'd finished, Megan was wide awake. Though not crying, she looked no more happy. Carlys's heart went out to her even as her own feeling of helplessness increased.

"If only you could talk better," she said softly, picking Megan up again and holding her close. "You could tell me what's wrong."

Megan sighed and leaned her cheek disconsolately against Carlys's shoulder.

"How about some milk? Does that sound good?"

Megan nodded without much enthusiasm.

"Well, no fever, your skin's cool. Stomach seems fine, which for the moment rules out any virus. I guess you could be hungry." Carlys let Megan sit on the counter while she poured her milk into her drinking cup. "Maybe it was just a bad dream," Carlys theorized at last, holding up the cup by the bottom.

Megan gripped the two handles, lifted the cup to her mouth. The narrow spout got no farther than her lips. Megan's face crumpled. She began to cry again.

Carlys immediately withdrew the cup.

Megan opened her mouth wide and sobbed even louder. Carlys knew immediately at the sight of red, swollen gums what the problem was. "A new tooth! It's almost through the gum! Oh, no wonder you're crying. Megan, that looks..." Painful, she thought, but didn't say it.

The problem was what to do next. Picking Megan up, Carlys carried her into the den, found Jason's baby book and thumbed through it. Megan sat on her lap, silent again, as Carlys told her what she had discovered. "Well, Megan, it says we need some benzocaine. The question is does your daddy have any."

He did. In a very short time, with the soothing paste rubbed on her gums and a half a cup of milk in her stomach, Megan was situated on Carlys's lap, holding her favorite stuffed animal and blanket. While Megan contentedly sucked her fingers again, Carlys read her a story about Big Bird and rocked her back to sleep.

She was still rocking Megan at twelve thirty when she looked up and saw Jason standing just inside the door, a look of admiration on his face.

Her first reaction was one of surprise. She hadn't heard him come in. Nor did she have any idea how long he'd been standing there watching. A long time, judging by his relaxed stance.

"Hi," she mouthed soundlessly.

"Hi." A slow, welcoming smile tilted his lips, telling her he was glad to be home. Then, as if drawn by forces he was unable to resist, Jason's eyes lowered from hers to her lips. His smile faded as slowly as it had appeared.

Carlys's heart fluttered. She tried to think of something to say, to alleviate the sensual tension between them. Instead all she could do was stare at him. It was as if all that had gone before, the time spent together, the confidences exchanged, was suddenly culminating in something beyond their control, which despite its intensity maybe neither of them was ready for emotionally.

Carlys was drowning in sensual confusion as Jason came soundlessly closer, his gaze still locked with hers. Try as she might, she couldn't look away.

Acutely conscious of the late hour and her dishabille, Carlys noted how dashing he looked in sports coat and tie. How rumpled she felt in contrast, in an old pale blue terry cloth robe and faded white flannel gown. Yet from the entranced way he was looking at her, she might have been wearing an evening gown.

Her heart tripped faster still.

Since that first kiss he'd kissed her again several times, but always under carefully controlled circumstances. The rational part of her knew that she had nothing to worry about. Jason wasn't some lothario out to seduce her into his bed against her common sense, and yet . . . In his presence she felt a pinprick of something akin to fear, as if every sense, every nerve ending, was sensitive to his feelings, yearnings. . . .

"Is she ready to go back into her crib?" Jason whispered.

Carlys nodded numbly.

Jason started for Megan's room. "I'll make sure everything's ready."

When Carlys tiptoed in, the room was dark except for the night light and the crib was prepared. She began to lay the child down, only to find that the toy and blanket were tangled in the front of her robe. Seeing what the problem was, Jason, careful not to disturb Megan, but unable to avoid touching Carlys, disentangled the blanket from her belt. Carlys sucked in her breath as his knuckles ghosted over her ribs and just narrowly missed brushing her breasts.

Jason finished tucking his daughter in.

Her heart pounding, Carlys moved soundlessly back to the living room.

"What happened? Why was Megan up?" Jason asked, coming in to join her. His voice hit her like a velvet arrow to the heart.

Carlys made her report, watching as Jason shrugged out of his sports coat and tossed it, along with his tie, over the back of a chair. Despite the long hours he'd just worked, he didn't look the least bit ready for sleep.

"Sounds like you really handled the crisis well."

"It was easier than I thought."

He grinned and nodded approvingly. "I said you had nothing to worry about. Taking care of children is mostly instinct."

An instinct Carlys had discovered she had in abundance. "Thanks for suggesting I stay here. I feel a million times more secure that I can do the job now."

"I was glad to have you here. After all, I've got a stake in that baby, Carlys. We'll do all right. We're doing this solely by choice—that's bound to make us stronger parents."

"I hope so." Involuntarily, her hand moved to her abdomen. "I want our baby to feel cherished."

Jason followed her protective movement. "Any baby would be very lucky to have you for a mother." His eyes met hers and stayed.

Carlys tightened the belt of her robe. Her throat was as dry as the Sahara, her knees weak as jelly. "Well, if that's all," she said, aware of the blush stealing into her cheeks. "I think I'll go to bed."

She was almost at her bedroom door when he spoke. "Aren't you forgetting something?"

Carlys knew a delaying tactic when she heard one; the lazy, faintly predatory low voice gave him away. "What?" She half turned to face him.

He strolled toward her, closing the distance between them to two feet.

"My hello kiss," he said in a husky voice that sent warmth sluicing along her nerve endings.

He couldn't have been more blatant about his intention to have her if he'd held up a sign. Shock held her motionless. Yet beneath that initial reaction excitement was trembling through her veins.

"Your hello kiss," she repeated numbly.

He grabbed her around the waist and walked her back to the wall until she was trapped between it and his body.

The fingers gripping her waist relaxed and began a rhythmic caress, but they sent her a message that she was his captive. "You didn't really think you'd get away without it, did you?" he asked softly. "Especially when you're looking so ravishing."

Ravishing. Despite the danger inherent in his embrace, Carlys liked the sound of that very much. She liked being ravishing for him.

"Ravishing." His mouth lowered to hers with an implacability that stole her breath. "Delectable. Desirable. The woman of my dreams. I missed you tonight, Carlys. I always miss you when we're apart."

His hand slid beneath the silky curtain of her hair, eased to the back of her neck. His fingers spread wide, he drew her against him, his mouth covering hers with passionate abandon.

He had never kissed her with this urgency and never with such unbridled feeling. Every inch of her trembled. "I missed you, too," she whispered against his mouth.

"Oh, God, Carlys."

His tongue sought hers in a fiery dance, slowly stroking her senses, touching her, taking, tempting, until she felt thoroughly possessed, wonderfully alive, yearning to be his.

His hands touched her shoulders, skimmed down the length of her arms to her waist, then inched their way luxuriously up until they framed the slender lines and the arch of her neck.

He kissed the hollow of her throat, then lifting her hair aside, strung satiny kisses across her collarbone. He kissed the notch of skin framed by the open collar of her nightdress and brushed another kiss in the shadowy cleft between her breasts. He was asking to touch her body, she knew.

"Jason—" She felt full of need, powerless to resist, and yet frightened that everything was suddenly moving too quickly.

"Carlys, don't, don't deny me. I won't hurt you. I promise." She had no more chance to protest. Driven by emotions held at bay far too long, he kissed her again, lingeringly, sweetly, until her heartbeat steadied, until she was relaxed and pliant, experiencing only the mesmerizing drift of soft, heady pleasure.

"You're so beautiful, so sweet." His hands glided over her, drawing her deeper into the realm of sensation. "I want to feel you against me," he murmured. "Tell me it's what you want, too."

"Jason, I—" She moaned, soft and low, as his lips stroked down her throat, barely touching her, yet creating ribbons of endlessly unfurling desire. Her legs weakened traitorously; she swayed against him; she gripped his arms.

His hands parted the deep front placket of her high-necked gown, then slid effortlessly beneath to stroke the softness of her breasts. In response her nipples budded against his palms; he tantalized them tighter still.

Dimly it came to her that she'd never been wanted so much. And then she realized he was making her want too much, too soon. If he'd said he loved her . . . But he hadn't.

His hands were on the belt of her robe. "No, Jason—" In a panic she swayed herself back from him. And yet even as she did so, part of her longed to yield. "No!"

Look what we've got for you:

. . . A FREE compact manicure set
. . . plus a sampler set of 4 terrific Harlequin American Romance® novels, specially selected by our editors.

. . . PLUS a surprise mystery gift that will delight you.

All this just for trying our Reader Service!

With your trial, you'll get SNEAK PREVIEWS to 4 new Harlequin American Romance® novels a month—before they're available in stores—with 9% off retail on any books you keep (just $2.49 each)—and FREE home delivery besides.

Plus There's More!

You'll also get our newsletter, packed with news of your favorite authors and upcoming books—FREE! And as a valued reader, we'll be sending you additional free gifts from time to time—as a token of our appreciation.

THERE IS NO CATCH. You're not required to buy a single book, ever. You may cancel Reader Service privileges anytime, if you want. The free gifts are yours anyway. It's a super sweet deal if ever there was one. Try us and see!

Get 1 FREE full-length Harlequin American Romance® novels.

Plus this handy compact manicure set

Plus a surprise free gift

▼ PLUS LOTS MORE! MAIL THIS CARD TODAY ▼

Harlequin's Best-Ever "Get Acquainted" Offer

Yes, I'll try the Harlequin Reader Service under the terms outlined on the opposite page. Send me 4 free Harlequin American Romance® novels, a free compact manicure set and a free mystery gift.

154 CIH NA9W

PLACE STICKER FOR 6 FREE GIFTS HERE

NAME _____

ADDRESS _____ APT. _____

CITY _____

STATE _____ ZIP CODE _____

Gift offer limited to new subscribers, one per household. Terms and prices subject to change.

Don't forget...

...Return this card today to receive your 4 free books, free compact manicure set and free mystery gift.

...You will receive books before they're available in stores and at a discount off retail prices.

...No obligation. Keep only the books you want, cancel anytime.

Her alarm and distress pierced through him, and he dropped his hands. "All right, Carlys, all right."

An instant later, her robe was retied and they were standing at a little distance from each other, their breathing harsh, shaky, erratic. In Carlys, feelings of humiliation mingled with wonder. How could she have behaved so wantonly! She couldn't look at him, could only lean helplessly against the wall, hiding her eyes.

"I'm not normally a tease." The words were halting.

"I know."

She couldn't stop trembling or stop thinking about what had almost happened, what damn well would have happened if he'd been only a tad more insistent, less gallant.

His arms wound around her, gentle now. "Carlys, I'm sorry. I shouldn't have..." He withdrew slightly. A hand under her chin, he forced her to confront him. His voice was soft as velvet, gently stroking her love-ravaged nerves. "I never meant to go that far."

"I know." Neither had she. The question was what happened now? Would he want her to move out? How would she feel if he did?

He regarded her silently, an unreadable expression in his eyes. "I still want you," he admitted raggedly.

She knew that. She couldn't give him what he wanted, not as things were now.

He saw she wasn't angry, only confused. It was a confusion he shared. Hands cupping her shoulders, he drew her close again.

His face sought refuge in the fragrant mass of her hair. "I need to hold you," he said simply.

"Please," she said tightening her arms around him, stepping closer into his tender embrace. "Please..."

WHEN HAD HIS FEELINGS for her changed? Jason wondered several hours later, unable to sleep, unable to do anything except stare at the ceiling and think of Carlys.

Was it when she first moved in with him, or when she became pregnant? Or was it earlier still that his feelings for her had begun to change, however subtly? The first time he took her to dinner? The day he held her as she cried?

How had he gone from simply looking on her as a prospective friend to feeling sorry for her and so becoming involved with her problems? Now she was living with him, albeit platonically. And he found he wanted to make love to her more than he'd ever imagined it was possible for him to want a woman. What would the next step be? Did he really want to know? No, he didn't think so, not when just the thought of taking a woman to the altar again gave him pause.

Maybe with Carlys marriage would be different, more giving. And maybe it wouldn't. He didn't quite trust himself to be able to handle it successfully. He wasn't ready to take a chance yet. She obviously had picked up on that, which had to be the cause of her skittishness about making love.

He understood. He admired her tenacity in holding on to her beliefs, holding out for Mr. Right. If anyone deserved to be happy, Carlys did. But then, he'd thought that from the very first.

Looking back, he realized he couldn't name a day or a time when their relationship had begun to shift from friendship and mutual purpose to something deeper and more intimate. He'd only known on a subliminal level that the change had been happening, not all at once but day by day, hour by hour, minute by minute. And this evening, when he'd walked in that door and found her with the baby in her arms, everything had simply fallen into place. He'd realized he wanted Carlys and needed her, and most of all he was determined to make her his, no matter how long it took or how difficult Carlys would be to win.

They were right for each other, he and Carlys. Judging by the way she'd looked at him, both before and after he kissed her, she knew it, too.

As for marriage... Well, marriage he still didn't know about. The age-old institution seemed full of pitfalls. He didn't want to chance losing Carlys simply because they were forced into a convention neither of them had been able to make work before—she, because she'd never been able to even get to the altar, he, because his relationship, fragile and ill-made as it was, had disintegrated almost as soon as the vows had been said.

On the other hand he could and would commit himself to a relationship. He'd even consider living with Carlys indefinitely.

The question was, would that be enough for Carlys, with her fairy-tale vision of hearth and husband and children.

He frowned.

She deserved better than that. Yet he couldn't offer her something he himself didn't want. Possibly day by day his feelings toward marriage with Carlys would change; possibly it was only a question of time.

The immediate question was what to do now.

Tonight, for all its triumph, had also been a disaster. Carlys had been frightened by passion slipping out of their control. He couldn't blame her; he'd been just as surprised by his own ardent response to her, his unprecedented unwillingness to end the embrace.

Jason stood up restlessly, strode over to look out his bedroom window into the night-darkened street beyond.

At that moment, he knew what his impulse was. He wanted to go into her bedroom, wake her and tell her how his feelings and wishes had changed and demand equal frankness from her. If she hadn't been pregnant, if their situation hadn't been so otherwise complicated, possibly a direct approach like that would have worked.

But their situation was complicated now, hopelessly so. And she was pregnant. Pregnant women were emotional and vulnerable, Carlys doubly vulnerable because her situation was so unusual. Did he have the right to rush Carlys into a sexual affair? He didn't think so. No, hard as it would be for him, she deserved his patience, his willingness to give her time to identify her own feelings.

And he needed to think about marriage. The one thing he wouldn't do was make any promises about marriage that he couldn't deliver; Carlys had already been left at the altar once. So until he did know his own heart, it was better simply to say nothing. Better to remain silent than raise hopes and later dash them.

Patience, Jason decided finally, for both of them. Willingness to let life unfold at a natural rate. That was the key.

"I DON'T KNOW ABOUT YOU, but I'm about to call it a night," Jason announced from the other end of the dining room table. "I'm going to have a couple of cookies and a glass of milk in the kitchen. Care to join me?"

Carlys looked up from the stack of papers in front of her. Since Megan had gone to bed, she'd been immersed in her work. Jason had been similarly occupied in his office most of the evening and had only just come out to join her.

Carlys stretched and smiled. "I'm ready to quit, too. A snack sounds great." Together they wandered into the kitchen.

Several days had passed since their erotic midnight encounter. To Carlys's relief, nothing had changed between her and Jason. If anything, they were closer than ever. Yet by the same token they were also both very aware now of how easy it would be for them to find themselves in bed together. As a result, Jason hadn't kissed her since. Abstinence was wise, indeed Carlys was relieved he was so practical and considerate. And yet in a secret corner of her mind she wished not for practicality and consideration but for a reckless, passionate love affair.

"Chocolate chip or iced oatmeal?" Jason asked, producing the cookie tin.

"One of each." Carlys poured milk into two glasses.

Jason sat across from her and reached for a chocolate chip cookie. "So what have you been working on?"

"The new business I'm trying to set up, Nannies Incorporated."

"Problems?"

"Nothing but." Carlys explained her attempts to get an innovative child-care training program with the local community college. "The red tape with city, state, and federal government, is impossible. It would take me years to get something going if I go through those channels. So I've begun going to the private vocational schools. I started last week. I've found one that wants to sponsor the program, but their tuition requirements are impossible." She named the fee. "Which is of course totally unaffordable for most of the people who would be interested in joining the program."

"So now what?" Jason asked, dipping another cookie into milk. Unlike Carlys, he could eat half a dozen or so at one sitting and never gain a pound.

"I don't know. I think my best bet is still the private vocational school. But then I have the problem of finding scholarships or perhaps simple grants to underwrite the program." Ultimately, she didn't want costs to run any higher than those at the community college, if she could help it.

"Is there any reason why you can't set up your own training program and run it privately any way you want?"

"A big one. If I have employees educated by an accredited institution, my insurance rates for the agency will be much less. If I set up my own program, just to break even I'd have to charge fees that would be far too much for most of the people who would be interested in hiring a nanny."

"Which would be self-defeating."

"Right. My idea is to serve as many people in as many income brackets as possible, not just a small elite. Two working couples each with a modest income and two children, should be able to pool their resources and hire a single nanny to take care of all four children at once. With a well-trained, professional sitter, backed up by substitutes from the agency, they could concentrate on their jobs in peace and the children would get more individual attention."

"Carlys, you're a great saleswoman."

"It's perfect for people who have to work but don't want to put their child in a center." Now, if only she could overcome the myriad of obstacles and get the business working! When she started she'd had no idea the organization would be so complicated. Her previous businesses had been relatively simple in scope and easy to start up. And she'd been able to rely on her parents' expertise. Now she was starting from scratch, venturing into foreign territory.

"Have you thought about asking big businesses to finance the educational program?"

Carlys hesitated. She hadn't gotten that far yet. "I wasn't sure they'd be interested. You work for a big company. What do you think?"

"I doubt you'd get any one company to underwrite the whole venture, but if you can get the program solidly put together, you might be able to interest fifty or so in underwriting it jointly. The trick would be to approach them that way—jointly, with all your facts already in place."

Carlys drank down the rest of her milk. "Good thinking, Jason. I'll give it a try."

"I hope it works out for you. You're really serious about this project, aren't you?"

Carlys nodded. "Good in-home child care should be more readily available, Jason. I'm determined to do something about it. As it is, from the business point of view, the situation's an entrepreneur's delight. Demand far outweighs supply, even with all the current educational programs for such help filled to the max."

Jason slanted her an admiring glance. "This sounds like it could take a long time to get off the ground."

"I don't mind. I'm determined to see this through no matter how hard it proves to be." On some level he seemed skeptical, or maybe just worried that she might be in for disappointment. "There are twenty existing schools for nannies nationwide, all with a thirty-week training program. So it's not as though I'm a pioneer venturing into uncharted territory. I have the benefit of other models, far-flung as they may be."

At that, he seemed to relax and put his worries aside. "You've studied their curriculums?"

"Sure, and I've got an idea of general costs and various improvements I'd like to see made in any program I set up." Thinking of all the parents and children she would help made her glow. "I have a chance to do something important here, something vital. I'm not going to fail."

Jason saluted her with his milk glass. "With an attitude like that, I'm sure you won't."

"ANOTHER GREAT CHECKUP!" crowed Jason after Carlys's two-month exam.

She grinned as they left the doctor's office together, unable to resist teasing him about his overprotectiveness. "It must be because I'm eating all my veggies."

He stopped dead in his tracks, looking as if he wanted very much to kiss her. She flushed to her knees.

"And because I'm around to give you tender loving care."

That he had. "You've been wonderful," she said sincerely, her blush fading as her eyes locked with his. She felt safe around him, secure and happy, as if nothing would ever go wrong again.

"I've enjoyed having you near me." He brushed a thumb lightly across her cheekbone. "And it keeps me from worrying about how you're doing, if the baby's all right, that kind of thing. You've been great about helping out with Megan, too."

She smiled. "I haven't minded. It's been a pleasure."

"I know. That's what makes the attention you give her all the more special."

There was a prolonged moment of awkwardness between them before he moved to help her into his car.

"Too bad I'm going home at the end of the week." Her three weeks' stay at his home had stretched to four and then five. She really couldn't put off leaving any longer—even if she was falling in love with him.

Because as much as she wished the feelings were mutual, she couldn't be sure yet how he felt. He desired her, liked her, even cared about her deeply. But love? That was an emotion that demanded much from two people, perhaps more than Jason could give her at this point in his life. And then, too, there was still the over-all precariousness of their situation. To ask for too much might be to ruin everything. She wasn't willing to risk that.

His hand lifted to the ignition key, then dropped. He turned toward her impulsively. "Carlys, do you have to go?"

The truth was that Carlys didn't want to go but was treading on dangerous ground every day she stayed. She was becoming too accustomed to living there, to depending on Jason to cheer her up when she felt down, to having Megan tumble into her room first thing in the morning and give her a wake-up kiss, to sharing equally in the grocery shopping and cooking and cleaning for three. Staying with Jason, she felt like part of the family, his family.

And yet romantically, sexually, everything was as it had been before that one passionate night: careful, friendly, but with a degree of aloofness that was necessary and yet not what she wanted at all.

Still, she sensed beginning an affair too soon would be the quickest, surest way to end a friendship and muddle their feelings about each other and the baby they shared.

"Jason, we agreed that—"

"You'd stay with me for three weeks, and I've already talked you into five. I know. But now that it has worked out so beautifully..." He leaned toward her persuasively. "Carlys, I like having you near. I like watching the baby grow."

Was that all?

"I've enjoyed being with you and Megan," Carlys said carefully. And it had been nice, having someone share her delight over the child growing within her. His child. Their child.

"Then stay with me," he pleaded softly, covering her hand with his, "at least until the baby's born."

Shock rendered her momentarily speechless and he hurried on, "Having you with Megan and me has been good for all of us. I never have to worry about being called out in the middle of the night. You have a child to practice on. Megan has a woman's presence in her daily life."

And they'd become close friends. More, she would miss seeing him every day. She would miss talking to him, laughing with him, even occasionally grumbling at him for hiding the sugar and forgetting where he put it.

"Jason, you're sure about this..." she said uncertainly. Her emotional reaction was to say yes, yes, yes!

"Yes. I'm very sure. Carlys, I need to be near you and the baby you're carrying right now."

Carlys didn't want to be alone at a time like this. Nor did she want to live with her folks. In her mind to do so would prove she couldn't handle pregnancy alone, as they had originally said. Still, he hadn't said he loved her, or even hinted he might feel the same as she did. And as for marriage, even if he loved her, he was bound to shy away from that.

She didn't want to be with a man just because they were friends, because they were sexually compatible, or parents to the same child.

Jason cared about her. He also cared about the child she was carrying, his child. If he had subconsciously lumped the two of them together, become enamored of them jointly, if he realized this only after the child was born, then his feelings about her might change.

If she were sure that it was really Carlys Holt he cared about, and not just the mother of his child . . .

She wasn't sure.

And as long as she was still confused . . .

"Say yes, Carlys," Jason pleaded. "Stay with me until after the baby's born. Then when you've had a chance to regain your strength you can go back to your own place."

The silence between them strung out for long heart-rending minutes. Put that way, it was such a sensible plan. What could she do? Forcing her qualms aside, she gave in to her heart's desire. "Yes, Jason. Yes. I'll stay."

"YOU'VE GOT TO BE KIDDING," the twins said in unison when they heard about Carlys's new arrangement several weeks later at a gathering at the Holts'.

Matt plunged on, "Living with him for a couple of weeks in order to get the hang of parenting is one thing, but to do so until after the baby's born is ridiculous. Hell, if you're going to do that, why not just get married? You can always get divorced later, and this way, at least the baby would be born legitimate.''

Carlys felt herself blush. Leave it to the twins to state flatly what everyone else thought but were afraid to express. Fortunately, Megan and Susie were both playing in another room, well out of earshot. Only Jason and she were witnessing her brothers' reactions.

''Matt, I don't want to discuss this with you.''

He folded his arms across his brawny chest. ''I don't know why not.''

''Because it's none of your business!'' Carlys snapped, avoiding Jason's eyes. He had to be as uncomfortable as she was.

''The hell it isn't! You're my sister! Dammit, Carlys, I just want the best for you.''

''I know that. I still want you to back off.'' Carlys felt she'd been backed into a corner with no possible way out. Damn them anyway for making her feel she was breaking all ten of the commandments. She'd done nothing wrong except start to fall in love with Jason a few days too late. As close as they were, and getting closer every day, she wasn't sure they would ever have a happy ending. Nor could she simply blurt out how she felt without jeopardizing everything they'd already built.

''I don't get it, either,'' Mark interjected quietly. He appealed to Jason. ''The two of you have obviously become close. Wouldn't you like your child to have your name?''

Jason turned to Carlys, trying desperately to read her mind. All she felt was embarrassment. She ducked her head.

"Of course I would," Jason answered calmly. He looked at Carlys steadily and without apology. "But Carlys and I had an agreement."

"So renegotiate," Matt interrupted heatedly.

Renegotiate. Sometimes Carlys looked at Jason and thought *I want to start over. I want to date him. I want to be his...girl...his love, anything and everything more than his friend.* And at other times, early in the morning, late at night, she felt that everything was so good between her and Jason, so right, that she didn't want to spoil what they had. Sex or dating would probably be ruinous. She had to face the fact that she was nearly three months pregnant, with a waist that got rounder all the time. Even if she started an affair with Jason, it wouldn't be likely to continue. Soon she'd look like a whale on legs.

"Enough, Matt," Carlys said irritably. "Jason and I are perfectly happy as it is."

"Oh, yeah? You really sound it," Matt replied under his breath, then at her scathing glance he left the room and walked outside with Mark to inspect the engine of Mark's new Jeep.

Knowing she needed time to collect herself, Jason walked Carlys into the deserted dining room. She stared at the flowers on the wallpaper, willing the hot tears scalding her eyes not to fall.

"Are you going to be able to handle this?" Jason asked her softly, searching her profile with a thoroughness that was both painstaking and tender.

For once, Carlys's willpower did the trick. Dry-eyed, once more in control, she turned back to face him. She took a deep, steadying breath and nodded decisively. She had wanted a baby too long to let anyone or anything ruin it for her. So what if she wasn't married! So what if people talked!

"Yes. I'll handle it. As for Matt, he's just doing his usual big-brother number. He and Mark have always been very protective of Susie and me. They still are." The amazing thing was that they hadn't scared Jason away. They seemed not to have bothered him in the least. He'd been irritated by their interference, of course, but that was all.

"I never meant to cause you pain."

"You haven't." She took a moment to count her blessings, was rewarded with a feeling of peace and a sense of fulfillment she'd never dreamed possible. When she spoke again, the words came straight from her heart. "This child has brought me only joy."

"To me, also," Jason said, visibly relaxing and squeezing her hand.

Later, Carlys's mother cornered her. "Mark told me what Matt said."

Carlys wouldn't have voluntarily brought it up. Now that Helen had, she asked her, "Is that what Daddy and you think, too?"

Helen hedged. "Your father and I want you to be happy. We don't like the idea of your living with Jason, even platonically. But at the same time, maybe under the circumstances it is good for you to be together. Having a baby is such a special experience." Her voice drifted off reverently.

"Jason said that," Carlys murmured. "He said there's a special closeness, a romance, an excitement."

"It's true. The two of you must feel it. Darling, it's obvious when people look at you that . . . well, that a certain intimacy has developed."

"I didn't realize it showed." Carlys stopped, shaken that her innermost feelings were so obvious to others. She'd never been that easy to read before. "Did you and Dad share the same sort of intimacy?"

"Oh, yes. With each pregnancy we got closer."

"What about after the baby was born?" Carlys asked, trying hard to hide the edge of anxiety in her voice.

"Well." Helen paused thoughtfully. "It's hard to remember. A new baby in the house brought about so many changes."

"You don't remember it being a magical time as well?" Carlys asked, disappointed.

"Busy. And happy, certainly. Darling, what is it? Are you afraid the intimacy between you and Jason will fade?"

"I guess I am." He'd only asked her to stay until the baby was born. "Sometimes I feel like Cinderella waiting for the clock to chime midnight. I was hoping you could reassure me otherwise."

"I wish I could, but those are answers only you can give. For what it's worth, I do like Jason. I think he's a wonderful man. He'll be a wonderful father to your child."

"You are happy about the baby?" The look on her mother's face gave her the answer, but Carlys needed to hear her say the word.

"Oh, yes." Helen smiled and gave her daughter a hug. "Very happy indeed."

Chapter Eight

"Jason, where's Megan's blue dress, the one with the two teddy bears appliquéd in front?"

"Uh, I think the hem's out of it."

"When did that happen?" Carlys advanced farther into the living room, thinking how handsome Jason looked in an open-necked polo shirt and shorts. His feet were encased in boat shoes; he wore no socks; and the effect of all that muscular, hair-dusted leg was evident in her heartbeat. Did he have any idea what he did to her, she wondered, or how much she had come to crave his closeness in the time they'd spent together? Carlys could hardly imagine her life without him. And Megan was just so much more joy.

"She caught the heel of her shoe in it on Tuesday when she was going down the slide." Jason looked up briefly from the computer magazine he was studying, then went right back to it.

"Why didn't you tell me? I would've sewed it for you."

"I didn't want to impose."

Carlys grinned. In the three months she'd lived with Jason, she'd come to know him well, better even than her brothers. He was a morning person, perky and lively before breakfast and inclined to be grumpy or short tempered only in late afternoon. Even at his worst, he was polite. And if on a rare occasion he was brusque, he never forgot to apologize later. Carlys liked that, finding both his lapses and his considerateness reassuring and endearing.

He liked televised sports with a passion. He read mostly nonfiction and computer magazines. He was terrible about writing letters, but not averse to picking up a phone. His only real flaw was that he couldn't sew worth a darn. Given a missing button on one of Megan's outfits or his own, he was likely to push the garment to the rear of a drawer and forget about it. Worse, he resisted all Carlys's efforts to reform him.

"It wouldn't be an imposition," Carlys said over her shoulder, leaving the room only long enough to gather up everything she needed, including Megan's ripped dress.

Returning, she sat beside Jason on the sofa, ignoring his slouchy posture and pointedly uninterested look. "However, you wouldn't have to ask me to do it if you could sew."

Jason shrugged and went back to his magazine. "I know." Knew but didn't intend to remedy it.

Men could be so stubborn! "Jason, let me teach you," Carlys said impulsively.

Jason sighed and sat up straight. "Carlys, we've been all through this. I know you mean well and have my best interests at heart but I just don't want to learn to sew." He took off his glasses, put them on the coffee table and rubbed the bridge of his nose.

He looked vulnerable without his glasses. Carlys couldn't help staring. She so seldom saw him unguarded these days. They were closer, true, much closer for having lived together, yet there was a new tenseness between them, a tenseness of the man-woman sort.

"Don't tell me you're afraid of a little needle and thread?"

"Not afraid, just clumsy."

Carlys looked at him in exasperation. Nothing made her more determined than an outright no or an assertion that something simply couldn't be done. "Jason, come on. Anyone who can fine-tune a television to the nth degree can sew on a button. You're just putting up roadblocks for yourself." Roadblocks he had to tear down. After all, she wouldn't be there forever.

He repeated with overstretched patience, "Carlys, I don't want to learn to sew."

She knew she ought to leave it. For some reason she didn't want to examine too closely, she couldn't. Recognizing his temper, she ignored it. With Megan in bed for the night, this was an excellent time for him to learn. And teaching him to sew was the one way she could repay him for having taught her so much about parenting.

He switched on the television. In his mind, the conversation was over.

A devil in her eye, Carlys reached for the remote control, turned the volume down low, then tossed it out of reach. He looked at her in amazement. Like an operating room nurse, she opened his hand and slapped needle and thread onto his palm. "Step number one..."

Deftly Jason jabbed the needle back into the pincushion top of the sewing basket and handed Carlys the end of the thread. He stated in clear, careful tones. "Carlys, I'm not learning."

Dimly, she was aware that this was their first real fight, even though it seemed to be only over a needle and thread. Excitement roared through her veins. All the politeness was being stripped away. It felt good, if terribly dangerous.

To emphasize his refusal to take a sewing lesson, Jason got up and stalked into the kitchen.

Sticking to her guns, Carlys followed him, taking with her thread, needle, Meg's dress, and the whole sewing basket. In for a penny, in for a pound.

"Jason, if you'd just—"

"Forget it, Carlys." With a warning look, he went to move past her. From the other room came the muted sound of a baseball game.

Carlys blocked his way. "Sooner or later Meg is going to need a hand-sewn costume for a school play."

"Then I'll hire it done."

"What if you can't find anyone to do it?"

A very male grin. "Then I'll ask you."

His sudden capriciousness invaded her soul. "What if I make you help?" she couldn't resist teasing back.

"I won't." Firm.

"Oh, yes you will." Her response was equally adamant.

"No, I won't."

"Will."

"Won't."

"W—" Carlys's words were cut off by an involuntary gasp for air as his hands closed firmly about her waist. Lightning quick, the sewing kit was snatched from the hands, put aside. The hands returned to her waist, lifted her and turned her around until their positions were reversed and she was backed up against the counter. His hips were aligned with hers, not touching. His eyes as they gazed down at her were dark with pique...and something else.

"Won't," he said firmly.

Her breasts rose in agitation as she took a quick, deep breath. Her head slanted back. And then his mouth was lowered to hers. With the mood between them, she expected fireworks; he gave her slow, gentle passion. His hands came up to cup her face. His thumb stroked across her lips again and again until they parted helplessly under the sensual onslaught. "Yes, you will," he whispered softly, ardently, and then his lips captured hers with a completeness that shattered her soul.

First, softness, tender searching; Carlys felt she had been waiting for that kiss an entire lifetime. Nipping love bites at the corners of her mouth that worked slowly to the center. She moaned soft and low in her throat, needing and wanting so much more. And he was vibrating with life, with suppressed need.

Standing on tiptoe, she pressed lips to lips. Never had she derived such pleasure from such a simple thing. Never had she felt she pleased a man more.

Pressure, he used it a thousand different ways, to say a thousand different things, first leading, then following, then taking the lead again. His tongue flicked out and dampened her lips, moved into her mouth to lay claim to the softness there.

She felt wanted, incredibly wanted; the need to dissolve into him was almost overpowering. Her tongue twined with his, passionately meeting wish for wish, touch for touch, desire for desire. A shudder ran through her, echoed in him, and all restraint fled. His touch demanded a response and she gave it gladly, wreathing her arms about his neck, yielding as he spread his hands low across her hips and dragged her close until her breasts were flattened against the wall of his chest, thighs touched thighs, and the hardness of his sex was pressed between them.

"Oh, Carlys, Carlys," Jason whispered, "what are you doing to me?" He buried his face in the softness of her hair. "Carlys, I want to take you to bed."

She drew back and away from him. This was crazy, totally unlike her. The chemistry was there between them and probably always would be, yet they'd made no commitment to each other beyond sharing in the parenting of a child.

She pushed hard against his chest and stepped back as far as she could, until her spine touched the countertop. There were all of one and a half inches between them.

Jason seemed ready to close even that small gap.

Jason, what you're doing to me is so nice but we can't go on. I can't let us, much as I might want to. Because in the end, knowing you don't love me as I want to be loved, I would be so hurt.

Swallowing hard, she looked up at him. The misty sensual glaze in his eyes had her immediately looking away. "We've become good friends. I don't want to lose that."

"And you think if we go to bed we will?" His voice was a harsh staccato in the silence of the kitchen.

"I don't know. Maybe. I only know it's a chance I can't take. Not now."

"And in the future?" For a moment, he was motionless, seeming not even to breathe.

She didn't dare open her lips. Silence fell between them. *Oh, please,* she thought, *don't let him hate me.*

Jason kissed her again, quickly, reassuringly. "I know what you're thinking. I don't mean to force you into promising anything you're not sure you want. I'm hardly some caveman, Carlys, who'd drag you off at the first opportunity. I just meant I desire you, that's all. I want you to know. I know we had an agree-ment—''

An agreement Carlys regretted with all her soul.

''But it's not enough for me, or you, either, judging by the way you just kissed me back. I'd like to have permission to court you. I know that's an old-fashioned term, an old-fashioned way of establishing a relation-ship.''

''You want us to become lovers?''

''Eventually, yes, very much.''

He was smiling, at ease with his sexuality and hers. Well, that was certainly adult. Jason had progressed from platonic friendship to a desire for an affair, whereas what she wanted was a marriage that would endure.

Swallowing hard, Carlys slid away from him. ''Jason, part of me would like that, but the other part says this can't happen again, that I should never have let it go so far. I don't want to lose you. But we've got to think of the baby we're going to have first.''

He withdrew, both hurt and baffled by her hot-and-cold attitude.

''I guess this has all happened at an inopportune time,'' he said uncertainly.

''Yes, it has.'' Carlys took a deep breath. Dammit, why did she have to be pregnant now? Was she really going to let herself throw away everything they had shared? ''Bringing sex into it just confuses everything all the more. Jason, I don't mean to hurt you or be coy, but I need a few days to think, to figure out what to do.'' To make sure that what she wanted physically now was right for her emotionally in the long run. ''I don't want to just jump into anything in the heat of the moment."

And she needed to figure out if she could continue living with Jason or not, if she wanted to chance the complications of a love affair.

Already her heart said she did. And if in a few more days she still felt the same, if Jason still felt the same...

"It would've been easier if we'd dated first, wouldn't it, rather than moved in together?" He suffered his own regrets.

"Hindsight's always better."

He studied her briefly before asking, "Carlys, are you sorry about the baby?"

"No, never. Only that we're thinking about getting involved now."

"It'd be easier if we didn't."

"Yes. Don't you think so?"

"Probably."

She knew by the expression on his face that she'd disappointed him by holding him at arm's length. Nonetheless, for the moment anyway, she was helpless to do anything at all differently. "I need time Jason, a few days," she reiterated with a calmness she didn't feel.

His voice was a soothing balm for her love-ravaged senses. "Take all the time you need."

WHO HAD HE BEEN KIDDING? Jason thought irritably, prowling the living room long after Carlys had gone to bed. He'd shocked the hell out of her, kissing her as passionately as he had, telling her outright he wanted them to become lovers. He'd shocked the hell out of himself.

The truth of the matter was that he wanted Carlys in ways he'd never wanted a woman and with a ferocity that amazed him. He'd come to count on her during the past few weeks and months. He'd loved having her near him and near Megan. But more than that, he felt she was a part of him now. He didn't think he could go on without her, at least not happily. He didn't think she could go on happily without him, either; whether she would admit that to herself, however, was another matter.

He knew now without a doubt he was falling in love with her. He was contemplating making their living arrangement a permanent one. Ironically, just as he was beginning to understand his own feelings, she was backing away from the intimacy hovering just within their reach.

Knowing how much she'd been hurt by her first engagement, he was not surprised by her reserve. When he'd first met her he had been averse to love and marriage, and yet for the first time he could recall since his divorce he felt the risk was worth it. Nonetheless, there were major problems.

Carlys still had to come to terms with her feelings about him and decide if she cared about him enough to take the next step, to become lovers. To woo her, to make her his, he would have to move slowly. With time, with caution and effort, he hoped to make her reciprocate all his desires.

Who would have thought he'd come to feel as enamored of her as he had? He'd thought he had no time for romance. Yet in ordinary, dull conditions of daily life, under which most love affairs dwindled and died, his affection for her had only grown.

She was closer to him, too; he knew it.

Jason smiled. Maybe there still was magic left in the world after all. With Carlys, he hoped to find it.

THE NEXT MORNING brought a surprise visitor, whom Jason had to admit he was glad to see, surprise or no. Not that Alice's timing couldn't have been better; it could've been a helluva lot better. Nonetheless, Jason decided to handle Alice's inopportune arrival as best he could, for Carlys's sake as well as Megan's and his own.

"I'm sorry for blowing up at you the last time I was here," Alice stated frankly, immediately upon her unexpected arrival on his doorstep, suitcases in hand. "But I've been thinking about what you said, Jason. I should spend more time with Megan. I still don't want her to rely on me, for all the reasons I've told you before, but at the same time, I don't want to hurt her, either, and I know if I continue to avoid her, I will."

It was clear that Alice meant what she said. Jason's response to her speech was simple; one didn't look a gift horse in the mouth. "How long can you stay?"

"A few days—I'm between assignments—if you don't mind my being here."

"I don't. But Carlys..." Jason stopped and swore mentally. Alice's visit couldn't have come at a worse time for his love life. He wanted to start courting Carlys immediately, if he could get her to agree, but that couldn't be done with Alice in the house. Yet he could hardly refuse Alice lodging, either, when it had been so difficult to get her to agree to do even this much for Meg.

"Jason?" Alice broke into his thoughts. "I may not be married to you, but I can still read your face as easily as a hand of cards."

"You can, can you?" he bantered back, buying time, wondering how he was going to explain Carlys's living there with him.

"Yes. Some bonds—between parent and child and parents of the same child—can't be broken."

He grinned. "I guess not." In that respect he always would be close to Alice, though what they shared was a far cry from the intimacy he already had now with Carlys. In contrast, his relationship with Alice, at the height of their ill-fated marriage, was with a stranger.

Carlys chose that moment to walk into the living room, dressed in trim white slacks and a pink jersey shirt, her handbag slung over her shoulder. She said hello to Alice then turned to him. "Jason, we're almost out of soap. Baby shampoo, too. I think I'll run to the market, maybe do some shopping later."

Alice glanced down at Carlys's slightly rounded belly, easily picking up on what Jason had yet to tell her. "You're pregnant?" she asked Carlys.

"Yes." Carlys grinned, unable to contain her happiness.

"When are you due?" Alice looked genuinely pleased for them both.

"February."

"Well, congratulations!" Alice hugged Carlys and then Jason. "I wish you all the best."

Jason thanked her, then changed the subject. Indicating Alice's suitcases, he asked, "Moving in with me?"

"Only for the weekend. Do you mind? I could go to a hotel, but I know so little about child rearing and Meg's so settled in here, I—"

"Of course you must stay," Carlys said.

Jason looked at her. She wanted to cut and run. He didn't want her going back to her house, even for a few days. He would miss her. I don't want you to go, he transmitted to her silently. To Alice, he said, "Carlys has been staying with me."

"Oh." Alice clearly didn't know what else to say. Jason was hoping she'd elect to spend her nights elsewhere. She didn't disappoint him.

"Look, if it's not convenient—"

As if reading his mind, Carlys met his glance then turned to Alice. "We want you to stay. It'd be better for both you and Megan."

Alice vacillated. "You're sure?"

"Positive. You can have the guest room."

"Right," Jason intervened. "Carlys can take the master bedroom and I'll take the couch."

At that, Alice, jumping to the wrong conclusion, shook her head in silent amusement. "Jason, c'mon. It won't bother me if you share a bedroom with Carlys. I'm an adult. I understand these things."

Jason found himself flushing with embarrassment, not so much for himself but for Carlys. As innocent as their arrangement was, it looked bad. He sensed that although she'd die before admitting it, Carlys sometimes felt keenly humiliated by the casual assumptions that other people made about her.

"It's not what you think, Alice. Carlys and I are still just friends."

Alice said nothing more. It was clear that she felt they were refusing to admit they were lovers.

Jason gave up. He and Carlys exchanged a mutually embarrassed glance. It was hard not to think about the kisses they'd shared and how much he wanted their relationship to deepen. He was already impatient for her answer after waiting less than twenty-four hours.

Jason picked up Alice's suitcase. "I'll just take this into the guest room."

Carlys turned to Alice as he was leaving the room. She explained, "It really isn't what it looks. We're not. I am living here, but our relationship is strictly platonic."

"Right. Well, good luck with the baby. I wish you both well," Alice replied gently. And then, in a more friendly tone still, "Are the two of you hoping for a boy or a girl?"

Jason sighed and leaned a shoulder against the doorway. He knew what he wanted. The question was, what did Carlys want?

Chapter Nine

"Hey, thanks for suggesting we go shopping today. I haven't had so much fun in a long time," Susie said later that afternoon. They'd stopped at a pizza place in the mall for lunch. Now they were lingering over their sodas.

"It's my pleasure. I haven't seen you much either. Dad says you've been busy. How are things at school?"

"Fine." Susie looked past Carlys at a fountain in the middle of the mall.

Carlys spotted her unease immediately. Knowing Susie didn't confide her troubles easily, however, she took a roundabout approach. "Seen Zach Sullivan much?"

"No." Susie's answer was too quick.

"Why not?"

"Because I . . . oh, cripes! I don't believe it!"

"What?"

Susie leaned sideways in her chair and tried to duck behind Carlys, who couldn't see what she was hiding from. "Zach must have heard me telling Patty I was going shopping with you here."

Carlys twisted around in her chair. Behind her, near the fountain, three boys were lined up facing their table.

Carlys stared at her sister, perplexed. She'd never seen Susie quite so agitated.

Susie grimaced and looked as though she was going to be ill. "Don't look now. Here he comes. I can't believe this is happening," she muttered under her breath.

"Hi, Susie." A cute boy with ebony hair and a long, rangy frame stopped at their table, his hand on the back of one of the spare chairs.

"Zach," Susie mumbled.

Carlys could have sworn she was looking at Susie's first good dose of puppy love. Which didn't explain Susie's trying to avoid the boy.

"Mind if I sit down?"

"Not at all," said Carlys graciously.

"Actually, we were just about to leave, weren't we, Carlys?"

"Well, no." Susie kicked her beneath the table.

Carlys rubbed her shin surreptitiously.

Zach clearly was enamored of Susie. "I heard there's a sneak preview at the Presidio tonight. The new Steve Spielberg flick. Supposed to be pretty good. Want to go?"

Susie hesitated. After a moment, she shook her head. "I can't. I . . . I've got to study."

"Saturday night? C'mon Susie, everybody takes a break now and then and I know for a fact you haven't been seeing anyone else over the summer break, not steadily anyway. So what gives? What did I ever do to you to make you not want to go out with me?"

Susie stood up abruptly, jarring the table. "Zach, you're a nice guy—"

"Don't give me this, Susie. Why are you avoiding me? I thought we were friends!" His hurt showed.

Susie had tears in her eyes. She looked at him helplessly. "We were . . . are."

"Then why do you treat me like some kind of leper at school? Hell, I can't get two words out of you anymore. Anytime I walk up, you run away. What's going on?"

Susie grabbed her purse. "I'm getting out of here!"

"Susie!" But Susie turned away toward the central walkway of the mall, then broke into a run.

Zach started after her, but Carlys quickly caught his arm.

"No, Zach, don't." Touched by the hurt on his face, she said, "I don't know what's going on with her."

"I just want her to talk to me. When she looks at me, she acts as if she's afraid! I haven't done anything to make her feel that way."

Carlys believed him. She also believed something was very wrong. "Let me talk to her."

Zach's friends, having witnessed the whole humiliating scene, were edging nearer.

Zach swallowed hard. "If you find out anything—"

"I'll call you, or better yet have her call you."

"Thanks."

Carlys found Susie in the car. She'd rolled down the windows and was sitting with both hands laced around the wheel.

"I'm sorry, Carlys. I just had to get out of there."

"What is it with you and Zach?" Carlys slid in beside her. "Susie, either you tell me what's going on or I'm going to Mom and Dad."

Susie sighed. "All right. I guess I need to talk to someone anyway. You know that day I came home late for dinner?"

"Smelling of toothpaste? I remember."

"I got jumped in the parking lot after practice. I was late getting out. I usually am. Zach and the others had already left."

"Who jumped you?"

"Naomi Phillips and a bunch of her girl friends. They're all pretty wild."

"Why would they do something like that?"

"She's Zach's ex-girlfriend, or at least she thinks she is. She only went out with him a couple of times. Anyway, she's still hung up on him and didn't want me going out with him. She said—she said if I went out with him again they'd get me again. And then they smeared toothpaste in my hair."

"And that's when you stopped going out with Zach?"

"No. I wasn't going to let anyone intimidate me. So when he asked me to go to a movie with him, I did. We came out of the show to find that one of the tires on Zach's car had been slashed."

"Naomi?"

"I'm pretty sure. Zach called the police to report it but they didn't come up with any clues."

"Did you tell the police what you suspected?"

"Not right away. I was afraid of what Zach and some of his friends might do in retaliation. And besides, I had no proof."

"But you did go to the police?"

"A couple of days later, alone. They told me that without proof there wasn't anything I could do."

"What about the harassment?"

"They told me to either level with Zach and go to the school authorities or stop seeing him. Because it was almost summer break and I knew I wouldn't be seeing him much anyway—he had a job as a camp counselor in east Texas—I chose to stop seeing him.''

"Why?" Carlys was shocked, angry. It wasn't like Susie to turn tail and run.

Susie's mouth was set grimly. ''Because I knew to pursue it would only make matters worse. Last year another girl reported Naomi and some of her friends for harassment. The principal expelled several of the girls. The person who'd turned them in was later jumped when she was off school grounds. I like Zach, Carlys but the harassment isn't worth it.''

Carlys was silent for a thoughtful moment. "If you weren't being harassed, would you see Zach?"

"Yeah. For whatever good it does.''

"When did the harassment start up again?"

"A couple of weeks ago, when school started and Zach started chasing me again.''

"Can't you at least tell Zach?"

"And do what? Start an all-out war between the kids in the band and Naomi and her gang? Believe me, Carlys, if Zach and his friends knew what was going on, there'd be trouble, plenty of it. All my friends are in extra-curriculars. Naomi and her friends aren't. If there was a fight, we'd all be banned from participating in outside activities for the rest of the year by the school administration, whereas Naomi and her friends have nothing to lose that way and they know it. They'd love to start a ruckus, just for the pleasure of seeing some of the good kids get suspended and have to sit out their senior year.''

"So you're resigned to the situation."

"Not really. I was hoping Naomi would start dating someone else over the summer and lose interest in Zach, and then I could go back to seeing him, but it hasn't

happened yet. She hasn't found another steady boyfriend."

Carlys was silent. "There must be something I can do
to help you out of this mess."

Susie sighed and admonished her wearily, "Carlys,
you and the twins have been coming to my rescue since
I was a baby. Over the years I've taken quite a ribbing
for it from my friends. I'm a senior now. Next year I'll
be away at college. It's time I stood on my own."

"Okay. I don't like it, but okay."

Susie started the car. She backed out of the space.
"So how's your life going? I never had a chance to ask.
You and Jason still getting along?"

"Oh, yes."

"But?" Susie intuited there was more.

Carlys grinned. One confession deserved another.
"Alice is staying there for a few days." Her voice trailed
off and her lips compressed with the depth of her frustration.

"Don't tell me you're jealous!"

"Honestly, yes I am and I hate myself for it." She
hated feeling irrational and overemotional. She supposed the cause was the pregnancy, the hormones, the
fact Alice still had her figure while she was losing hers.

Susie slanted her an inquiring glance. "Should you
be?"

"No." With an effort Carlys recovered her common
sense. "That's the worst of it. Alice is a friend to both
of us. I think she might even get the hang of motherhood one of these days." Though no television-perfect
parent, Alice was at least making more of an effort to
get close to Megan and had even been sitting on the
floor and playing with her when Carlys had left the
house.

"Then what is it? Is it Jason? You're sweet on him, aren't you?"

Carlys turned to her sister as they stopped at another light. "Does it show that much?"

"Mom and Dad—" Susie stopped and bit her lip.

"What?" Carlys demanded. She hated sentences that were left hanging.

"They're hoping the two of you will become... more than friends."

"I thought they didn't like my living with him."

"Oh, they don't. But I don't think they'd mind it so much if you married him."

Married him!

"Not yet, hm?"

"No, not yet. Definitely not yet." But soon? Carlys wondered.

"AND THE WORST OF IT IS," Carlys confided to Jason later that evening, as they left a concert in the park, "I can't do anything to help her."

Jason shrugged and captured Carlys's hand with his. He turned her around to face him. "Sounds to me like Susie's already solved her own problem. You can't live her life for her."

"I know that. But Susie's miserable. It's not right what those thugs are doing!" In frustration, she pulled away from Jason and took a few steps into the darkness, away from the pebbled path and into the shelter of trees. The September night was warm, the breeze softly caressing.

"Does she want to see Zach again now that school's started?"

"Oh, yes. You should see the way she looks at him. I know he cares about her."

Jason sighed. He put an arm around Carlys's shoulder, drawing her near. "So tell me about this Naomi. What do you know about her?"

"Not much."

"Well, find out whatever you can. Ask Susie or maybe even the school's guidance counselor. Maybe if we put our heads together, we'll be able to come up with a solution."

"I hope so."

"But that's not why I wanted you with me tonight," he confessed. "Having Alice stay with us the past few days has been a strain for all of us, I think."

"She's doing better with Megan."

"Yeah, she is. I wanted the two of them to have some quiet time alone tonight. But that's not why I asked you to go to the concert with me."

"Why did you?" Sitting under the stars with Jason, listening to the strains of Stravinsky and Ravel, had been one of the most romantic times of Carlys's life.

"Because I want an answer from you about dating me."

Carlys had been about to agree to his courtship idea when Alice had appeared. Now all her doubts had resurfaced.

"Carlys?"

"I don't want it to happen just because of the baby."

"Is that what you think? That the only reason I'm pursuing you is the child?"

"Not consciously. Jason, it is possible. You yourself have talked about what a special, almost romantic time pregnancy can be."

"That's true, but it wouldn't be this special for us, this compelling, unless there was something more between us."

Carlys was silent. She wished she could be so sure, but she couldn't help but remember her brothers when their wives had been pregnant. There had been a special closeness between them, which had intensified right up to the baby's birth and after. On the other hand, what she felt for Jason didn't seem to be dependent on her having his baby. The truth was that she liked everything about him, even his few foibles. Still, because of the faulty decisions she'd made previously where romance was concerned, she hesitated.

"I don't know, Jason. On the surface our dating sounds like a reasonable idea, but with us living together already..." Would she be able to leash her own passionate nature? She was already attracted to him more than was safe. To see him continually at his best and then to go home to the same house, their bedrooms just down the hall from each other...

"It'll work if we want it to. Besides, married parents do it all the time. They set aside special private time, just for themselves. I don't know why we single parents-to-be can't do the same."

"You read this in one of your magazines I suppose?"

"Hey! The *Ladies' Home Journal* has some great articles in it."

Carlys shook her head exasperatedly. "Now I know what to get you for your birthday. A subscription."

"Just don't forget *Popular Mechanics*, too."

They laughed together, their voices blending as softly and agreeably as they kissed. She looked up at him, her eyes aglow. He did make her feel special. And she loved being with him. Maybe she was being overcautious, paranoid. Jason wouldn't be pushing for this so strongly unless it was really what he wanted. And yet

Carlys had the feeling he wanted much more from her, guarantees that her feelings would never change. She knew she would always care for him. She felt he would care for her, too. But she couldn't guarantee that the magic would continue.

She'd thought at the time her love for Drake would last forever; it hadn't. She'd thought she'd be married to her own Prince Charming by now; she wasn't. Not to mention that it seemed their real intimacy, Jason's real interest in her, had come only after news of her pregnancy. Had she not conceived, had she not had reason to move in with him, however temporarily, what would have happened then?

And yet never had she wanted a man so much. Never had she felt just being with any other man was so right.

"All right," she said cautiously at last, finally giving in to her heart's desire. "We'll date. But let's limit it to two or three nights a week." She needed time to sort out her feelings, time for her to be sure of his.

Two or three nights a week wasn't the answer he'd wanted. She felt his disappointment.

Nonetheless, he nodded his agreement. "You're probably right. We don't want it to be too intense."

"ADMIT IT, you loved the boat show." Jason had come back from driving the sitter home for the night to find Carlys waiting for him in a chaise on the patio with the two glasses of wine he had ordered in advance.

"Boats are okay." Carlys tried not to giggle as she sipped at her wine.

"Okay!"

"Mediocre," she confirmed with a lazy drawl designed to provoke.

"I saw you eyeing the speedboat. You liked those controls. And when you sat behind the wheel," he teased, moving to sit next to her on the chaise, "you liked the power."

"Maybe just a little."

"A lot."

"A little."

Both fell silent, remembering the last time they'd gotten into a similar debating game. Jason set his glass aside and took both her hands in his. "The last three weeks have been the best three weeks of my life," he confided.

"For me, also," Carlys said softly. They had found out they liked many of the same things and disagreed on little. They had identical needs for private time and companionship. They knew when to talk, and when to be silent.

More important, Carlys had come to realize that her engagement to Drake had never had a chance. A relationship wasn't made out of fleeting passion or surface compatibility; it took love and a depth of caring that surpassed everything else. She and Jason had that; she and Drake never had it. So she was beginning finally to unlock the most vulnerable part of herself, to open herself up to Jason.

True, her feelings about Jason were still faintly muddled and new, but she also trusted her love completely, trusted him. He would never do anything to hurt her, never desert her. He had more than proved that. Whatever doubts she'd had about his devotion to her and the reasons for it had disappeared. She knew that they were absolutely right for each other and always would be. That was all that mattered. Jason was all that mattered.

Their days together had been wonderful, their dates both exciting and heartwarming. He'd been the perfect escort, the perfect friend. But he hadn't gone beyond that and she had to admit she was a little disappointed.

He saw the look on her face. He studied her relentlessly for long moments, then seemed to come to some decision of his own.

He stood and wordlessly pulled her to her feet. "I guess you're wondering why I've been so physically aloof lately. I haven't kissed you because I wasn't sure that if I started I would be able to stop." His luminous gaze told her how much he adored her, wanted her. He took a short, halting breath. "Carlys, I want to kiss you."

She felt her heart jump and her breath stall in her throat. The touch of his hands on hers was at once commanding and compellingly sensual.

Suddenly she had nothing to decide. She had only to go with what she was feeling, what they were both feeling. "So kiss me," she whispered, her eyes never leaving the dark depths of his.

Pleasure and relief lit his face. "You're sure?" he said solemnly. His hands tightened possessively over hers.

"Oh, yes, Jason, yes . . ."

She glided into his embrace with a dancer's grace. When his arms slid around her, pulling her close, she felt she had finally come home. His mouth moved on hers, tenderly at first, then more and more insistently. Pleasure rippled through her, weakening her knees, making her lean shamelessly into him until she no longer knew where her body ended and his began, only that they were together, and that nothing had ever felt so good or so right.

And still he kissed her, until her mouth was hot and open and yearning beneath his, until she was giving back as good as she got. Over and over, his lips curved to hers. Their breath mingled, they tasted each other. They learned how to please.

And still he wanted more. His hands smoothed over her back, his slightest touch creating rivers of electric sensation. His lips coveted and caressed by turns, energizing her with a fierce, desperate need. When she cried out with mingled impatience and pleasure, his mouth absorbed the sound; he gave a low guttural moan and drew away. His breath was warm against her temple, his pulse, erratic and swift, matching her own. "Carlys, I love you," he whispered tenderly, his low voice underscoring every word. "Do you hear me? I love you."

She laced her arms tighter about his neck, loving his strength and the gentle way he held her. Tears brimmed in her eyes. "I love you, too," she whispered back fiercely, knowing at last it was true.

"If you want me to stop—" His voice was husky, etched with restraint.

She met his searching glance with a woman's desire freely expressed. "I don't," she said quietly. "I need you, Jason. I want to be with you."

"You're sure?"

"Never surer of anything in my life."

He took her by the hand, slid aside glass doors and led her into his private, masculine domain. From the moment his lips touched hers in the shadowy expanse of his bedroom they were making love. Her mouth open to the bold conquest of his tongue, she kissed him back fervently, discovering that the taste and feel of him was just what she wanted. Had always wanted. Deep inside her, fires began to curl, and she yielded against him on a wave of deep, mindless pleasure.

"I want to feel all of you against all of me," he whispered huskily at last, zipping her dress open. Cool air assaulted her as clothing was discarded, his and hers. Heated fingers roved her skin, followed by the warmth of his touch and the moist softness of his mouth.

There seemed no end to his patience, his tenderness. He lingered at the soft underside of her breast until he felt her tremble, explored her soft curves and deepest secrets, the curve of her belly, the slope of her hips. Her legs were trembling as he lowered her to the bed.

She was restless, an ache burning in her middle. Though equally aroused, he was content to take his time, to draw out every moment. Stretched out alongside her body, he stroked with the tips of his fingers, the flat of his palms. She was helpless against the assault on her senses. She arched her back, stretching sinuously, her legs moving restively on the sheet. His tender explorations, sensual and delicate, weren't nearly enough. Her breasts were aching, the nipples beaded with longing. Lower still, she throbbed, needing, wanting to be filled. She rolled over onto her side and pressed against him, silently asking for a stronger touch.

"God, you smell good," he murmured, clasping her to him and burying his face in her neck.

"Jason, I—"

"I promised myself when the time came I wouldn't rush. Carlys, it's a promise I mean to keep."

Before she could protest, she was flat on her back. He was kissing her again with an insistence and mastery not to be denied. Only when she was limp with longing did he let his mouth leave hers to trail scalding caresses down the slope of her neck to the rounded globes of her breasts. Once there, he tantalized and tasted until her whole body began to quake, only to drift down.

She thought she would shatter from the pressure building inside her. She discovered he had only just begun.

She was wet and soft, open to his need, the passion a never-ending rainbow of sensation piled upon sensation.

She touched him where he touched her, kissed where he kissed... He sucked in his breath in surprise, moaned and slid his leg up and down the length of hers. Then without warning, their positions were altered. He was moving her up and over him; he was hard against her, his manhood pushing against her softness, his hands kneading her hips.

The moment of joining was the most intimate sensation she had ever known. She was amazed she could bring him to this just by existing, that he could make her feel so wild and free. And yet she had always known that they were meant to be together, meant to take each other to the depths and heights only lovers reached.

Faster and faster everything moved, until the world was spiraling out of control. Their senses narrowed only to the passion, to the sweetness of release. Only gradually did she become aware again of her own soft sighs, his low murmurs, their joy and wonder over what they'd discovered, the more tangible sensations of skin against skin, the warmth and love she felt in his arms.

Long moments passed, moments to treasure. Endearments were exchanged, drowsy compliments given. And still they held each other, their embrace the only reality for her in the dark, silent night. They were together, really together at last, and that was all that mattered, all that would ever matter.

Chapter Ten

"Eggs or cereal?" Carlys asked happily the next morning when Jason entered the sunny kitchen. Since it was her turn to cook breakfast, she'd gotten up first. Jason had followed ten minutes later. Dressed in pajama bottoms and a loosely belted thigh-length robe, he looked rumpled and sexy. The faint shadow of a beard and mustache lined his face.

"Neither," he pronounced, helping himself to a cup of coffee. "We're having breakfast in the park this morning."

This wasn't so much a proposal as an order. Never having seen him so serious and inexorable before, Carlys wasn't quite sure how to react. Slowly she put her coffee cup aside. She'd expected their becoming lovers to change things, true, but not this much, and certainly not after just one night.

She stared at him, her heart pounding.

"Carlys, we need to talk, just the two of us. I've already called a sitter for Megan. She'll be here in half an hour. We can leave any time after that, as soon as you're ready."

So she really didn't have any choice in the matter. Whatever he wanted to discuss with her was very important. Whether it was happy or sad news she couldn't tell; the expression in his eyes was unreadable. *Let him do this his way,* she thought. He'd already given her so much; their lovemaking the evening before had fulfilled her every fantasy. Surely whatever he had to say couldn't be all that bad.

"Can you be ready to go in fifteen minutes?" Jason asked, a hint of mystery in his face.

"Sure."

At last they were settled in a shady spot, a picnic basket of take-out goodies between them. Her curiosity killing her, Carlys nonetheless had waited until the time was right. No serious discussion could be had if they were constantly being interrupted by a precocious two-year-old or distracted by traffic.

Jason doled out coffee, juice and the danish they had picked up on the way. "I'm sorry I was so mysterious this morning, but I couldn't see any other way to get us out here alone without an argument."

The newly intimate light in his eyes told her he wanted to talk about how their relationship was bound to change now they'd made love. She exhaled her relief. She was glad he was tackling the dilemma head-on, instead of ignoring it and just trusting to luck everything would work out all right. She shifted on the blanket, until she sat facing him, cross-legged and at ease in her jeans and smock top.

Ruefully Jason rubbed his chin and ran his thumb over the bow-shaped lines of his mouth. He took off his sunglasses so she could better see his eyes and stuck them by one side into the buttonhole of his plaid madras shirt. "If I've been over-dramatic, and I guess maybe I have, it's because I'm scared."

"Scared of what?" Carlys echoed in an astonished tone. She took a sip of coffee, feeling it scald her throat. Yet the burn was nothing compared to the sudden emotional tears stinging her eyes. She loved Jason fiercely; she didn't want him hurting, not for any reason.

"Losing you."

Carlys was silent. It really wasn't necessary for him to say any more. She had suffered the same doubts and anxieties. They'd started out on one path, only to change direction halfway. Sometimes it was hard to know where they were going. But last night had been a commitment for her and for him; she was sure of it.

"Carlys, I want to marry you."

Surprise mixed with happiness rendered her momentarily silent. She'd dreamed of this for weeks. She had wanted Jason to propose to her, but only for reasons that would enable them to have a lasting relationship that would endure decades of hardship and bliss.

"Are you asking me this because of what happened between us last night?" she asked carefully at last, putting her coffee aside. It was her turn to hide her feelings.

"No."

She nearly sagged with the depth of her relief. "The baby, then?" But already she knew the answer.

Jason leaned forward to her and gripped her hands hard.

"I'm asking you because I love you and I can't imagine living a life without you." He spoke with the authority of a man whose opinion cannot be changed. "I've known it for a long time, Carlys, I just didn't want to face up to it or the possibility you might not feel the same about me as I do about you. But now I know that you love me. I know I love you. It's past time we took that next step. I guess I need to know you're mine, that I'm yours, that we're a partnership, a team, for more than just the moment. I would've loved you without the baby. In fact, if you hadn't wanted a child, if I hadn't offered to be the donor, then we probably would've gotten together a lot faster."

She thought of all the barriers her decision to have a child alone had caused. "You're probably right there."

"I'll be a good husband, I promise. Faithful. Loving. Patient."

"And what do you want from me in return?" Although Carlys was already tempted to say yes, she needed to know his expectations of her, to make sure she could meet them.

"That you be a loving mother to Megan, a partner to me, that you put our family first, above everything else."

"Meaning my work?" That sounded simple enough.

"Yes. And I'll do the same."

Well, that wouldn't be hard. Carlys had always intended to put family first.

"I know I'm asking a lot . . ." Jason continued hesitantly.

Carlys found suddenly she wanted to give a lot. "Yes, I'll marry you, Jason."

He smiled broadly. "Soon?"

"Next week if you want." Her parents would be delirious, not to mention her brothers. And her baby…her baby would have Jason's name and a real family, parents who loved each other fiercely. Yes, it was happening fast, but waiting would be pointless. She and Jason were already living together. She'd become an unofficial stepmother to Megan. She was carrying his child To marry quickly would be best for all of them.

"You don't know how long I've waited to hear you say those words," Jason said, hugging her close.

Carlys reveled in his affection, the strength his arms offered. Never had she felt more cosseted, more secure. "I can't believe it," she murmured, tears of bliss sliding down her face. "All my dreams are coming true."

His thumbs gently erased the salty wetness. His mouth moving to capture hers, he kissed her passionately. "And more will come true yet, you'll see."

"No DOUBT ABOUT IT, we picked the perfect place for a honeymoon," Carlys murmured contentedly two weeks later.

They had been married in the Holts' backyard under a latticework canopy woven with flowers. All their close friends had been there as well as Jason's immediate family and her own.

Carlys had been misty-eyed and highly emotional through most of the ceremony, but she'd managed to repeat her vows in a clear, steady voice. Jason had spoken his vows solemnly and flawlessly and faltered only once, and then very briefly, when slipping the wedding band on her hand. It had taken him two tries to get the ring over her knuckle. He kissed her tenderly at the conclusion of the ceremony; she'd remember for the rest of her life the passionate promise in his eyes. Later, it had been all champagne and cake and laughter. Jason had removed her lacy blue garter with ease. Susie had caught the bouquet. And then it had been time for them to go.

After receiving many hugs and good wishes, they'd set off for a few days alone. Now Carlys had never been happier or more content; Jason was feeling and looking the same.

"Think we can capture some of this Caribbean sunshine and take it home with us?" Jason asked lazily, sipping a tall glass of pineapple juice with an elaborate parasol stuck on top. Since arriving in Nassau, they hadn't been able to get a drink, alcoholic or otherwise, without some decoration perched on it. Jason, amused by the touristy atmosphere, used every fancy straw and stirrer, whereas Carlys found them a nuisance and discarded them promptly.

It was the differences between them, she thought tenderly, that made theirs such an interesting match.

They were lounging side by side on padded chaises. Directly to the north of them, some fifty feet away, was a shimmering turquoise sea. In the other direction, beyond the spotless white sand surrounding them, was their modern red-brick hotel, complete with dramatic fountains, man-made grottos with waterfalls, lots of little footbridges, little wooden walkways and a profusion of landscaped greenery. Nearby, in the pool area, a steel band was playing.

She stretched luxuriously, answering his rhetorical question with one of her own. "Why would we want to take Bahamian sunshine back with us when Dallas has plenty of its own, not to mention Texas-sized blue skies?"

Jason lowered his dark glasses and slanted her an interested glance. "Not getting a little homesick there, are you?"

"No." Though she did wonder how her businesses were going. There'd been a small problem with one of the diaper-service dryers before she left—which had been fixed, she reminded herself firmly.

She turned to Jason, grinning. "You still haven't told me why it is you want to take that sunshine home."

"Simple," he said softly. "Because of the way you look in it." Sliding his glasses all the way up to the bridge of his nose, he settled back in his cushioned chaise.

Since their arrival, the weather had been ideal, the temperature had been a balmy seventy-five degrees, the single rainstorm gentle and brief. "Hey, lady," Jason teased, "anyone ever tell you you look utterly gorgeous with a tan?"

"Only you." Carlys smiled. "About a thousand times."

"That's because you do look gorgeous," Jason drawled, giving her a comic leer.

Carlys laughed softly. "Don't you think you might be just the tiniest bit prejudiced?"

"No, not at all." Jason shook his head decisively.

"Jason, come on—"

"Hey!" He thumped his suntanned chest. "I'm not the only one sneaking a look at the most beautiful woman on the beach."

Carlys had noticed the glances they were getting. "I think it's because, aside from the fact we make such a handsome couple, we're obviously on our honeymoon."

"You think they know that?"

How could he even ask? She groaned. "C'mon, Jason, every time you look at me I—"

"What?" He ran a hand down the side of her thigh, eliciting tingles wherever he touched.

"I melt." She blushed, running a hand through her hair, which had gotten even blonder and wavier in the damp tropical heat.

For a moment she stared out at the sea. She had changed in the brief time she had known him. She felt she belonged to him, and that was new to her. In the past she'd belonged and answered only to herself.

She sighed, hearing the echo of what she'd said. "God, that sounds so corny." To melt whenever your husband looked at you, touched you.

"But true," Jason said. "For me, as well."

The spell cast over them had thoroughly engulfed them both. Jason bent to kiss her and Carlys sighed her contentment, at peace with herself and with him. "I never thought I'd feel this loved, Jason, or this sexy." She laughed softly. "And certainly not when I was almost five months pregnant." She'd expected pregnancy to be an asexual time; it had turned out to be anything but.

Thus far she'd only gained ten pounds. She had ten more to go, and a comfortable four months to do it in. Her stomach was still flat enough to make her look chunky rather than definitely pregnant. The street clothes she wore were stylish and loose, not all of them even maternity clothes. Only in her bathing suit, a sleek black one-piece suit with a band of camouflaging teal blue slashed diagonally across the front, could one definitely tell she was pregnant.

Jason watched her lovingly for long moments, his eyes lingering on the sun-kissed color in her cheeks, on the tip of her nose. "I'm glad I make you feel sexy," Jason confided huskily, taking a love bite out of her shoulder, "because you send me crashing right over the edge."

Carlys shook with laughter, remembering their first night, when they'd both gotten so carried away they'd almost fallen off the bed.

"Love me?" he asked softly, remembering what she was remembering and loving her all the more.

"More than life itself."

Jason rolled onto his back and put his forearm across his brow. "Ah, Carlys, I don't want to go home."

She sighed. "Neither do I."

Since arriving in the Bahamas, their life had been sheer paradise. Their accommodations were private and perfect. They even had their own triangular terrace overlooking the ocean.

Because of her condition they'd passed up the water sports, electing instead less physically taxing activities such as a carriage ride through Rawson Square and the picturesque old section of Nassau, a fascinating trip in a glass-bottomed boat over a coral reef and a shipwreck, and lazy mornings spent swimming and sunning on the beach. At nights they'd dressed up and gone dancing, attended a sizzling floor show at a local hotel, and enjoyed a cruise under the stars. Still ahead of them was a trip to Fort Charlotte for their first encounter with a moat, dungeons and battlements and a shopping expedition to the open-air Straw Market. Not to mention several more long passionate nights, nights in which Jason couldn't get enough of her or she of him.

"Except to see Megan."

At the thought of the energetic little girl, Carlys got all misty. "I miss her."

Jason's mouth crooked up ruefully as he teased, "I know. I call her at night to talk to her and you end up talking even longer than me!"

She laughed, knowing Jason didn't give a hoot about the phone bills. "Can I help it if we have a lot to say?"

He sobered, studying the oval lines of her face and her clear blue eyes. "She loves you so much, Carlys."

The tears of bliss that had been sparkling in her eyes began to fall.

Jason stood and pulling her to her feet, held her close. "We're very lucky to have you, Carlys." His voice caught briefly, then steadied. "In so many ways you're our guardian angel."

"And you're mine," Carlys whispered, holding him tighter still, the words coming straight from her heart. "For now. And forever."

"I TAKE IT you two had a great honeymoon," Susie remarked, when Jason and Carlys arrived to pick up Megan several happy days later.

"The absolute best. It was heaven on earth," Carlys and Jason said in unison.

With shouts of glee, Megan ran for her daddy. Jason picked her up in his arms and cuddled her close. His other arm around Carlys, he lifted his thumb in the high sign.

Hugs were exchanged all around.

Knowing Jason was anxious to get home, Carlys went upstairs with Susie to gather up Megan's belongings. "So how's your love life?" Carlys asked her. "Seeing much of Zach?"

Susie's face fell. "No. He asked me out again."

"But you're afraid to go," Carlys guessed.

"Naomi's still not dating anyone else."

Carlys frowned. "There must be some way to get her mind off Zach and onto something or someone else."

She rested the suitcase on the bed. "What are her interests?"

"Besides boys? I don't think she has any."

"Nothing? She's not in any clubs."

"Unfortunately, no." Susie let out a heartfelt sigh of regret.

Undaunted, Carlys thought a moment. "Does she work? Have a job?" Surely the girl must have some other pastime. She couldn't cause trouble twenty-four hours a day and not be in jail or a juvenile detention center.

"Who would hire her? She's got such a chip on her shoulder, and it's even worse since Zach refused to see her again."

"I think it's a problem with self-esteem," Carlys told Jason later, recounting her talk with Susie. "If only there was a way to make her feel better about herself."

"Get her mind off her troubles," Jason agreed. He stretched and sighed, tired after the long day and the hours it had taken to get reacquainted with Megan and then settle her down enough to put her to sleep. "The only thing I can think of are work and school, and she's obviously not interested in school."

Carlys nodded in agreement, muttering as an idea began to take hold in her mind, "You're absolutely right, Jason. If you can't beat them, join them." Carlys would solve this problem for Susie yet!

"So what exactly would I have to do?" Naomi Elliott asked early the following week. Dressed in tight black leather miniskirt, revealing black sweater, and thigh-high boots, she was sullen and suspicious, with a bored edge to her. In addition she was wearing too much makeup and her hair was ratted straight up. Yet there was a vulnerability about her, too, a part of her that craved attention, would do anything to get it. Despite the way she'd terrorized Susie, Carlys's response to her was mixed. Though this girl was far too streetwise for her age, she had possibilities.

Carlys also knew now that Naomi had a rough time of it, and not just where Zach and her other boyfriends were concerned. Her father had walked out on his family four years previously. He'd taken off with another woman and they hadn't heard from him since. Her mother had been running around with a number of men.

Naomi, the school guidance counselor had surmised, expected to be hurt in all her relationships yet was simultaneously afraid of being abandoned again.

Carlys wanted to remedy all that, to make a difference in this child's life. She wanted to mother her, to tell her everything was going to be all right. She wanted to take her in hand and change her wardrobe, her view of life, her view of herself.

One thing at a time, Carlys, she thought, forcing herself to cool it. After all, she had only just started her mission to win Naomi over that very morning by going to school to see the guidance counselor. After a brief but satisfactory talk between the two women, Naomi had been called into the office. Carlys had proposed that Naomi work for her service.

Having decided not to sugarcoat the offer, she explained plainly what Naomi's duties would be. "You'd have to fold diapers and stack them in bundles of a hundred. The job isn't hard. It pays the minimum wage."

"How many hours a week would I have to work?"

"Twenty. I'm flexible about how you fit them in. It can be four days of five hours, five days of four hours each, whatever you prefer, as long as I know in advance when to expect you in."

She was tempted; Carlys could see it in her face.

"I don't know." Naomi bit her lip.

Carlys waved away her doubts nonchalantly. "Look, if it doesn't work out, it doesn't work out. At least give it a try."

Naomi stared at her belligerently. "Why me?"

Carlys met her look for look. "Why not?"

NAOMI EVENTUALLY TOOK the job with Carlys. Though they had a rather wary start, they soon became if not best buddies, at least casual friends. Her other employees at the diaper service hadn't been exactly thrilled when Naomi started, but eventually they also realized what a nice girl Naomi could be—when not threatened. They'd begun to accept her, and Naomi them. In addition to doing a good job, Naomi was beginning to show some initiative so when Carlys decided to take a few hours off to go shopping with Jason several weeks after Naomi started working for her, she felt no qualms about having Naomi answer the phones in her absence.

Relaxed and at ease, Carlys browsed through the stores with Jason at her side. She felt incredibly happy and content as they leisurely debated the merits of various kinds of transportation for the new baby. "So what do you think, Carlys?" Jason asked. "Should we get a stroller or a carriage?"

"I think a stroller's really more practical in the long run. Megan's still riding in hers and she'll probably use it for quite a while. Whereas a buggy'd be kind of short-term."

"I suppose a comfortable stroller would be better." Jason turned back to the strollers. He read the tags on every item, finally narrowing the choice down to two with scientific precision. He turned to her for the artistic part of the decision. "The rainbow stripes or the navy blue?"

For Carlys, having mothered enough to know, this was an easy choice. "The navy, I think. It'll be easier to keep clean."

The stroller having been crossed off their list, they moved on to the next store, a baby boutique where he bought many of Megan's clothes.

"The clothes are all so tiny," Carlys murmured happily as she and Jason prowled the racks and aisles, studying the variety of pastel-colored outfits.

Just looking at the baby clothes seemed to bring back a wealth of memories for Jason, all of them good.

"Newborns are tiny," he replied with a smile that told her just how much he was looking forward to the birth of their baby. He reached for her hand and squeezed it tightly.

"If only we knew now if the baby was going to be a boy or a girl—"

"At least then we'd know what colors to buy," Jason finished for her. "Little slugger suits or pretty little pink dresses."

"Couldn't we just wait?"

"I wish we could, but I don't think it'd be a good idea. Right after the birth is bound to be a crazy time. We'll have Megan on our hands, too. I'm going to have to work. We'd better be as prepared as we can."

He was right. She was putting on more weight by the day. There were tons of things to do, and time was flying. Carlys sometimes felt stressed for the first time in her life, pulled in every direction, wanting to do so much. Yet she was able to do far less than she was used to, responding to all the new demands on her, and slowed down by her pregnancy. As busy as she was, though, she loved every minute she spent on her new family. And when the new baby came, life would just get better.

"You're right," Carlys said finally. "The more we can do now the better."

An hour later, when they left the mall, they knew they were set for at least the initial period after the baby's birth.

Carlys was quiet, wrapped up in thoughts about the immediate future.

"Why so quiet?"

"I was just thinking about my maternity leave."

"Are you going to have trouble going back to work?" Jason asked, shooting her a curious glance.

Carlys sighed heavily, admitting. "I think I might. Six weeks doesn't seem very long."

"So take off longer," Jason counseled as they put their packages in the car. "You're the boss."

"It's not that simple," she said reluctantly. "I can't just walk away anytime I want for however long I want when I've got all the responsibility of seeing that everything runs smoothly."

"Maybe it's time you considered hiring a full-time manager, then."

"I wish I could but I can't afford to if I still want to pay myself much of a salary."

Jason hesitated, knowing how important independence was to her. Since they had been married she had paid a full fifty percent of every expense, right down the line. He admired her willingness to help; he'd also made it clear that he didn't expect her to go on contributing money to the household if it wasn't feasible. "Carlys, you don't have to work if you don't want to," he said slowly, repeating an offer he'd already made several times.

"Jason, I want to work. I wouldn't know what to do with myself if I didn't."

Obviously not wanting to get into the subject, yet knowing they had to, he took the plunge, choosing his words with utmost care. "Things are bound to be tough after the baby's born. I'll do my best to carry as much of the workload at home as I can, but I've already taken off the maximum time allowed by my company for Megan's birth. They made an exception for me there. Now I'm not a single parent. Except for my usual vacation time, I don't have any more time off coming and I can't ask for any if I want to stay at DTI. And I do. I couldn't make the salary anywhere else that I make there, and after all they've done for me, I feel I owe them, Carlys."

Carlys was silent, reading the worry she saw reflected on his face. Surely there must be a way they could both have what they wanted if they just tried. Plenty of other couples did. Together, they could do anything. "I'm sure we can handle it, although it probably will be a little hectic at first."

Jason relaxed. The worried look left his face as he promised, "We'll do whatever it takes to make it work."

Carlys stood on tiptoe to give him a hug. He truly was a man to cherish.

"THE NEW NURSERY looks great, doesn't it?" Carlys asked Jason happily as they viewed the finished room.

Jason gave a sigh of satisfaction. Moving to stand beside her, he laid an affectionate arm about her slender shoulders. Had it been only a blissful six weeks since they married? He felt he'd been with Carlys a lifetime. He could barely remember a time when she hadn't been part of his life. He didn't even want to contemplate what he would ever do without her.

"It looks terrific," he agreed.

Carlys wrinkled her nose. "The only question now is what do we do with the old guest room bed?"

Jason had known she was going to bring that up. They couldn't keep the bed in their bedroom forever, especially with an inquisitive Megan forever toddling around. He shrugged. "We'll put it in the attic, I guess."

"Can we fit it up there?"

"I think so." Jason scowled thoughtfully. "But I'll need Matt or Mark to help."

Carlys was quick to disagree. "Jason, I can—"

"Oh, no. Don't even think of lifting anything heavy," he warned. Nothing was going to happen to Carlys while he was around. And he knew how ambitious she could be, how motivated to get things done.

Her full, sensual mouth, soft and smooth without lipstick, made a belligerent moue. "Yes, Mother," she teased, giving him an utterly self-possessed look.

Jason tried to summon up a fitting degree of indignation and instructed her firmly, "Make that Mr. Mom."

She threw back her head and laughed. "Okay, Mom."

Jason shook his head in exasperation. Lacing an arm about her waist, he reeled her in to his side. Pale blond hair flew over her shoulders in soft, shimmering waves.

Nearly seven months pregnant, she still had gained only fifteen pounds. Her belly got curvier by the day. Her skin glowed with health. Never a moment went by when Jason didn't marvel that this beautiful, energetic woman was his wife who was madly in love with him.

"You're too sassy for your own good, you know that?"

"So are you!"

"I know," he said softly. "We make quite a pair." With Megan, they were a wonderful family. The new baby would only add to that. He couldn't wait for the happy day.

Carlys looked around her distractedly. "Jason, am I only imagining it, or do you think this house is getting a little crowded?"

Jason's lips compressed unhappily. "No, you're right. But we can't sell yet. I've only just bought it."

"I know. To put it on the market now would be a colossal mistake financially."

But maybe there was another solution. He began hesitantly, "Carlys, have you ever thought about selling your house? I know you use it for an office, but we could build on an office here." Jason could think of nothing better than having them both under the same roof all day. For a moment, he thought Carlys was going to agree, but then she sighed deeply and gave her head a shake.

"I don't think it would be feasible." Disappointment clouded her perfect features, telling him she'd obviously given the matter a lot of thought. Pacing restlessly, she fetched up at the window looking out on the backyard.

"If we did that, we'd have no backyard at all. As much as I'd like that, I can't do that to Megan. You know how much she likes her swing set and sandbox, and anyway kids need a place to run and play."

"You're right." Jason sighed, wishing he'd never bought the place. Why hadn't he rented? Because he hadn't guessed someone like Carlys would come into his life and steal his heart, that's why.

Picking up on his frustration—he longed to give her everything her heart desired right now—she soothed it gently. "Jason, I know it's going to be tough, but really, it won't be all that bad even after the baby's born. I think we can make it work here for another year or two. Then, when this house has had enough time to appreciate in value, we'll put both properties on the market at once and buy a home that's big enough for two offices and all of us."

"I like the sound of that."

"I'm just sorry that we'll have to wait to do it. On the other hand—" Carlys moved back into his arms, as usual finding a bright side to their problem "—I can't imagine trying to put a house on the market now. Having people trooping in and out's just too stressful, and with the baby due in another couple months..."

Jason held her closer, inhaling the flowery scent of her skin and hair. "You're right."

"Who knows, maybe the setup we have now will work out even better for a while."

"How so?" Jason asked, holding her away to get a clear view of her face.

"Well, I know there'll be times when I'll be running back and forth between home and the office. So I can take the children with me when need be, give you a chance to work here undisturbed from time to time. In fact, it might be a good idea to set up a combination nursery and playroom over there. That way our schedules, would be much more flexible—yes, our entire situation would be helped.''

Jason sighed his relief. He'd thought for one ridiculous, paranoid moment she wanted to keep her house as a refuge or escape hatch—but she was simply being practical. ''You don't mind that things will be a little rough for a while?'' he asked her, still holding her tight. Crazy as it was, he still wished he could make everything perfect for her, that they had the financial wherewithal to make their ultimate move *now*.

''No, I don't mind,'' Carlys said, hugging him tight. ''Not as long as I have you. All that matters, Jason, is that we're together.''

Chapter Eleven

"Merry Christmas, darling!"

"Jason, it's beautiful." Carlys took a gleaming silver charm bracelet out of the box. Christmas had been bountiful indeed. In robes and slippers, they were sitting by the Christmas tree. A fire was burning warmly in the grate behind glass doors; the woodsy scent of evergreen lingered in the air. A thrilled Megan was contentedly playing with a wooden train set.

"I didn't know what to get you," Jason confided, fastening the bracelet around Carlys's wrist. "You're a woman who wears many hats and wears them well. So I decided to get you a bracelet that spoke to them all."

Overcome by his thoughtfulness, Carlys examined each tiny silver charm. "There's a pair of running shoes—"

"To symbolize your boundless energy."

"A heart—"

"For the warmth you've shown Megan and me from the beginning."

"A briefcase—"

"For the successful businesswoman you are by nature."

"And a baby." Her smile grew even wider.

"For the child we're going to have."

"Oh, Jason." Tears of happiness in her eyes, Carlys threw her arms around his neck. "This is the best present I've ever had."

"I'm glad." He stroked her back with a warm, loving touch. "I wanted our first Christmas together to be very special."

"It has been. And now for your present." Excitedly, she handed him a ribbon-tied package. This year the joy was truly in the giving. She'd never enjoyed shopping as much as she had when she'd chosen gifts for Jason and Megan.

Jason opened the box. Inside was a collection of expensive software games for his computer. He'd been wanting them for months, but with the baby coming wouldn't buy them.

"For all the men you are," she teased, trailing a finger down the rugged profile of his face.

"BASEBALL—"

"For the summer sports nut in you."

"PILOT—"

"For your superb navigational skills."

He grinned and totaled her with a sexy, inviting look. "In bed or out?"

Her pulse quickened, but she gave him a gentle poke in the ribs, a silent reminder to behave himself. They had an audience, and a newly gabby one at that; Megan was learning more new words every day. There was nothing she'd like better than to go back to bed with Jason, but right now was not the time. And she and Jason had all the time in the world.

"Keep reading," Carlys advised him levelly.

He made a great show of clearing his throat. "WISHBRINGER—"

Carlys smiled and resumed her commentary. "That's for the magical way you have of making all my wishes come true."

He scanned the printed description of the game, not only liking it, but also identifying with it. "There is something medieval and mysterious about me, isn't there?" he teased, unable to resist the chance to give her a gentle nudge.

He lifted the last game from the box. "And MOON-MIST."

"I've always wanted to spend the night in a haunted English castle. I thought we could play that one together."

"Sounds good to me." Jason had a faraway look in his eyes, obviously recalling the first time they'd played a computer game together, the kiss they'd shared later. He returned his attention to the game in his hand. "Does it have ghosts?"

"You betcha." Shivering, Carlys snuggled closer to his tall frame. "You're going to have to protect me."

"Don't mind if I do." Encircling her in his arms, he drew her to him for a tender, romantic kiss. "Daddy, baby doll! Carlys, come see!" Megan was tugging them excitedly toward the tree.

Delighted, they followed her lead. For Carlys, it was the best Christmas she'd ever had. She had her dream come true, she had her family; it was only going to get better.

"CARLYS, can I talk to you a minute?" Naomi asked one afternoon early in January.

"Sure, Naomi, what's up?" Carlys gestured to the chair beside her desk.

Since coming to work at the diaper service, there had been subtle changes in Naomi, inside and out. She was no longer as sullen and mistrustful as she had been. And although she still wasn't as open as Carlys would have liked, she had taken to the work and had moved from just folding and sorting diapers to answering the phone from time to time and doing a little of Carlys's filing. Inundated with paperwork for her newest venture, Nannies Incorporated, Carlys appreciated Naomi's presence; in time she might even prove indispensable. Recently, she'd been the first to spot trouble with one of the dryers and had promptly, if nervously, urged Carlys to get it repaired not just sometime soon, but that very day, that very minute. Impressed, Carlys had praised her initiative lavishly and was still delighted over the sense of responsibility Naomi had shown.

"I want to ask you a question," Naomi continued, biting her lip.

"Okay." Carlys could see something was troubling Naomi greatly; she put down her pen.

"I heard you had a sister. Susie. Susie Holt."

Carlys took a deep breath, sensing trouble. "That's right."

"You never mentioned her." This, half accusingly.

"I knew the two of you didn't get along, or didn't used to anyway." Susie had started dating Zach again with no repercussions. Were the threats and harassment about to start up again? Carlys wondered. Naomi looked as if she felt her back was against the wall.

"Did you know about Zach Sullivan?" Naomi asked pointedly.

Carlys decided to take the bull by the horns. "Yes. I knew you harassed her, made threatening phone calls, put toothpaste in her hair, and perhaps you were in-volved in some tire slashing.''

"Hey, I didn't want that to happen," Naomi inter-jected quickly, standing up. She sat down again and said sullenly, "It just . . . kinda got out of hand.''

Carlys nodded her understanding. Since Naomi had come to work for her Carlys had realized she wasn't bad or vicious, just insecure and badly in need of guidance, which Carlys had tried to give her, with some degree of success.

Silence fell between them.

"Does Susie know I work for you?''

Carlys nodded. "Yes. She was against it, but after meeting you I felt it would work out.''

Naomi studied her boss with a streetwise bluntness that would have been guilt-invoking under the best of circumstances. "You hired me to get me away from Susie, didn't you?''

Carlys saw no reason to evade the charge. She shrugged, her eyes never leaving Naomi's face. "I thought if you were busier there might not be so much of a problem.'' Carlys had also wanted to get Naomi away from that gang of girls she'd been running with and so far had had a partial success.

"So now what? Am I out of a job?'' Naomi asked belligerently.

"No.''

Naomi folded her arms truculently. "I oughta quit, the way you tricked me into working here.''

Carlys knew there was a grain of truth to that. "I wish you wouldn't,'' she said honestly. "I've come to rely on you. But I won't beg you to stay, either.'' If Na-omi were to remain angry with her for any length of time, she would lose all influence with the girl.

Naomi said nothing for a moment. Carlys knew she could jump either way. She decided to level with her. "Look, I have to be honest with you, Naomi. My first loyalty is to my family. My second is to my friends. I don't want to choose, but I'm not going to let any group of girls terrorize my sister."

"So either I stay away from Susie or I lose my job," Naomi paraphrased bluntly.

Carlys nodded. "That's about it. Unless the two of you wanted to be friends." Now she was reaching for the moon.

Naomi didn't even consider that a distant possibility.

"I like my job here," Naomi said finally.

"For what it's worth, I want you to stay. I care about you."

Naomi looked away, her lips set, a suspicious moistness shimmering in her eyes. "Yeah, well, you'd mother anything that came through the door."

There Carlys disagreed. "Don't kid yourself, Naomi. You're a good person, well worth having around."

Naomi gave her a testing glance. "Zach didn't think so."

The hurt was still there. "Zach wasn't right for you," Carlys said gently, her heart going out to the girl. She paused, then decided to add, even if she did sound faintly preachy, "You've got to stop thinking the worst about yourself. You have a lot of strengths." To lighten the tension between them she joked, "I'm not saying you couldn't make improvements in some areas, you understand, but on the other hand who among us couldn't stand a little improving? Me, for instance." She thumped her chest lightly with the flat of her hand. "Sometimes I meddle too much."

Naomi grinned. "You can never find your pencils, either, mostly cause they're always buried under huge stacks of terminally messy papers! Geez!"

Carlys raised both hands in self-defense. "Guilty as charged on both counts," she admitted with a laugh, happy to see Naomi smiling once again.

Now, if she could just get her to do something about that ratted up hair...

"So how was your day?" Jason asked as Carlys came through the front door.

"A mess of problems," Carlys answered, removing her key from the lock with one hand, almost dropping her overstuffed briefcase with the other. "But I had some good news, too. I talked to Bio Tech Labs today. They're going to think about becoming a sponsor for Nannies Incorporated."

"That's great," Jason said enthusiastically. "When will you know for sure?"

Carlys kicked off her shoes and put her briefcase aside. "They've promised to get back to me by March first. They want to talk to their professional employees first and see if there's enough interest to warrant their underwriting the pilot program at the college."

"I hope their people clamor for it."

"So do I," Carlys said wearily, accepting the soothing massage he bestowed on her shoulders. "The sooner I can get this off the ground, the better. But either way it's going to fly sooner or later. I've already got three other companies signed as sponsors. They've agreed to donate five thousand dollars each. If Bio Tech Labs signs on for another five, we'll be able to hire college-educated teachers, set up a curriculum and go ahead with the pilot program of twenty students. Oh, yeah, and one more thing. The vocational school is also arranging for a private scholarship fund to help students who don't have the tuition money.''

"Any chance you'll get more companies on board before you begin?"

"I'd like to think so, but I really don't know. I've approached over fifty companies in person in the past few months. So far only three have signed on to help, so we'll just have to see. So how was your day?'' Carlys walked into the kitchen to help with dinner.

Jason sighed. Carlys suddenly noted how tired he looked, how stressed. She hadn't paid him enough attention during the past few days, she realized guiltily. But she couldn't help it. She was rushing to finish up as much as possible in order to make her maternity leave run more smoothly.

"It wasn't the best day I ever had,'' Jason admitted succinctly. He looked up at her, lines of worry bracketing the corners of his mouth. "Alice called. She's thinking of taking a job here in Dallas as an early-morning anchor, in the six to six-thirty spot. She wants to be closer to Megan, or so she says.''

His troubled expression went straight to Carlys's heart. There was more here than Jason was letting on. "You don't believe she'll really take it?'' she asked gently.

"No, I don't think so,'' he confessed in a discouraged tone of voice. "I think Alice is going through the motions. Eventually she'll decide against it. She's never slighted her career or her ambitions before. To think she'd do so now, even for Megan, isn't very realistic. Dammit, Carlys, I worry about Megan being hurt. She's too young to be aware of what's going on now, and I made Alice promise not to tell her, but in the future it won't be so easy. I don't want her to have her hopes built up and then dashed.''

''Alice did that to you?''

''When we were married? Time and time again. She'd say I'll be home on Friday, absolutely nothing will stop me. Then a story would come up...''

''And she'd break her promise?''

He exhaled roughly. ''The worst of it is I knew she didn't mean to. But that didn't change the outcome. As an adult, I had a tough time handling it. To think of putting a child through that—'' His hands flexed and unflexed at his sides. ''Sometimes I wish she'd never started to become closer to Megan.''

''But she has,'' Carlys interjected, more objectively. ''And now you can't just go back to the way it was.'' To the way Alice had originally wanted it.

Jason whirled on her, his face set, angry, as if she had betrayed him by not taking his side.

''You think I'm being too rough on Alice again, don't you?''

Carlys shrugged, unable to defend all of Alice's actions, yet understanding what drove her all too well. Carlys had felt the same intense yearning for success in her work; in fact she was experiencing it now daily as she tried to set up her new business, which she hoped would eventually benefit many mothers and children. ''I know she's trying. Jason, in the past six months she's called several times, just to speak to Megan. She's written letters, sent presents, even visited two more times.'' A phenomenal commitment from someone as busy and well traveled as Alice.

''I know that. Even so...'' In Jason's view, what Alice was prepared to give wasn't enough for his daughter. He didn't want her to have to settle for anything less than she deserved.

Carlys empathized with all of them.

"Alice's job is very important to her," Carlys pointed out calmly, trying to help Jason ease up in his anger.

His face remained set as he snapped back unforgivingly, "More important than her child? I'm sorry, Carlys, but I can't help it. I still resent her lack of involvement. And for her to dangle this job in front of me—and Megan—like some carrot when I know she isn't going to take it in the end anyway! I could throttle her, I really could."

Carlys knew how he felt, sometimes she shared his sentiments, but telling Jason that wouldn't help Megan. This family needed peace and mutual understanding, tolerance, if the child was to thrive. "Alice is doing as much as she's able at the moment, Jason. Be thankful for that. Accept her the way she is, stop trying to change her. At least she came for Christmas this year and saw Megan in person."

Her differing opinion and forthright advice catching him unawares had sobered him slightly. "Yeah, she did that, didn't she?" he said slowly, thinking how very much things had changed in a year.

"She loves Megan, and Megan will love her. With any luck they'll just get closer and closer as the years pass. Whether they do or not, though, we ought to be supportive. For Megan's sake we should help Alice along, not put roadblocks in her way."

The anger drained out of him. He looked as though he'd been through the mill. "You really do understand her, don't you?"

"I identify with her in a lot of ways. We're both in that generation of superwomen who are expected to have it all—fabulous careers, husbands, homes and children. I've often felt inadequate because all I had was a job. At the same time, I was always afraid to slow down. I thought that if I did ease up, I'd fade away into nothingness. No one would want me. Without my work, my business success to validate me, I'd be nothing but a dull caricature of a woman, a pale creature when compared with all the dynamic working women out there in the world.''

"And you think that's the way Alice feels?" Jason studied her, an unreadable expression on his face.

Carlys nodded. "I think she's afraid to slow down, yes. I also think she might, given time. Her even considering this job is an indication that something new is developing. So what if she doesn't take it? At least she's thinking of Megan now, trying to fit her child into her life. That's a hell of an improvement over last year at this time."

"I guess you're right."

"When does she have to make up her mind?" Carlys asked, encouraged by his gentler demeanor.

"By mid-February."

"Let's keep our fingers crossed everything works out."

Jason took her into his arms and held her close. "What would I ever do without you?" His voice was sensuous and low, a potent aphrodisiac to her work-weary senses.

Carlys couldn't resist teasing as she snuggled deeper into his embrace. "I don't know. I hope you never find out, though."

"Lady—" he lifted her face to his and kissed her earnestly. "—I don't intend to."

Chapter Twelve

"Is there anything like SuperBowl Sunday?" Matt asked Mark as he settled next to Jason on the sofa. Surrounding the three men were five children. Megan, the smallest of the lot, was the most vocal, often to comic effect and the giggling delight of her new cousins.

"Not that I can see, no," Carlys murmured. It had been Jason's idea to entertain her family during the game. So far, everyone was having a rousing good time. It looked as though the Cowboys were going to win.

The timer went off in the kitchen. "Whoops. I'd better get that." Jason stood up.

Matt said, eyes on the television, "Let Carlys get it."

"Thanks a heap, Matt," Carlys shot back. It wasn't that she minded missing the game—at best she merely tolerated football—but her lower back was killing her. It had been aching off and on all day, and no matter how she stood, sat or walked, it still throbbed. Carlys decided that if the ache kept up, she would have to call her doctor in the morning. If she felt then the way she felt now, she wouldn't be able to work. And with two days left to her due date...

Jason shook his head, also vetoing Matt's idea. "Carlys, stay put. It's my day to cook." He took his half of the housework very seriously, never failing to come through for her.

Matt and Mark exchanged amused glances. In their houses, unlike their father's, they ruled supreme, simply because they were men. Carlys groaned silently, steeling herself for what was bound to come next: Matt and Mark's philosophy on how to handle women. Fortunately, at that moment the Cowboys completed a pass and ran for a forty-yard touchdown. Jason watched the play, dashed into the kitchen, rescued the hot ham-and-cheese rolls from the oven and raced back into the living room, serving dish in hand, just in time to see the instant replay. Deciding to give Jason a hand—after all, she was as much the host as he—Carlys stayed in the kitchen with her mother. Enjoying their respite together, they fixed fresh drinks for everyone, poured more salted nuts and chips into bowls and whipped up a new batch of dip.

Later, content to talk removed from the game, they lingered in the kitchen on the pretext of tidying up. "You really are happy, aren't you?" Helen said.

Carlys nodded blissfully. "I've been married four months and now I can't imagine not having Jason in my life."

Helen smiled her approval. "Jason seems to feel the same about you. And Megan loves you, too." She shook her head, disbelievingly.

"What?" Carlys demanded.

"I just can't believe it sometimes," Helen confessed. "You are so happy, Carlys, and so lucky. The odds against this arrangement of yours and Jason's working out so well were very great."

Carlys sobered. She knew. She thanked her lucky stars daily. "I love him, Mom."

Helen smiled. "And you're going to have his baby."

Life couldn't have been more perfect.

"HONEY, YOU'RE TIRED. Why don't you go on to bed? I'll finish up in here."

"You sure?" Carlys hated to leave Jason alone with the mess from the party, but her back was still aching. She was dead on her feet and feeling more fragile with every passing moment.

"Positive." With a hug and a kiss he promised, "I'll join you as soon as I'm done here."

Carlys fell asleep almost the instant her head hit the pillow. The next thing she knew it was three o'clock and she was wet between her legs. "I don't believe it," Carlys grumbled. "Wetting the bed at my age." And then, as realization hit her and simultaneously she was gripped by a pain: "My water! Oh God, it's my water!"

"Wha'?" Jason mumbled sleepily and rolled over, still exhausted from the party.

Carlys breathed slowly and rhythmically, as she'd learned in childbirth classes, until the pain passed. The minute it did, she grabbed Jason's arm and shook him roughly. "Jason, wake up."

"What's wrong?"

"My water broke."

"When?" he demanded, shaking himself awake the rest of the way.

"About five minutes ago." Another contraction gripped her. Carlys lay back against the pillows. To Jason's frustration, she was unable to speak until it was over.

"How long between contractions?" he demanded, worry permeating his voice.

Carlys shrugged. "I don't know. Three minutes. Five." She only knew the contractions themselves seemed to go on forever. Suddenly she wanted to be at the hospital—now!

Breathlessly, she asked, "Can you find my shoes and clothes, get my suitcase out? Maybe you'd better call the doctor. Mom, too, to come and get Megan."

"Right." Jason leaped from the bed, raced to the closet. His hands were shaking so badly that he could hardly get his shirt on and buttoned. "Just as soon as I get dressed."

Carlys said nothing. Another contraction had hit her. They weren't regular yet, were they? Because if they were . . . There'd been only sixty seconds between these two.

Jason raced out to the living room to call the doctor—why, Carlys had no idea; there was a phone right next to the bed. In the meantime, Megan, awake now, crawled out of her crib—her latest trick—and strolled in to see what was up. "Hi, Carlys," she said, climbing up on the bed next to her.

"Hi, Megan." Carlys patted her head affectionately and briefly cuddled her close. The worst thing about going to the hospital was that she had to leave Megan. Just thinking about being away from the child she'd come to think of as her own brought tears to her eyes and a lump to her throat.

Jason, mistaking her show of emotion for pain, became even more frantic. Carlys tried to explain the reason for her mistiness, but she was too choked up to make much sense or get through to her husband.

Thinking she was only trying to reassure him, he came racing back with a maternity dress and running shoes, nothing else. Between contractions, Carlys managed to go to the bathroom, and grab a sanitary pad and some clean panties. That trip alone exhausted her; she wasn't up to much else. Who said first babies came slow and easy?

"Jason, some socks?" she said weakly, looking at the running shoes. So she'd go in dressed eccentrically. Panty hose were out of the question. The contractions were coming harder and closer. She was beginning to feel very shaky. Scared. She was glad he was there with her. Very glad.

"I called your Mom." Jason knelt before her, putting on her socks and shoes, now very efficient. "She's on her way over to watch Meg."

"Good."

He helped her on with her dress and a jacket. "I'll just put your suitcase in the car, and we'll be ready to go as soon as Helen gets here."

He strode out before Carlys could say a word.

When he came back, she was doubled over with laughter, the tears streaming down her face.

"What?" Jason demanded, knowing without a doubt that her burst of hilarity had something to do with him, but unable to figure out what he had done.

"Daddy funny." Megan pointed at him and giggled.

Jason looked down at himself, then back at Carlys. "What?" he demanded impatiently, now exasperated with them both beyond measure.

"Jason, the pajama bottoms are real cute. Especially with the socks, shoes and regular shirt. The leather bomber jacket adds a nice touch, too. But don't you think you'd be more comfortable in jeans?"

For a moment, he froze. "Oh, sh—ucks." The last was amended for Megan's sake. Flushing bright red, he looked at his legs and sighed. Both hands were raked through his hair. "Good thing you noticed or I probably would have forgotten my wallet."

"Not to mention the entrance we would have made at the hospital."

Jason grinned, sharing in the joke, calmer now.

"Try not to laugh too hard," he advised dryly.

He was dressed correctly when the doorbell rang. Jason helped Carlys to her feet. Though she was trying hard to suppress her mirth for the sake of Jason's ego, it kept breaking out.

"You're never going to let me live this one down are you?"

What a story to tell their grandchildren! "Not on your life, Jason, not on your life."

"BREATHE, HONEY. That's it. Nice and slow. In through your nose, out through your mouth. Now pant. He-he-he-he, whoooo. He-he-he-he, whoooooo," Jason patiently mimicked the sounds she was to make.

Carlys did as ordered, glad he was there. The breathing was helping, yet the pain hurt more than she had ever imagined anything could.

Long moments passed. The pain grew unbearable. "Jason," she whispered wearily at last.

"What?" He was close to her, as close as he could be. Tears were misting his dark eyes. He felt frustrated and helpless, she knew. Try as she might, she couldn't be brave anymore. She had to tell him, as tears rolled down her face, "I can't take much more..." Her voice was barely more than an agonized whisper.

"I'll get the doctor," Jason said firmly, his mouth set.

"Please."

"THE SHOT HELPING?" Jason relaxed as Carlys relaxed.

"Yeah." Carlys was exhausted. Perspiration beaded her face. The worst of the pain had been dimmed by a slight dose of Demerol, but had been replaced by intermittent bouts of shivering she was helpless to battle or contain. She huddled under the extra blanket the nurse had brought for her. "It still hurts, but at least I can rest between contractions now."

"I hate seeing you in pain." As he spoke, Jason looked more tortured than she had felt at the height of her agony.

"Think of the baby," she soothed, gentling him as he had gentled her.

"The baby," Jason repeated.

"A GIRL, can you believe it?" Jason repeated wonderingly for the fifteenth time.

Happiness was bubbling up inside Jason from a wellspring of joy. "All eight pounds and seven ounces of her," she recited the vital statistics of their new daughter tenderly. "You bet I can believe it. You've got to remember I carried her around for nine months. I know exactly how heavy she was."

Jason grinned, his bliss apparent. "I'll remind you both of that when she gets old enough to sass."

Tears of happiness slid down Carlys's face. She'd been crying on and off since the baby's birth and couldn't find the switch that would turn them off. "You do that."

A long moment passed in which they couldn't stop looking at each other. "Carlys," Jason said softly at last, "I love you."

Carlys sighed her happiness and gripped his hand hard. "And I love you."

They were both too choked up to speak.

"I never thought it would be this wonderful," Carlys said.

Jason knelt beside her bed, and careful of the IV line running into her arm, hugged her tight.

"Try and get some rest now," he said warmly. "I'm going home to shave and shower and check on Megan."

"Give her my love. Tell her I'll call her later, after we both have a chance to nap."

"I will. Anything you want me to bring you when I come back?"

"Just you." Carlys smiled, thinking, *And your love.*

Jason bent and kissed her again. "That you got, darlin'. That you got."

"SHE'S SO TINY," Jason noted solemnly.

"She has your eyes."

"And your nose and your chin."

"And curly blond hair like Megan's."

Jason preened like the proud papa he was. "The nurse said she gained half an ounce today," he observed with scientific accuracy.

"She's hungry. I'll attest to that."

"How's the nursing?" Jason's gaze roved his wife's face anxiously. "Do you like it?" He only wanted them both to be happy.

"The truth, Jason?" His presence filled the private hospital room with a masculine presence that engulfed her. "Being here with the two of you I feel like I've gone to heaven."

"No regrets?" His eyes met and held hers seriously.

"None," Carlys was able to say honestly, her eyes never wavering from his. "Except I miss Megan. Do you think you could bring her in during special family hours tonight?"

"I know she'd like that. She's been asking a lot of questions about the baby."

"Think she'll feel jealous?" Carlys felt disloyal even mentioning the possibility.

"Yes." Jason was able to be more realistic. "I also think she'll adjust and come to love her new sister very much. She knows how much you—we both—love her. It won't take her long to realize that won't change. Besides, I think she'll like having a playmate."

"Jason, it won't be possible for them to play blocks together for quite a while."

"They grow up sooner than you think, Carlys. Much sooner."

"Too soon for Daddy?" she asked gently, knowing full well how he felt.

He grinned, shrugged sheepishly. "Can you blame me for wanting this utopia to last forever?"

No, Carlys didn't. "How can I when I feel exactly the same?" she asked softly.

"MEGAN, THIS IS JULIE." Jason handled the introductions with pride and the utmost sensitivity.

"Ju-lee," Megan repeated.

"She's your new baby sister."

Fingers in her mouth, wide-eyed, Megan stared at the bassinet through the viewing room window. Hospital regulations forbade closer contact.

The three of them went back to Carlys's room. Megan walked between the two adults, holding tight to their hands and adjusted herself instinctively to Carlys's careful pace.

Carlys settled herself in her bed, drawing the covers up to her waist. Jason lifted Megan in his arms and put her on the bed. "Meg, do you want to watch a little TV? *Sesame Street* is on."

Megan nodded solemnly, showing none of her usual excitement at mention of her favorite show. She scrambled across the bed to climb up into Carlys's arms and snuggle against her shoulder. For the tenth time that day, Carlys's eyes filled with tears of sheer bliss.

She hadn't been wrong; this was what life truly was all about.

Chapter Thirteen

"Bad day?" Carlys asked, coming in the door and reading the disgruntled look on Jason's face.

"The worst," Jason reported succinctly. "Megan refused to take her nap. Julie had colic and spat up twice."

For a second Carlys's heart seemed to stop. She knew she shouldn't have gone on outside appointments today, she just knew it! The whole time she'd been gone she'd been worried sick about both girls, barely able to concentrate on her work. Yet she wouldn't admit it to Jason. Did she want him to know she was a worrier and a softy, especially since she hadn't been there when they all needed her? No, not when Jason thought her so inept and occasionally even unmaternal. Forcing her voice to calmness, the same calm she tried to project at work even when everything was at its collective craziest, Carlys asked, "Is Julie okay now?"

"Yeah, both girls are sleeping."

Score two for Jason. Not only was he more adept in a parental crisis than she, but also he'd been at home to solve it. *He* had no reason to feel guilty. Whereas she could barely cope with being torn between two beloved worlds, home and business, and so had reacted by shutting off as much of her incessantly overflowing emotion as possible.

"How did you manage that?" Carlys asked, going into the kitchen for a glass of milk.

For a moment, Jason was unhappily silent.

If he was trying to make her feel guilty for going back to work, Carlys thought, he was succeeding. Anger filled her. This, she didn't need. She was struggling enough with the part of her that wanted simply to stay home and tend her children all day. But she couldn't do that; people were depending on her, and their families on them. She couldn't watch all that she'd worked for come to nothing.

Other women combined work and family. She would do it, too. Already she was doing absolutely as much as possible from Jason's place. She left the house only when she absolutely had to.

Jason passed her on his way to the window, offering her his back. She could see the tense set of his shoulders. Long moments stole quietly by. "I rocked Julie and read to Megan."

"What happened to the sitter?" Carlys asked curiously when he turned around to face her again, his expression unreadably calm. When she'd left him four hours earlier, all had been well. He'd even had extra help, a grandmotherly woman with twenty years of child-care experience.

"Mrs. Flannery had an emergency of her own. One of her grandchildren got sick at school. She went to pick her up."

"And left you alone." Now Carlys understood. No wonder he was grumpy! If she'd been in his shoes, she, too, would be grumpy and probably resentful.

Jason's face relaxed. He continued less harshly, "I understood why Mrs. Flannery had to go, of course. If it had been me, I'd have done the same."

He looked so discouraged and wrung out. Carlys asked sympathetically, "Get any work done yourself?" The moment the words were out she knew it had been a stupid thing to ask.

"None whatsoever." He jerked open the refrigerator and pulled out a can of soda.

Her heart was stung by a thousand well-aimed arrows. She paused, unsure what tack to take when he was behaving more like a moody stranger than the affable man she had married. Maybe it was not being able to work that had made him so irritable. "Would you like to work now?"

"No. What I have can wait until morning."

"All right." Carlys put her glass in the dishwasher and went back into the living room, where she sat curled up on the sofa with a thankful sigh. Maybe Jason just needed some tender loving care. That, she could give him, and maybe it would make up in part for her having given him an unproductive work day. When he drifted in to join her after a while, she asked, "Anything else happen today?"

"Alice called." His voice was rough with restraint. He popped open his can and took a generous swallow. "She isn't taking the Dallas job."

"I'm sorry."

"So am I. Megan will be also." His words were hard as granite. He took a second swallow of soda.

Carlys's heart picked up speed. Now she was almost as on edge as Jason. She asked levelly, "Did she say why?"

Pained by what he saw in her eyes, Jason turned away from her, reciting contemptuously, "She can't give up her career. She's worked too hard for everything she has."

Carlys was silent. She could understand Alice; she knew Alice's reasoning was deeply offensive to Jason. She decided to let him be.

Eventually, as she hoped, he pulled out of his depression on his own, dropped into a chair and asked her about her day.

"So how did your work go? What happened at Bio Tech Labs?"

His voice could have indicated more interest, but at least he was asking. Carlys smiled her pleasure. "I've got great news, actually." She tried to downplay her excitement but she didn't entirely succeed. "They've agreed to sponsor a grant. So the pilot training program at the vocational school can start next fall."

Months before, Jason would have reacted with more enthusiasm than she; now he stayed moodily silent. "That's a lot of work between now and then."

"Yes, but it'll be worth it," Carlys said confidently. And just think what a service she'd be providing for other working mothers. If only she could have a fully trained nanny for her girls.

"I wonder."

At his grimly speculative tone, Carlys felt another knife prick to her heart. She said nothing, deciding to weather his bad mood in silence. This wasn't like Jason. It was just the stress talking, and the stress would pass.

Jason looked at her directly then, no longer mincing his words or sparing either his feelings or hers. "I'm well aware this probably isn't the time to bring it up. I'm sorry. I can't help it."

Carlys flinched.

"I had a lot of time to think today while I was walking the floor with Julie. I think you should take a longer maternity leave. I can't do it all by myself. I can't be expected to work and take care of two babies simultaneously."

"I'm not asking you to do that," Carlys said defensively. She'd walked the floor with Julie plenty of times, also.

"I know that."

"Jason, we can manage if we stagger our work hours."

He ran a hand around the back of his neck. "We've already tried that, Carlys. So far it hasn't worked."

Only because in her opinion he hadn't wanted it to. "Jason, it's only been five weeks."

"Yes, and from the number of hours you're putting into your businesses, you might as well be back at work full-time. Dammit, Carlys, you promised me you'd take off a full six weeks."

His criticism stung and was right on target. She hung her head in shame. "I know. I'm sorry. I couldn't help it." He also knew there were extenuating circumstances for her every action. Damn him anyway for loading her down with more guilt! Carlys was beginning to feel as if there was an albatross hanging around her neck, put there by Jason. Patiently she reminded him, "If I hadn't gone to Bio Tech today, they might have changed their minds."

Jason was unmoved by her logic, however gently offered.

"And maybe they wouldn't have."

"Either way, I couldn't risk it. I've worked too hard and too long on this project. Jason, please try and understand."

At the pleading note in her voice, his face changed. He seemed to come to his senses. "I know you had to go. I'm sorry I'm grumpy. It was just a bad day."

"I'm sorry I wasn't here to help." Carlys got up and went over to him.

He pulled her onto his lap. "You're here now."

For a while they just held each other. Gradually both felt better. The tension that had been with them earlier left both their bodies. Yet with Jason a residual depression remained.

Carlys knew how he felt. She herself had been up and down a lot lately, full of joy at one moment and at the next full of quiet desperation, wondering how they were ever going to manage. She sought to comfort him as best she could. "I know there's been a lot of confusion lately but I really think in a few more weeks everything will settle down. Julie is already sleeping eight hours at a stretch every night."

Jason sighed. "If you could only take off a few more weeks until we can get into a reasonable routine."

Carlys met his pleading gaze. "I wish I could, but I can't. Like it or not, I have to go into the diaper service at least three times a week." She bit her lip. "Jason, you knew all along I planned to keep on working after Julie was born." Was he identifying their situation with his previous one, subconsciously lumping her into the same category as Alice?

"I never thought it would be this hectic."

"I didn't, either." Carlys smoothed the hair away from his forehead. "And you have been a saint." She on the other hand had often been preoccupied with worry about how the diaper service was progressing without her and how Nannies Incorporated showed signs of not progressing at all. Being an entrepreneur had its down side, and now was definitely a down, she thought. Yet professionally she wouldn't have wanted to do anything else; Jason knew that. In the past he had even respected and admired her tenacity and optimism.

"Agreed, I have been a saint," Jason said after a conciliatory moment, with a rumble of laughter.

The trouble was that they were both frazzled by the demands of two children under three years old.

"Look," Jason sighed, "maybe we just need a change of pace. The weather tomorrow is supposed to be warm and sunny. We haven't taken Megan to the park since Julie was born. Let's both just take the day off, go on a picnic, make a real family day out of it."

What he was describing sounded heavenly. "Jason, you've got yourself a deal."

He hugged her close. "I think I feel better already."

"DIAPERS. Treats for Megan. Extra clothes for both. Oops, where's that pacifier?" Jason said, looking around him on every side.

"Maybe we should just put the house on wheels and take it with us so that we don't have to pack up all this stuff."

In response to her droll tone, Jason turned to Carlys and tweaked her nose. "Trust me. I'm the pro here. The first rule of parenting is that if you don't have it, you'll need it, and vice versa. Are we all set? Okay. I'll take the first load out to the car."

"I'll gather up the kids."

A tiny voice piped up between them. "Megan wants to go with Daddy."

"Honey, my arms are full." Jason turned to Megan apologetically. "Stay with Carlys and I'll come back for you in a minute."

"No!" Having too often been put on hold during the past few weeks, Megan grabbed on to Jason's leg and held tight. "Megan wants to go with Daddy," she repeated in an adamant voice that was loaded with unexpressed tears.

Jason and Carlys exchanged glances. Since Julie's birth, Megan had demanded a little extra tender loving care while continually trying to ensure that her place in the family was sacrosanct. Once she knew in her heart she wasn't going to be abandoned, Carlys and Jason both felt, her behavior would go back to normal.

Take her, Carlys mouthed. If sticking to Jason now was so very important to Megan, so be it.

Jason, willing to reassure her, not willing to encourage temper tantrums, deliberated just long enough to make Megan know her behavior was not exactly of the recommended type. "All right," he said finally, getting down on one knee to talk to Megan at her own level. "You can go with me. But only if you'll be a big girl and help Daddy. Think you can carry your teddy bear and your blanket?"

"Yes, Daddy."

Megan and Jason set off hand in hand. He would have to triple the number of trips out to the car, she would have the pleasure of having been included in the family arrangements.

"Don't forget the strollers," Carlys called on their second return to the house.

The phone rang just as Jason and Megan walked back into the house for the fourth time. Already exhausted before they had even left, Jason looked at

Carlys, flashing his impatience like a neon sign. "Don't answer it."

She wanted to do as he directed; she never had been able to ignore a ringing phone. "I have to. What if it's something important?" Someone they knew could have been in an accident or had a heart attack.

Carlys picked up the receiver.

"What? I can't. Naomi, slow down! I can't understand what you're saying. Oh my, yes! Call the fire department! But first get everyone out of the building, including yourself. You can call from across the street. I'll be right there. Now go!"

Carlys hung up, already striding toward the door. "Jason, I've got to go. There's a fire at the laundry. I'm sorry about today. Try and explain this to Megan. We'll make it up to her tomorrow."

"Carlys, wait—"

"I'll call you as soon as I can."

Megan in his arms, Jason followed her to her car. "Carlys, dammit, wait a minute. I'll go with you. I'll—"

"There's no time for that, Jason. Just stay here!" In her anxiety her voice was sharper than she intended. She couldn't help it. There was simply no time. A vision of her building in flames was already in Carlys's mind. What if Naomi or Jill or any of the others got hurt because of this? No, no, Carlys wouldn't let that happen, she wouldn't!

Aware that Jason was still right behind her, Carlys jumped into the driver's seat, ignoring the bereft look on his face, the hurt and bewildered expression on Megan's, and from inside the house, the beginnings of a wail from Julie. So she felt guilty as hell for having to miss the family outing. There were lives at stake, property, a business that helped to support them all. She was responsible for all that. Jason, Megan, Julie would have to understand.

But even as she drove away, she knew they wouldn't.

Putting out the fire, checking the wiring, determining where and how the conflagration had started all took time, lots of it.

Three hours later, Carlys called Jason from the store across the street. After the way she had left, she didn't expect him to be receptive to her attention now; he wasn't. Nonetheless, she continued doggedly to describe what had happened, sure that if he knew all the details he would understand why she hadn't wanted to waste a minute in explanation when Naomi had called, but instead had left the house as swiftly as possible.

"It started in one of the dryers. The entire laundry room was in flames when I got here. Fortunately the fire department came quickly and we were able to save our files and most of our office equipment." Still, it had been an abominably close call. She got sick just thinking about what might have happened. "Only Naomi's quick thinking saved our entire building from burning down," Carlys finished in a voice that trembled.

Jason was silent, taking it all in. More cordially, he said, "She must be pretty proud of herself."

Carlys sighed her relief. She hated having Jason mad at her. "She is. I am, too. Naomi really saved the day." And for that Carlys intended to give her a bonus as well as all the praise and thanks she deserved.

There was another pause. "When are you coming home?" Jason asked softly, in a voice that gave them a chance to avoid a fight.

"I don't know." Carlys raked a hand through her hair. "Hours from now, probably. There's still a lot to do."

Silence. "Can't someone else handle it?" This, less politely.

Carlys cringed and steeled herself for the worst. "I've got to meet with the insurance people, get estimates on new dryers, get the existing laundry farmed out and call customers whose service has been delayed. No one but me can do any of that."

"I understand."

The response was formal. Beseechingly, she said, "Jason, I know today was ruined. I'm sorry. I'll make it up to you."

At that, his temper blew. "When?" he snapped, giving full rein to the irritation that had been plaguing him for days. "When will you make it up to me, Carlys? Tomorrow? The next day? And in the meantime what *the hell* am I supposed to tell Megan?"

His anger hit her like a blow to her midsection. Exhausted, on edge, Carlys heard herself snapping back before she could stop herself, "Dammit, Jason, be reasonable! You know I can't give you a definite commitment this instant."

Another silence, this more potent and chilling than the last. "Then don't bother to come home."

Shock radiated through Carlys, rendering her momentarily speechless. Her hands and knees were trembling; she felt very close to fainting. She whispered, "What?"

"You heard me." His voice was like a whipcord on her already shattered senses—flat, final.

Turning her back on the crowd in the store, Carlys tried to get a leash on her tumultuous emotions.

"Jason, I know you're upset with me, but this is no conversation for us to be having over the phone." She finished on a steadier note.

"I agree," he snapped back, riding the wave of his temper. "But since this is the only way I can talk to you, it'll have to do. So what's it going to be, Carlys, your work or us?"

He's angry, tired, hurt. He doesn't mean any of this.

Tears pricked her eyes. "I can't believe you're saying this."

And now of all times. Didn't the months they'd shared count for anything?

"And I can't believe you don't know in your heart what you're doing to us."

His voice dropped a notch. "We need you, Carlys. We need to be a family. Especially now." In a tone full of threat he continued, "If you can't do that for us, put your work on hold—"

"Jason, my work isn't like yours," she interrupted him placatingly. "I have a business to run. It's just me. No one else can do this for me."

"Then sell the damn business! We'd get along without the income for a while."

Carlys had been afraid he would say that. It was the one demand they both knew she could never, would never meet. And for him to be saying this now, of all times, could only mean... Was it over between them? Was this really the way Jason felt? Maybe it was time they got everything out in the open and discussed what she realized, in passionate retrospect, he had been discreetly hinting at for months. "I see," she said with icy resentment. "You'd prefer I didn't work at all, wouldn't you? Wouldn't you?"

"You're damn straight about that much."

Without warning, memories closed in on her, memories she'd tried hard to forget. Drake had done the same thing to her during their engagement. One day he'd tell her it was commendable for her to work, resent the hell out of her for it the next. She couldn't get back on that merry-go-round. She wouldn't be made to feel guilty for being a success, for caring about what happened to her business and the people who worked for her.

"And if I don't sell, then what?" What would happen to Naomi, who was starting to come along nicely but who still ratted her hair sky-high and wore tons of makeup and therefore wasn't bound to be easily or quickly employed anywhere else? What would happen to the part-timers, to the college students and mothers, to the sixty-six-year-old accountant who still did a damn fine job on her books yet at his age was hard-pressed to find work anywhere? Carlys couldn't, wouldn't, turn her back on these people. Nor did she like Jason's demand she do so.

"If you don't sell," Jason said slowly, emphatically, weighting each syllable heavily, "then there's really no reason for you to come home at all, is there?"

He sounded like a stranger. He was a stranger.

No, he wasn't, Carlys reminded herself firmly. He was just tired and overwrought; so was she. They were both saying things they didn't mean. "Jason, we'll talk about this when I get home," she said calmly.

An unbridgeable silence fell. "Which will be when?" he snapped finally.

Carlys looked across the street. The fire trucks had left, but water was still streaming from the inside of the building onto the street. All that would have to be mopped up. Customers expecting delivery still had to be called. "I don't know," she said tiredly. Silence. "Jason?"

Her only answer was the click of the receiver. It hit her like a lethal blow to the heart.

"SO YOU JUST LEFT HER THERE with both kids and walked out?" Alice faced Jason incredulously from across the table in the trendy New York City bar. It was full of yuppies, and she and Jason fitted right in.

Jason shrugged. Going to his former wife for consolation was a peculiar thing to do, yet he hadn't known where else to turn. Also he figured that if anyone would be willing to help him understand Carlys's side of it and make him feel like a jerk for acting the way he had, Alice would. She'd been his friend first and last, and had never been above giving him a swift kick in the pants, which was, he suspected through the haze of Seagram's penetrating his brain, what he needed right now.

He reiterated his excuse in a surly tone. "I needed some time alone."

As usual, Alice ignored the red flag. "Like hell, Jason. You wanted her to know what it was like to be stuck with two kids and no way to get *her* work done."

"Hey, I had a job interview here."

"And you no more want to live in New York than I want to live in Dallas. Stop playing games with yourself. Face up to it. You love Carlys, have since you met her, and you always will."

"So I love her," Jason said heavily. "Does that mean everything will work out?"

"You'll never know if you stay here, will you?" Alice responded tartly.

To that, Jason had no reply.

"CARLYS, you must be mistaken," her mother soothed. "Jason is just angry. I'm sure he doesn't mean to walk out on you. And he would never leave Megan."

Carlys stared sourly out the window, aware she had never felt more lost or alone in her life. More hurt. "That's what I thought, until he did."

Helen paused, unsure what to say. "Did he leave a note?"

"No, nothing." Carlys bit into her lip. If she could cry, maybe she would feel better. But she couldn't. The tears wouldn't come. A glacier had settled over her heart, freezing her tears.

"Do you have any idea where he is?" Helen asked gently, touching her arm.

Carlys's jaw jutted out furiously. "Yes, unfortunately, I do. Alice called."

"Isn't that—?"

"His ex-wife. Yes." What an act of friendship that had been! How could she ever have been jealous of Alice even for one moment? She turned back to her mother, explaining practically, "She said she'd seen him, that she was sure he'd come back to me sooner or later, and that I should give him bloody hell when he did."

Helen grinned. "Whoever would've believed it. Your life has gone from dull to soap opera."

"Tell me about it," Carlys said glumly. For the past two days it had been all she could do to get dressed. In retrospect, she was beginning to see what Jason had coped with while she'd escaped to work. Admitting that she'd taken him too much for granted wasn't easy, but she had. The question was would he listen to her now if she told him she'd mend her ways? And knowing how he felt about her working at all, did she really want him back? Sooner or later, Carlys knew, she would want to go back to work, maybe even full-time.

"He wants me to give up my work."

"Would that be such a bad thing if you had to do so in order to preserve the marriage?"

"Mother!" Carlys whirled on her, reacting as she would to any heresy.

Helen lifted propitiating hands. "You've wanted a home and family for a long time, Carlys. You love Jason. He did love you. Chemistry like that, the oneness, isn't easy to find."

"So I should do what?" Carlys snapped temperamentally. "Go crawling back to him on my hands and knees?"

"No. I'm just saying don't throw it all away on a whim."

Was that what she was doing? Carlys swallowed hard. "What if he doesn't want to come back to me?" Like it or not, she had to face her fears.

"It's up to you to make him want to do that, isn't it?"

Carlys glared at her mother through narrowed eyes. "I don't believe this," she muttered from between tightly gritted teeth. Any minute now she was going to jump out of her skin.

"Why not?"

"Because this advice of yours sounds suspiciously like it's come out of some snazzy little how-to book entitled *How to Catch that Special Man*."

Helen laughed, amused by Carlys's uncharacteristic jaunt into sarcasm. She watched her speculatively and with a wisdom as old as time, hit the nail right on the head. "Carlys, have the two of you ever had a fight before this?"

"No," Carlys reported sullenly. "Why?"

A light had been switched on in an area that heretofore had known only darkness.

"Because, darling, it would seem your honeymoon, extended as it's been, is finally over." She held out her hand, greeted her daughter formally. "Welcome to the real world, darling, the world of compromise."

"YOU WERE A JERK to walk out on me without so much as a word." Carlys threw down the gauntlet the moment Jason walked in the door late on the evening of the third day.

Steam practically rolled from her mouth and spouted from her ears, she was so angry. She wanted to damn him to dirty diaper washing for all eternity. And if the turkey thought he had a warm welcome in store for him, he had another think coming. She'd been on a roller coaster ever since she'd discovered he'd left town, one minute ready to kick him out on his tail if he showed his face, the next ready to take all blame and give up everything just to keep him in her life. Now, seeing him again, all her original anger surfaced; she was ready to give up nothing. Rather, she wanted to make him pay for hurting her so.

Whatever his mood when he'd entered the house, it quickly changed. Jason angrily accepted her challenge.

"I think *you* were a jerk to run out of this house without so much as a word."

"My store was on fire!"

"And Megan's feelings were hurt."

What could she say to that?

Carlys lapsed into glum silence. Ten o'clock at night and she was still in the bathrobe she'd worn all day. She was grumpy and out of sorts and hurt more than she ever wanted him to know was possible.

Was it necessary for them to go through all this again? Suddenly she didn't think so. Exhaustion swept through her, and with it resignation.

"Jason, we've been all through this—"

"Not that it seemed to help any."

She knew she couldn't bear one more sarcastic remark from him. It simply hurt too much. As it was, she thought she'd never recover.

"You're right," she said, struggling to keep her voice even. "It didn't help and I don't want to go over it again. I think...I think maybe you were right on the phone, maybe we should just call it quits." There, it had been said. He'd gotten from her what he no doubt wanted to hear, what he'd hoped to goad her into saying by leaving town.

He looked as if he'd been slapped in the face. He hadn't expected her to capitulate so fast. "You won't even try to work things out, find a reasonable solution?" Clearly, he didn't expect they would be able to work out anything at all.

Carlys's last tiny shred of hope fled. It was time for her to face up to the situation between them, as Jason had done already. "I don't see how we can," she said tiredly. More than anything she wanted the hurting to stop. He had been miserable enough to walk out on her and leave both children behind, to drink himself into oblivion in New York City, by Alice's report. And she was unable to sleep or eat, never mind think about work. It was time for them to cut their losses.

"I see." His face was carved in stone.

Unbearably weary, Carlys sat down. If there was one thing she could do, she decided, it was exit from this marriage gracefully. They had to remain friends. Enough accusations had been flung both ways.

"When we made plans for the baby, you told me I could have sole custody of Julie, that you'd be content with just visitation rights. Does that still hold true?" *Please God*, she thought, *let him say yes*. Because if she had to endure a custody fight on top of losing Jason and Megan and her dream of a happy family life, she thought she might break down.

For a second he seemed not to breathe. He blinked, looked down at his hands for a long moment, then back to her face, "Yes, it holds true. Carlys, I have no intention of divorcing you."

Her hopes rose. He didn't want to break up with her after all. Then, looking at his face, remembering all the unhappiness they'd been suppressing and hiding for weeks on end, the resentments that had simmered and come to a boil, she knew it was no good.

"Jason we can't go on as we have, bickering back and forth. What's the point of staying married if everything else we've built between us is destroyed?"

His voice was rough with restraint. "If I really thought you wanted a divorce—" He stopped, unable to go on.

There was a lump in her throat the size of a walnut. "I just know I can't take this fighting."

"Neither can I." He stood up restlessly, prowled the house they'd shared so happily. Coming back to her, he said, "Dammit, Carlys, I didn't want it to end this way."

"Neither did I." Unable to bear the anguish and indecision on his face, she dropped her head into her hands. "But considering how we started out . . ."

"What?" He turned toward her, his expression stark, bleakly disbelieving.

She lifted her face to his. Feeling fragile and helpless, unable to stop the tears streaming down her face, she said, "My mother made a remark about our having had a long honeymoon and it was time we joined the real world. It's been going through my head ever since she said it. I know what she meant, but—" she stopped and took a deep, halting breath "—I got to thinking maybe she was right in a different way. Maybe the baby did draw us together. Even Matt and Mark, who are real male chauvinists, admit pregnancy is a very romantic time. It's very special." She choked back the constricting emotion in her throat. "Maybe we just read more into that than there was. What if we just thought we were in love when really all we had was friendship and joy over the child was all that bound us together?"

Jason stared at her. She could tell he didn't want to believe the idea but it wasn't new to him.

"You really believe that?" he asked quietly.

Carlys didn't want to believe it, but it was easier to accept than the possibility he had never really loved her at all, but instead had been in love with the idea of having a baby with her. There was quite a difference between the two. If he'd never loved her, she couldn't stay married to him. "Can you give me any other explanation for what's happened to us?"

Now fighting desperately to keep her in his life, Jason said firmly, "Yes. It's postpartum stress. I think we're both suffering a delayed reaction."

"Jason—" Talk about grasping at straws!

"Listen to me, Carlys. I was wrong to walk out. And you're wrong to give up on us now. *I want this marriage to work.*"

Then why had he walked out? Why had he been so dissatisfied lately, then so quick to walk out on her? She wanted to believe his love for her had brought him back; in her heart she knew he had come back for the children's sake. For although he never stopped caring about them, he had stopped caring about her, however briefly.

"I'll quit my job entirely, if necessary. One way or another I want us to stay together," he finished on a passionate note.

"Why?" she asked suspiciously. "Why do you want us to stay together?" If only she could be sure that he loved her for herself, by herself, and not just for the child they had or the love she could give Megan.

"Because home and family are important. We're important."

Not I love you.

Did he love her? Carlys wondered miserably. Did he even know? Carlys only knew she was more confused and unhappy than she had ever been in her life, tired to the bone.

Jason attempted to take her into his arms. She stepped away from him before he could touch her. If they brought passion into this, she would be lost.

She couldn't afford to be vulnerable now.

His expression grimly accepting, Jason dropped his hands to his sides. "I'm willing to make some compromises. I think you should make some compromises, also."

He spoke so...efficiently, like a robot representing *Father Knows Best*. "I don't know, Jason," she said bewilderedly, aware he was watching her in the hope that she would agree to do things his way. Part of her wanted a reconciliation. The other half, the half that remembered the angry stranger on the phone, his moodiness of late, the man who had walked out on her three days ago, didn't trust him.

Jason's expression softened. Apparently he realized she was too exhausted to think straight. "Look, why don't you get some sleep. I'll take care of the kids," he said, at his persuasive best.

"Jason—" She put up a weary, resisting hand to his chest.

Blocking her move easily, he pulled her forcibly into his arms. "It's very clear nothing is going to get settled tonight."

"Jason—"

"Everything will be brighter in the morning, you'll see." Hand on her shoulder, he propelled her to bed.

"HEY, JASON." Matt Holt's familiar voice coasted across the grocery-store parking lot to assail him. "Heard you were having a little trouble with the wife."

This he didn't need, Jason thought on a weary sigh. Silently, he crossed the last six feet of blacktop to his station wagon. While Matt and Mark Holt watched, he began loading groceries into the back. As to Carlys, this morning she still wasn't saying much to him. In fact, he'd never seen her so down. Worse, he knew it was all his fault for walking out on her. Yet if he hadn't forced her to realize what was happening to them, would the situation be any happier now? In truth, he doubted it. She would have gone on her merry way, insisting there was no problem, whereas in reality there were plenty.

"Listen, guys, I know you mean well." Jason shut the door with a thud and twisted the key in the lock. "But everything's under control." Megan and Julie were both with Mrs. Holt. Carlys had gone to her house to work this morning. "Everything's going to be fine."

"We don't think so." Matt was all confidence. "We just stopped by to see Carlys."

So she was still that down, even at work. "She's been experiencing postpartum depression," Jason informed his brothers-in-law politely, knowing even as he spoke that this was the flimsiest of excuses for the enormous problems they'd suffered in recent days. "Yesterday, she saw her doctor, who assured her she's simply experiencing the normal postbirth fluctuations of hormones. All she needs is a little rest—" Which Jason intended to see she got.

"Right. We know all about that," Mark interrupted.

"Our wives both had it."

"Take it from us, Jason. Women in this stage are always overemotional. If you're smart you won't listen to anything she says, because they don't mean half of it."

Jason felt Carlys had meant what she'd said.

Mark continued. "My wife said she hated me."

"Mine said she wished I'd go fall off a cliff."

"You gotta roll with the punches."

"Give it time. The sooner Carlys gets her rest, the sooner everything and everyone will be back to normal."

Jason had to admit that for the first time since he'd known them Matt and Mark were making complete sense. The question was, was that a good sign or a bad sign?

"Right," Mark continued emphatically. "The two of you have been doing too much."

Jason nodded curtly. "I'll agree with you there." Oddly enough, he was glad they'd made a point of talking to him. Having been through the mill themselves, they could sympathize. "But as for her getting more rest, she's not being very cooperative. And until the kids are both a little older, or her work schedule and mine ease up, or I can talk some sense into her, I don't see how—"

"We know, Jason, we know how stubborn our little sis can be," Mark interjected with a knowing grin.

Matt slapped him on the shoulder. "Not to worry, Jason, m'boy, it's all taken care of. Mom and Dad are moving in for the weekend to take care of the babies. Megan feels real comfortable with them, ditto Julie, so you don't have to worry there."

Mark added, "And Matt and I are going to deal with Carlys's diaper service. We all agree the fire's too much for her to handle right now."

Jason grinned from ear to ear. He might not have realized before that being taken care of by family was so nice, but he'd been through enough during the past week or so to realize he and Carlys couldn't keep on managing alone and both work as well. The first order of business was getting her to rest. Now that he didn't have the children to worry about, he felt certain he could manage the care and understanding his wife required.

"And where am I going to be while all this is going on?" he asked dryly.

Matt opened his arms wide. "Off with Carlys, of course, at some hotel. Your choice. Here in Dallas or anywhere you like."

Jason kicked a tire thoughtfully. What they were describing sounded so wonderful. But knowing the mood Carlys was in, knowing her loss of faith in him, he didn't think he could so much as get her to go through a doorway with him, let alone spend a few days with him in a hotel, short of kidnapping her. Maybe in a few weeks. When things settled down. Then he would call on the Holts once again.

"Nice try, guys," he said, shaking hands with them, genuinely pleased. As much as he hated to do so, he leveled with them bluntly. "But I don't think Carlys is in the mood to go anywhere alone with me now."

Matt and Mark exchanged exasperated looks and turned twin angry glares on him.

"That's not surprising after the way you walked out on her," Mark said stiffly.

At that, Jason became angry. Did the twins really think he didn't know he had botched things up? No one was more aware of the insane way he and Carlys had both been acting. Much as he wanted to blame everything on the postpartum adjustments, he knew he couldn't. They had problems to work out, problems that had been swept under the rug. Carlys was still trying to avoid dealing with them.

"Hey! No one's more aware than I am that it was dumb of me to leave town."

"All right, all right," Mark interjected smoothly, cutting Jason off before he could launch into a long explanation. "The trick is to get her in hand now."

"Just tell her what you're going to do," Matt instructed firmly, "and don't take no for an answer. I guarantee once the two of you are alone and she's had some rest, she'll come around. She loves you. She loves the kids. It's up to you to make it work, Jason. I know you believe in all this equality nonsense, but there are times when a man has to take charge and exert his authority."

Jason knew what the twins wanted from him. He'd be damned if he'd go in there like some macho he-man and make her go away with him. Number one, Carlys would never go for it. "Carlys would never go for it."

"Sure she would," Mark interrupted. "We know our sister, Jason, and unless you do something dramatic to snap her out of it, this depression could linger for weeks."

"Months, maybe."

"Even years."

Matt slapped him on the back. "Think about it, Jason. Let us know."

All he had to do was say the word.

Chapter Fourteen

"Okay, Carlys, I've had enough of this cold war between us. It's going to end and end now."

Carlys stared at Jason, fascinated. He had blazed into her house without warning. She'd never seen him quite like this, so determined, so hellbent on having his own way. Part of her, the softer, feminine side, wanted to give in to him. The more rational half, the half that had been hurt by his departure, wanted to throw him out on his ear.

She stood up, both palms flat on her desk, eyes flashing, chin lifted. Steadily, in a smooth, unperturbed voice, she informed him, "You can't just burst into my office like this—"

"Still working?" He sauntered closer, ignoring everything she'd said and gave the myriad of papers and scrawled phone numbers on her desk a careless flick with his finger.

"Obviously."

Jason crossed his arms over his chest. "Well, wrap it up. Time's awastin'."

This was all so...strange. "Jason—" Exasperated she tried to make her tone sound harsh; it came out more like a laugh.

"Carlys."

She narrowed her eyes in speculation. Her pulse was tripping along too fast. "Have you been drinking?"

He grinned and circled closer. "What do you think?" There was more than a hint of challenge in his tone.

She studied him silently, aware that she was tingling all over. He was standing in her way, showing no inclination to get out of it.

No, he hadn't been drinking. She'd never seen him in more sober control of himself or his emotions. More to the point, he was acting like a predator suddenly, as if he had designs on her, erotic designs. Carlys gulped, involuntarily stepping back a pace and guessing slowly, "Something's happened...."

He nodded, taking a step closer so that if he swayed forward just a quarter of an inch more their bodies would meet. She had on high heels; they didn't give her nearly the height nor advantage she needed to fight him properly. He was still several inches taller than she and looking indomitable; whereas she felt fragile, bruised and spent.

"Matt and Mark finally set me straight." His voice was low and seductive. "I know just how to handle you."

Carlys's breath flew out of her lungs in a furious if amused whoosh. Now that she knew what he was up to and why, she knew exactly what to do. Leave. Promptly. "Like hell you do!" she spat out, whirling away.

She made it one step before the hand that clamped down on her shoulder spun her around and danced her back. With the toe of his shoe he kicked her swivel chair back, lounged on the edge of her desk and dragged her between his spread legs. "I think this is the part where

I tell you I like your spirit." His voice was teasing; his grip on her not to be denied.

"Jason, honestly!" Carlys tried to twist free of him, failed. "Will you stop!"

"Stop what?" All of a sudden he let her go.

Flushing, she moved back quickly, but he was still between her and the door.

"Stop chasing me around my office!"

"Am I?" he asked lazily, rolling to his feet with a lithe economy of motion.

"You know you are," she said breathlessly as the last of the oxygen left her lungs. Hurriedly, she tried to edge past him toward the door. Where she danced, he followed, repeatedly, easily blocking her moves. He was having fun!

"I mean it, Jason." Carlys had to fight hard to keep the laughter out of her voice; there was no disguising it in her eyes. "Enough." She hadn't felt like this since she was in first grade, being chased by the boys at recess.

"But Carlys," he drawled lazily, "I haven't caught you yet."

She raised both hands to ward him off, too late realizing she'd backed herself up against the door frame. Immediately he pinned her to it with the length of his body. Their hearts were beating together. Then and there Carlys knew that she was fighting a losing battle.

Breathless, she tried to figure a way out of his passionate clinch, which was threatening to undo her every previous resolve to keep them apart. "If you want me home, I'll be glad to go."

"When you're done here?" he asked softly. The man she had first gotten to know had suddenly returned.

"Y-yes." What was happening to her and to him?

His hand traced her profile, tilted her face back so that she had no choice but to look up into his mesmerizing eyes, which told her that they belonged together, just as they always had. They had been forced apart by fatigue and stress, but it wasn't too late for them after all.

"I want more than just having you home, Carlys," Jason said quietly. "I want you all to myself for the weekend. I want a fresh start. No, I want more than that," he continued emotionally, drinking in the love in her eyes, "I want what we had before. We still have it, Carlys. I know it—" he touched his heart "—in here. I love you, Carlys." He hugged her close, and she clung to him, needing him in ways she couldn't even name.

"Oh, Jason," she whispered, "I still love you. I never stopped."

Jason drew back to face her. When he spoke again, his words were solemn and heartfelt. "I've made some mistakes."

"We both have."

"I know you need to work. And I want you back in my life all the way. I'm tired of us living in the same house, but being little more than strangers, withholding more than we say. We can't keep trying to spare each other's feelings. Like it or not, if there's a problem, we're going to have to work it out, even it if means fighting, which I know you hate."

Tears flooded her eyes at the revelation he still cared so much for her, still wanted to try, and hadn't given up. "Sometimes my optimism does get in the way, doesn't it?"

"Only when you won't admit there's a problem."

She knew that in recent weeks she hadn't dealt willingly with problems and conflicts. Instead, she'd left everything to Jason, or worse, just insisted that with time difficulties would work out on their own, which hadn't happened. Yet through it all, until that last terrible fight, Jason had stood by her, trying to understand.

Carlys realized anew what a wonderful man he was and how much she needed to be with him. She took a deep breath and said seriously, the words coming straight from her heart, "I want to try again."

"Exactly what I wanted to hear." He offered her his arm. "Shall we go?"

SOME HOURS LATER, over a leisurely room-service lunch, they began to talk again, not about the babies, who were being well taken care of at home by the Holts, but about themselves, about their own needs.

"I felt that you were pulling away from me," Jason said, "that, in a sense, I was pushing you into marriage."

"I wanted Julie to have your name. But everything was happening so fast. I was afraid later you might regret marrying me, that you'd realize you'd done it in the euphoria of the moment, of becoming lovers, finding each other..." Her voice trailed off softly.

"That was one of the best times of my life, even though I was scared, too, Carlys, scared to wait, scared that if I did you might change your mind and decide you could manage just fine on your own. I was afraid you'd believe that a husband wasn't necessary. I knew that as your lover and part-time parent to our child I'd find a certain joy, but also that it would be nothing compared to what we could eventually have together as one family unit."

"So you plunged ahead and proposed to me?"

"Yes, hoping and praying you wouldn't say no." He paused reflectively. "Would you have felt better about it if we'd had a long engagement?"

"After my disastrous first attempt?" She shuddered just thinking about it. "No, the way we did it was fine. But you're right about me being reluctant to marry, I was scared of the depth of the commitment."

"But not anymore."

"No. I realize in retrospect that I have kept one foot out the door—by refusing to sell my house, for instance—that I haven't let myself trust you or our love completely. Oh, Jason, I knew the first time you kissed me you were the one, and yet I think I must have been scared that I wouldn't measure up and that if you knew the real me, how ambitious and restless I am deep down, you wouldn't love me anymore. I'd be miserable if I wasn't active in some business venture, and I guess that without realizing it I thought that if Drake felt threatened and left me, why not you?"

Jason nodded understandingly. "I realize that, Carlys. I've been at fault there. I know now that managing your own business carries a special responsibility. There'll be times when you'll simply have to drop everything and go, just as you did with the fire. I was wrong to expect you to go on with our outing when your whole livelihood was at stake. If anything like that happens in the future, I promise you I'll make things easier for you. You know, I should have taken the children to the park that day even though you had to go."

"It's wonderful to hear you say that, but you couldn't really have managed both Julie and Megan alone."

Jason shrugged, not so sure. "Perhaps not easily, but I could have done it. Or I could have asked your mom or dad to fill in. In a pinch they'd be glad to help out.

All we have to do is ask. And next time I intend to ask. I'm a part of your family now.''

"Jason, do you mean that?'' Carlys's eyes filled with tears.

"Yes. As difficult as it is for me to admit this, even to myself, I guess that all along I've been worried that a life with me, with home and children, just wasn't enough for you. There was always a chance that we— I—couldn't compare with the pleasure you got from your work, and that one day you might leave me.''

Alice had left him, Carlys thought.

"Or worse, you'd stay married to me and just not be there much in spirit or love or commitment. After the baby was born, we were both so busy. It seemed we never had time for each other.''

"And I didn't make time,'' Carlys admitted sadly.

"You were hard to slow down.''

Carlys was quiet, thinking. "Looking back, I think initially I was afraid that if I didn't start doing something soon, really force myself to go back to work, I'd never be able to return at all.''

"Would that be so bad?'' Jason asked curiously, and Carlys saw that he really did want to understand her. He wasn't trying to get her to quit any longer.

"For me, yes,'' she admitted. "I'm not sure I can explain it, but I've always been a person who operated at high speed. I'm always chomping at the bit. I'm impatient and restless, too much so for my own good, yet I can't do anything to change it, it's just the way I am.''

"Did you think I expected you to give everything up?'' Jason asked, aghast. "Carlys, when I suggested a longer maternity leave, that was all I wanted from you. I was just asking for more time to let us get organized. I wanted more help from you now, not forever.''

"What you wanted wasn't half of what I demanded from myself. I've wanted children for so long. There's a part of me that wants to just let everything else go and enjoy every second of it, not let them ever grow up."

"That's natural," Jason empathized readily.

"Another part of me wants to get down to work."

"Oh, yes, I understand that. When I was home with Megan, on a paternity leave, it drove me crazy sometimes wondering what was going on at work."

Carlys laughed softly. "And yet when you're at work you're wondering what goes on at home."

"Exactly." They looked at each other and grinned in mutual understanding.

"Do you think we really can have it all?" Carlys asked.

"Yes, if we start working together more instead of separately."

She sighed. "Guilty as charged. I was so busy trying to make sure I hadn't lost ground in the weeks I had been out that I didn't give much thought to your feelings. When I had to go to work, I just told you I was going and went."

"Meanwhile, I was grappling with my own secret demons, afraid our marriage would simply fade away from lack of nourishment."

"I just shut you out and hurt you. Oh, Jason, I behaved miserably. If we had just talked about it . . ."

"Sometimes the deepest fears are the hardest ones to voice."

They stared at each other in recognition of all they shared and had nearly lost.

"I *do* love you," Jason said softly.

"And I love you." They clasped hands. "We're going to make our marriage work."

"We'll have to make some changes, both of us," Jason cautioned.

"In terms of work and family."

"Right. And none of it is going to be easy."

"I know. I'm ready to do that now, though. In those three days without you I realized just how important you are to me. When I said before that my family would be my top priority, I had no idea really what I was promising. This time I mean it. If ever again I have to choose, it's going to be family first. And I'm going to start by hiring a manager for the diaper service. It'll cut my profits down enormously, but it'll be worth it in the extra time I have to spend with the children and you."

"As long as you're sure."

"I am."

Carlys looked up at him and felt sunlight burst in her soul. Jason was looking at her with such tenderness, suddenly she knew everything was going to be all right. And not just for the moment, but forever.

Carlys savored the warmth of his embrace. From the first touch of his mouth to hers, she felt cherished and safe and loved.

His fingertips trembled and twisted in her hair. His lips whispered over her forehead, her eyes, her cheeks. She was vibrating all over, wanting him, and longing to show him her newly slim shape. "Jason," she whispered, "the doctor—"

"I know. You can't," he interrupted, giving her a fierce hug, telling her with every fiber of his being that he could wait to make love; all that mattered was that they were together again.

"No," she said softly, lifting her eyes to his. "I can, I—it's all right."

It took a moment for the impact of her words to sink in. "You're sure?" he asked softly.

His hesitation made her smile. "Absolutely."

Ever so gently Jason drew her back. "Well, then..." He kissed her until they were both breathless and yearning.

"Oh, Jason," Carlys whispered. "I've needed to be with you for so long."

"And I've needed you."

"It seems like years."

"Instead of just days," Jason agreed huskily, all the pain of separation in his voice, all the joy he felt now.

And then suddenly they were beginners again. Everything was new, different and unbearably tender. Carlys felt the slow glide of his mouth moving over her throat. With an explorer's curiosity she smoothed her hands over the warm, strong muscles of his back, down his ribs; she felt his whole body tense. Jason was undoing the first buttons, dropping kisses where her blouse parted. He touched her as if he'd never touched her before. The pleasure she felt then was sweet and thrilling; and as her body responded he made a husky sound of masculine satisfaction deep and low in his throat.

Jason drew her to him again, fitting hardness to softness so they were intimately aligned. They trembled together, kissing and holding each other, yet he was in no hurry to undress her further. He was prepared to take all the time in the world, to give as well as take. Carlys knew she would never want anyone the way she wanted him. At first she kissed him gently, then with building passion, wanting to please as he pleased. "Jason, I love you," she whispered, joy floating through her, lacing her voice, wrapping around them both like the softest, warmest cloak.

He held her tighter still. "And I love you, Carlys," he murmured back emotionally, "so very, very much."

Epilogue

Carlys was sitting on the sofa reading to Megan, now five, and Julie, two and a half, when Jason walked in the door. As she'd predicted to herself, he dropped his briefcase and headed straight for her, an expectant, almost nervous look on his face. "So what did the doctor say?" he asked anxiously, foregoing all other greetings.

Carlys stood up to give him a warm welcome-home hug, so excited she could hardly speak. She swallowed hard, looking up into his eyes. "The news is just what we wanted to hear."

"Meaning?"

She smiled happily, glad to be able to confirm their highest hopes. "We can expect the next addition to the family in late December."

"Carlys, that's wonderful!" He hugged her again.

She felt tears of happiness flood her eyes; Jason wasn't the only one overcome with emotion. Girl or boy, she didn't care, having Jason's baby was enough for her, this time made the old-fashioned way.

Jason bent to give her a celebratory kiss. Carlys returned the caress tenderly and felt a sensual thrill slide down her spine.

"This calls for a real celebration," Jason said jubilantly.

Carlys said demurely, "I was hoping you'd say that."

"Feel up to a little dancing?"

"Always."

"The slow, sexy kind." His eyes glimmered invitingly.

"Just what I had in mind."

"Eight o'clock?"

She squeezed his hand. "You've got a date."

Meanwhile, Megan and Julie, never ones to sit still for very long, had abandoned their storybook and tumbled off the sofa. Carlys, aware they were on tiptoe to greet their daddy, stepped back to allow them to get to Jason. Before turning his attention to the girls, he gave her a long, affectionate look that told her they'd do their real celebrating later in private.

Carlys was already anticipating the evening. No matter how busy they were, she and Jason always found time to spend with each other as well as time to spend with their children. In the three years they'd been together, it was an arrangement that had worked out very well.

As Jason squatted down with his daughters to hear all about their morning preschool classes, Carlys reflected on the practical changes they had made in their lives.

She'd sold her home, Jason had sold his. The financial setback had been nothing in comparison with the advantage of a home large enough for two offices and all the family. Currently, Jason and Carlys both worked at home, though Jason went into the plant for four hours daily, on flex time.

They had hired a part-time nanny, one of the first graduates of the Nannies Incorporated vocational training program, and she was working out beauti fully. She also stayed with the girls whenever Carlys and Jason wanted an evening out alone.

Carlys had hired a manager for the diaper service and so was able to concentrate entirely on running Nannies Incorporated.

"Have you heard about the Houston deal yet?" Jason asked, when he'd pacified the girls and left Megan "reading" a book to Julie.

"Yes. The vocational school there is definitely interested in starting a nanny training program. They've asked me to help oversee it, and I've agreed to guarantee jobs with my firm for those who finish."

"That's great! Congratulations, Carlys."

Carlys was as thrilled as Jason, but she had also done a lot of soul-searching so as to be sure the new venture wouldn't interfere with her family life. "This program won't be as hard as the first one," she reassured Jason worriedly.

"I haven't a qualm about you accepting the opportunity," Jason commented calmly. "You've learned to handle work and family like a pro."

"Teamwork, that's what it's all about," Carlys agreed as they strolled into the kitchen to prepare dinner together.

"Teamwork and a lot of love," Jason said, drawing Carlys into his arms for a kiss full of promise.

She couldn't have agreed more.

PAMELA BROWNING

...is fireworks on the green at the Fourth of July and prayers said around the Thanksgiving table. It is the dream of freedom realized in thousands of small towns across this great nation.

But mostly, the Heartland is its people. People who care about and help one another. People who cherish traditional values and give to their children the greatest gift, the gift of love.

American Romance presents HEARTLAND, an emotional trilogy about people whose memories, hopes and dreams are bound up in the acres they farm.

HEARTLAND...the story of America.

Don't miss these heartfelt stories: American Romance #237 SIMPLE GIFTS (March), #241 FLY AWAY (April), and #245 HARVEST HOME (May).

HRT-1

MAIL-IN-OFFER
OFFER CERTIFICATE ✂

I have enclosed the required number of proofs of purchase from any specially marked "Gifts From The Heart" Harlequin romance book, plus cash register receipts and a check or money order payable to Harlequin Gifts From The Heart Offer, to cover postage and handling.

002

CHECK ONE	ITEM	# OF PROOFS OF PURCHASE	POSTAGE & HANDLING FEE
	01 Brass Picture Frame	2	$ 1.00
	02 Heart-Shaped Candle Holders with Candles	3	$ 1.00
	03 Heart-Shaped Keepsake Box	4	$ 1.00
	04 Gold-Plated Heart Pendant	5	$ 1.00
	05 Collectors' Doll Limited quantities available	12	$ 2.75

NAME _____

STREET ADDRESS _____ APT. # _____

CITY _____ STATE _____ ZIP _____

Mail this certificate, designated number of proofs of purchase (inside back page) and check or money order for postage and handling to:

Gifts From The Heart, P.O. Box 4814
Reidsville, N. Carolina 27322-4814

NOTE THIS IMPORTANT OFFER'S TERMS

Requests must be postmarked by May 31, 1988. Only proofs of purchase from specially marked "Gifts From The Heart" Harlequin books will be accepted. This certificate plus cash register receipts and a check or money order to cover postage and handling must accompany your request and may not be reproduced in any manner. Offer void where prohibited, taxed or restricted by law. LIMIT ONE REQUEST PER NAME, FAMILY, GROUP, ORGANIZATION OR ADDRESS. Please allow up to 8 weeks after receipt of order for shipment. Offer only good in the U.S.A. Hurry—Limited quantities of collectors' doll available. Collectors' dolls will be mailed to first 15,000 qualifying submitters. All other submitters will receive 12 free previously unpublished Harlequin books and a postage & handling refund.

OFFER-1RR

GIFTS FROM THE HEART
from Harlequin

FREE BY MAIL

With proofs of purchase
plus postage and handling

A. Hand-polished solid brass picture frame 1-5/8" × 1-3/8" with 2 proofs of purchase.

B. Individually handworked, pair of heart-shaped glass candle holders (2" diameter), 6" candles included, with 3 proofs of purchase.

C. Heart-shaped porcelain keepsake box (1" high) with delicate flower motif with 4 proofs of purchase.

D. Radiant gold-plated heart pendant on 16" chain with complimentary satin pouch with 5 proofs of purchase.

E. Beautiful collectors' doll with genuine porcelain face, hands and feet, and a charming heart appliqué on dress with 12 proofs of purchase. Limited quantities available. See offer terms.

HERE IS HOW TO GET YOUR FREE GIFTS

Send us the required number of proofs of purchase (below) of specially marked "Gifts From The Heart" Harlequin books and cash register receipts with the Offer Certificate (available in the back pages) properly completed, plus a check or money order (do not send cash) payable to Harlequin Gifts From The Heart Offer. We'll RUSH you your specified gift. Hurry—Limited quantities of collectors' doll available. See offer terms.

401R

GIFTS FROM THE HEART
ONE PROOF
OF PURCHASE

To collect your free gift by mail you must include the necessary number of proofs of purchase with order certificate.